Praise for Karen Gregory's

Skylarks

'This moving romance, with its well-drawn working-class heroine, its examination of power, politics and protest, and its clarion call to make courageous choices, represents all that's best in British YA'
Guardian

'Wonderful family dynamic, believable voice. About love, identity, and the power of standing up for what you believe in and not letting others put you down. Highly recommend!'
Katherine Webber, author of
Only Love Can Break Your Heart

'An authentic, hopeful-but-not-saccharine account of contemporary life'
Irish Times

'An elegantly written, page-turning story of two girls falling in love, interwoven with themes of wealth, injustice, protes͟ ͟ ͟ ͟ ͟means to be free. But most of all it's

Je͟ ͟ ͟ ͟ ͟ ͟ ͟ ͟ ͟ ͟ ͟ ͟ *ly*

I hold
your
heart

Books by Karen Gregory

Countless
Skylarks
I Hold Your Heart

I hold your heart

KAREN GREGORY

BLOOMSBURY

LONDON OXFORD NEW YORK NEW DELHI SYDNEY

BLOOMSBURY YA
Bloomsbury Publishing Plc
50 Bedford Square, London WC1B 3DP, UK

BLOOMSBURY, BLOOMSBURY YA and the Diana logo
are trademarks of Bloomsbury Publishing Plc

First published in Great Britain in 2019 by Bloomsbury Publishing Plc

A catalogue record for this book is available from the British Library

ISBN: PB: 978-1-5266-0916-8; eBook: 978-1-5266-0917-5

2 4 6 8 10 9 7 5 3 1

Typeset by RefineCatch Limited, Bungay, Suffolk

Printed and bound in Great Britain by CPI Group (UK) Ltd, Croydon CR0 4YY

To find out more about our authors and books visit www.bloomsbury.com
and sign up for our newsletters

For Nikki

Part One

Chapter One

Gemma

'We're going to miss it.'

Dad's hopping next to me on the touchline, face contorted in agonised suspense.

Mum's not doing much better, but she attempts a weak, 'It'll be fine.'

'He's not focusing, he's—'

Mum gives him a worried 'shhh' face; 'words' have been had with him before about shouting out during matches. I can sense rather than see Dad grappling with the stream of advice he wants to yell at Michael, swallowing it back down. I know how he feels. My brother looks suddenly small, positioned a few paces back and to the side of the ball, facing off the goalie a few feet away. The goalie is about six foot, even though he can't be older than fifteen. He's staring right at Michael, his gigantic gloved hands resting on his thighs, knees bent.

Don't let him psych you out, I think. It's not long since the summer league cup, and we all want *that* particular weekend wiped out. Like Dad said again on the drive here, this season's make or break for Michael's chances at the Academy. He needs to score a goal – preferably in the opposing team's net this time.

I take a long breath in and let it out gently, trying to send positive vibes over on the breeze. It's seriously warm for September and I can feel the sun on the backs of my shoulders, smell cut grass and suncream and sweat, courtesy of Dad, who's been leaping about as ever through the whole match. Michael got some good touches in, a few shots on goal, but the match has gone on, vital minutes to impress tick-tocking themselves away. And now we're nearly at time and he's got a free kick just outside the penalty area. This is his chance.

The whistle goes. Michael flicks a look up at the goalie, assessing. Then he puffs out his cheeks, makes a sharp shrugging movement and starts his run-up. I sense Mum and Dad tense beside me as the solid thwack of Michael's foot connecting with the ball echoes around the pitch. I feel my fists clench too, willing it on.

The ball rises, and the lads forming a wall leap high in the air. Sunny Patel is running down the left wing. I hear Dad sucking air in through his teeth in a sharp hiss.

Go in, go in, go in.

It's going too high, too fast.

Come on …

And now at the last second, the ball's curling round, dropping like a bird of prey. The keeper dives, but even I can see he's way too late. A split second later the ball smashes into the back of the net.

I let out a massive whoop, Dad's roar practically deafening me.

'Get in! Superb,' Dad's shouting. He turns and envelops Mum in a massive bear hug, swinging her off her feet, all of us laughing.

A moment later, the whistle blows for time. We've won, one-nil.

I stop cheering and watch my brother, who's still zipping around the pitch on a victory lap. Short he may be, but he's super fast: even Sunny can't catch him until he stops and then all his team-mates pile on top of him. I spot Jim, the coach, pumping his fist in victory. Another parent claps Dad on the back.

I've still got a massive grin on my face as Michael looks over and gives us a thumbs-up, then the team start jogging off the pitch.

At that moment I get the sudden sense I'm being watched. I shift my gaze and see a tall boy, maybe a couple of years older than me, a golden Labrador at his calf. Technically, he's not supposed to be here, but there's a public footpath running across the next field and sometimes dog walkers stray over. He's only about three metres away, and as my eyes meet his, I get this weird sense I know him. Or that he knows me. An odd feeling flutters in my stomach, halfway between nervousness and interest. I wonder how long he's been there. He's about the best-looking boy I've ever seen – I suspect he knows it too. This is confirmed by the smile he flashes me: all overconfident, slightly teasing. I'm suddenly uncomfortably aware that I'm probably bright red with the heat and the cheering, and my fringe is sticking to my forehead.

The boy holds my gaze for a beat longer than generally

considered socially acceptable, then his smile widens. Something about it makes me smile back too. The next moment, Dad's saying, 'Come on then, Gemma,' and the boy twitches the dog's lead and begins to walk on.

I hesitate for a second, feeling oddly disappointed, then follow my parents out to the car, listening to them going over the goal for what I know will be the first of many times. Just as we get to the edge of the field, I can't help turning my head to check if he's still there.

He totally is.

I'm about to turn away, embarrassed, when he lifts one hand, as if in greeting and I swear I can feel his smile even from this distance.

I grin and give a small wave back, then jog over to the car.

Later, after lunch, Mum drops me off at the Beach Cafe for my afternoon shift. I've been working here all summer, but now college has started, I'm down to weekends only. Esi's already here, and so is Dora, who owns the place. When she sees me, she gives a big smile before wiping her hands on a tea towel. 'Right then, I'll leave you girls to it. I'll be back later to lock up.' She bustles out.

I slide behind the counter next to Esi and stash my bag. The place is only half full, now we're into September, mainly retired people and a couple with a young baby. Cucumber sticks litter the floor under their table. The whole cafe is filled with light, slanting through the huge windows and bouncing off the floorboards, which Dora has painted white. There are seascapes on the walls, a model ship in a huge bottle up on a high shelf and tea lights wavering in jars on each table, surrounded by artfully scattered shells.

I go to the little CD player at the back of the counter. 'Whose turn is it?' I say to Esi. Not that there's much of a choice. Dora doesn't 'hold with' useful stuff like docking stations, and we're not allowed to use our phones, which might be for the best, given Esi's taste in music, so we're stuck with the same ancient ten CDs.

'Yours. But please can it not be – oh, *Gemma*,' Esi says, as I pick up a copy of *Country Greats* and shove it in the CD player, holding my thumb on the Skip button until I get to a Dolly Parton track. A moment later, the familiar opening melody of 'Jolene' starts.

'You love it really,' I say.

Esi raises her eyes to the ceiling.

'It's a classic,' I add. I sing along for a few bars, but a couple of the old ladies look over, and I remember I'm not supposed to be belting songs out. Not even Dolly.

'Can we at least skip this one?' Esi says, pushing the sleeves of her shirt up to reveal a couple of bracelets. She looks at me. 'I'll never, and I mean never, understand why you love all this stuff.'

I lean over to flick to the next song, and grin; if there's one thing bound to annoy Esi more than Dolly, it's Shania Twain. She may have a point there – even I hate half of the songs on this CD, but it's worth it for the look on her face.

Esi grimaces, but she lets it drop. 'How did the match go?' she asks as she leans into the chiller to swipe a spoonful from a tub of sherbet lemon ice cream.

'We won!' I say happily.

Esi breaks into a warm smile, then gives the ice cream a lick and pulls a face. 'Who voted for this?'

Dora has a suggestion book for ice-cream flavours, and whichever one has the most votes each week gets made, which has led to some interesting taste combinations over the summer. The worst one had to be scampi. I rock-paper-scissored Esi for who got to try that one – and lost.

'Who knows? Those kids down from Bristol I think. Michael scored a goal from a pretty damn awesome free kick.'

'Cool,' Esi says neutrally. She's also not the biggest football fan.

'Yep, he's just got to keep it up now,' I say, echoing Dad. I go over to the coffee machine. The milk container needs filling up. 'Also,' I say, leaning into the fridge under the counter to grab a bottle, 'I saw a guy at the match.'

'A guy?'

'Yeah.' I find the milk and start to straighten back up, still talking. 'Didn't get to speak to him, but he was really ho— uh …'

It's like that moment in films when there's the sound of a record screeching to a halt. Because now I'm standing, I can see who's just come into the cafe, and for a second I can only stare, clutching the milk to me.

'He was what?' says Esi as the guy from this morning begins to walk towards us.

I elbow her with the milk.

Did he hear me? Hard to tell. He doesn't seem half as surprised to see me as I am to see him though. I watch him walk between the close-packed tables. He's wearing shorts and a T-shirt that's tight enough to see his pecs. Which I am totally not staring at.

'Hey,' he says, all casual like he's never seen me before.

I lengthen my spine, push down the clenching in my stomach that's definitely escalating into something approaching full butterflies.

He's just a boy, Gemma. Like millions of other boys. Amazing cheekbones do not make him the Messiah.

And suddenly I'm not nervous at all. I'm me, Gemma, and I know exactly how to handle myself. I raise one eyebrow. 'You're going with "Hey"?' I leave a beat as he colours the tiniest amount, then say, 'Where's the dog?'

He blinks twice. 'Outside. I didn't think you'd recognise me.'

There are two ways to play that, and I wonder which one he's expecting.

'That must be the longest walk in history. Are you in training for something?' I say. We're miles away from the football pitch.

He laughs. 'Nah, I drove.'

'Well, what can I get you?'

'Some water? For the dog? This is empty.' He holds out the bowl we usually have outside and I realise he's had it in his hands all along.

I pass an open-mouthed Esi the milk and reach over the counter to take the bowl. I fill it with water and hand it back. Both times, I avoid touching his fingers.

'Thanks.' He takes the bowl, gives me another killer smile – seriously, those cheekbones – and suddenly it's over, he's walking away. I wait until the door is closed, then turn

9

to Esi, who's staring at me with a bizarre combo of half-smile and one raised eyebrow.

'He *was* hot,' she says. 'Bit too muscle-man if you ask me, but still …'

I look at her. I look at the door.

Then I say, 'Bugger it,' and grab a glass of water.

Outside, the boy's looking at the sea, shielding his eyes against the sun.

'Here,' I say and thrust the water towards him.

He takes it, like he's not surprised at all, and gulps the lot down. 'Thanks.'

'Well, don't want you getting heatstroke. You don't realise how hot it is with the wind.'

He nods, but kind of leaves it hanging.

'So … cute dog,' I say.

'She's called Moonshine.' He reaches down to pat her and she gives a doggy grin, her tail wagging like crazy.

I laugh in disbelief. 'Like the bootleggers?'

'Just like that.' He gives me that smile again, the one that says Little Boy Lost with a hint of something much more adult underneath.

I keep my face straight. 'You're not supposed to walk dogs on the football pitch, you know,' I say.

'Yeah?' He's still patting Moonshine.

'Yeah.' Now for some reason I'm starting to get irritated; with him, with myself for whatever the hell the ridiculously intense reactions he's setting off in me are all about.

'Will I be in trouble?' he says, one side of his mouth going up. And now I can't get a read on him at all. He holds my eyes for a second, then says, 'I'm Aaron, by the way.'

'Gemma.'

He puts out his hand suddenly, and I feel mine come up automatically to take it. His hands are large, his grip strong but not like a bone crusher or anything. He's still holding my gaze, and it feels odd. My stomach does another butterfly thing, one that actually feels more like a flock of seagulls, if I'm honest. I can feel the sun on my face, the sound of the waves breaking along the shore as the moment elongates.

Then he drops my hand and thrusts the empty glass at me. Again I take it, like my body's still on autopilot. 'Well, it was nice to meet you, Gem.' He unties Moonshine's lead.

'That's Gemma to you,' I say, but my voice doesn't come out quite as full of snark as I was aiming for. I overcompensate. 'Nice to meet —' I pause for a fraction of a second, then look down at the dog — 'you. I'm sorry about your ridiculous name.' I reach to give her a pat and she lolls her tongue out at me, tail going like a motor.

He laughs, but doesn't say anything. I watch him as he walks away, heading for the beach, the dog trotting obediently by his side.

I wait for a few moments, until he's almost out of sight, but he doesn't turn around. It's not until I go back in to where Esi is waiting with a questioning look that I realise I'm super disappointed.

Chapter Two

Gemma

I should've given him my number. My shift has ended and we're on our way to a celebration dinner with Michael, but I can't help running through the conversation with Aaron one more time in my mind, even though I've already gone over it with Esi in between making coffee and wiping tables and mopping floors.

'Well, maybe he'll come in again,' Esi said, a bit optimistically if you ask me.

'But do you think I should have asked him out?' I said. Again.

'Gemma. Unless you've got a time machine, I think you're asking the wrong question,' Esi said, in a tone that indicated I'd used up all my dissecting a brief interaction with a hot stranger points for the day.

All of a sudden, I realised how dumb I was being. I mean seriously, who cares? He was probably a tourist anyway, due to disappear next week. I decided to shove him out of my mind. I even let Esi change the music to a *Now … !* CD, which she claimed was 'fractionally more bearable than your rubbish'. Anyway, I can't help it. I've always had a thing for country music. I like the instruments, and that special twang to match in the singers' voices. Most of all, I love the way country songs are all story and emotion. Something real.

The talk turned to other things, like college. It's been weird not having Esi in my tutor group any more, now we're doing different courses. We still see each other in the refectory though, along with the rest of the crowd from school, and on the bus.

'I've got so much homework already,' Esi groaned. 'And Mum wants it all done before church tomorrow too.'

'Well, that's what you get when you sign up to four A levels.'

'I'm seriously thinking I should've stuck at three, but then everyone else applying to medical school will have four.' Esi's a future doctor: she's had it planned out since nursery, and so far, she's right on track. 'I spoke to Mum about it and she said I should cut back on something else.'

'Like what? Not here? Or your martial arts?' I didn't mean to sound a teensy bit hopeful about the last option. It's just that if Esi was going to be quitting anything, I'd rather it was her three-times-a-week training sessions than working in the cafe with me. We've had such a laugh all summer.

'I don't know. I want to do everything,' she said.

I kind of knew what she meant. Starting college feels like such a massive step, like suddenly the world's got that much wider and there's all these options you can choose from. A time to fly. Do something amazing. Or different, at least.

For a moment, looking at Esi, it felt like life was full of possibilities.

That was earlier though. Right now, sitting in the car, things feel pretty much the same as always. Dad drives us along the winding, narrow roads leading from the clifftops inland. A few times, when the road curves around, gaps open up to reveal flashes of the sea, a shining smudge on the horizon, but mainly it's the same boring hedges rushing past my window.

Dad parks the car up at the restaurant and we get seated at our usual table. We come here whenever there's a win to celebrate, which means the waitress already knows what Michael's going to order before he says anything: a plain chicken breast, steamed veg and a mountain of rice. Luckily for me, I don't have to be match fit at all times, so I go for the double-decker burger with bacon, cheese and barbecue sauce, while Dad has a steak and Mum a salad.

Mum's salad looks a bit pathetic when it comes out, compared to our portions. I lean over and dump a handful of chips on her plate. 'Go on,' I say, with a grin, before she can say, 'Ooh, I really shouldn't.'

'Well, maybe one or two,' Mum says. Dad's tucking right into his steak, but he gives her a quick smile.

'You treat yourself,' he says and she beams at him and the whole thing's so mushy yet cute that I hold back on the sarky comment about getting a room. If Esi was here, she'd push back her twists with that look she gets when she's about to start on feminism. She reckons food is political, especially when it's women feeling guilty over chips, but I don't know if it's exactly like that with Mum. It's more …

14

an approval thing, maybe. Whatever, I leave it and catch Michael's eye instead, making him smile.

Michael's only a year younger than me, which I'm not sure was 100 per cent planned, or maybe it was: Dad's always joked he wanted a football team, but something went wrong after Michael was born and Mum couldn't have any more kids.

Dad continues the post-match analysis he started in the car. 'That Arley midfielder couldn't get near you, but you need to watch your turns …'

I eat my dinner as Dad and Michael talk tactics and what's coming up next, me and Mum chipping in every so often. Then, when Dad goes to the toilet, Michael says to me, 'You want this?' It's the rest of his chicken; Dad told them to bring out two breasts because he reckoned Michael needs the protein. I'm pretty full, but I nod and say, 'I'll shove it under my bun,' and swipe it off his plate. Mum doesn't say anything. If we had a dog – and believe me, I begged my parents for years – then I could've saved it for him, or her. I could have a dog like Moonshine, all joyous tail and grinning mouth, who loves you just because.

'How was work?' Mum asks.

'Oh yeah, good,' I say vaguely, half my mind still on the golden Lab. And her owner.

'Do you have much homework?' Mum says.

'A bit. We're still doing all the introductory stuff. I've got an essay on the origins of psychology.'

Michael leans forward. 'Is it about Freud?'

'Uhh …' I haven't actually started it yet, but I'm pretty sure the teacher wants us to go a bit further back than that.

15

I love that Michael's interested though. It's like he tries his best to de-football when he can, which is not right now because Dad's coming back to the table. He picks up where he left off, in between bites of steak. When he's finished, he raises his glass of beer. 'To Michael, for a fan–bloody–tastic opening match. I'm proud of you, lad.'

We all chink glasses and I watch my not-so-little brother as he smiles, sending a quick thanks to whatever power might be lurking up there, that the bad run he had in the summer seems to be finally over.

Dad has another pint, so Mum drives us home. She takes the twisty track up to our house in first gear, even though Dad tells her she can go a bit quicker. The car lurches over a couple of potholes as we climb. Our house stands almost alone, apart from Esi's, perched at the top of a cliff over-looking the sea. It's so close to the cliff edge that we don't have much of a garden and the only reason we could afford it was because there's a fair chance our whole house is going to end up at the bottom of the cliffs one day. But I love living up here. Well, most of the time anyway. Sometimes I wish we lived in a city, or at least closer to pretty much everything, but then where else can you lie in bed and smell sea-salt air, or lean out of your window and watch the waves? Once I swear I saw a whale. No one believes me because the closest they've ever been spotted to us is in Lyme Bay, but when I was younger, I used to spend ages staring out of that window with a pair of old binoculars, making songs up in my head. That was before I got my first guitar. And I know it was a whale I saw, despite what Dad says. So yep, just occasionally there's magic in our house, despite the fact it has no central heating and rotten window frames.

When we get in, Michael says, 'Grabbing another shower,' and jumps up the stairs three at a time while Mum and Dad settle down in the living room, Dad's arm slung over the back of the settee behind her. Dad got that settee last year so he and Michael can watch their matches on the TV that takes up one wall, and we're not allowed feet on it, even in socks. If I brought a drink anywhere near the shiny leather, Dad would probably have a heart attack. It was pretty funny watching him pace around as the delivery guys tried to squeeze it through our tiny hallway though.

I go up to my room, past the rows of pictures lining the stairs. Lots of Michael holding various trophies, family holidays and Mum and Dad's wedding. My room is my little oasis. On one wall I have the Kacey Musgraves poster where she's holding the peach fan. It cost loads to ship from the US but it was totally worth it, even if Esi disagrees. I've given up trying to get her to see the genius of Kacey, or any country music. The only exception I think she's ever made is Iris DeMent's 'Wasteland of the Free', but that's just because she likes anything political. Anyway, my heart belongs to The Greenwoods, who are possibly the most perfect country duo in the UK. And 'Greenwood' is their actual surname – how awesome is that? Like some things are just meant to be.

Next to my desk is my guitar and amp. I've also got an electric piano covered in sheet music, my works in progress. It was a squeeze to fit the piano into my room but there was nowhere else for it once The Settee arrived and anyway, I prefer having it up here, even if it means my stereo and recording equipment are now in a jumble under my desk. The piano was a gift from my nana when I was twelve and it's what got me into music properly – learning to play and write songs myself as well as just listening and singing all around the house. I've only had a couple of years of lessons, but I'd already taught myself to read music before that and there's loads of stuff on the internet too. I know Nana would be proud of me. She died not long after she got me the piano and I still miss her sometimes. We didn't see her much – I don't think she got on well with Dad, who incidentally wasn't impressed about the piano, especially when we had to lug it up the stairs – but she got me. What I mainly remember about her was that she gave the warmest hugs, but her eyes were always a little sad, because Grandad died before I was even born.

After I get into my PJs, I sit at the piano and plug my headphones in. I've been working on a song for a while now, a duet. I try out some new harmonies, thinking about possible lyrics as I play. The story of a girl on the edge of the world, gazing out to sea. A boy by her side who takes her hand. Together they lift off and head towards the horizon, their toes skimming the waves, while overhead the sky bursts into colour.

I stop and scribble a couple of notes down, but I already know I won't forget this song. I'm dying to try the whole thing out loud without headphones, or on my guitar, but Michael always goes to bed early after matches and he's got training tomorrow. I can't resist going over it one more time, fingers flying on the keys, and don't hear the knocking at my door until it opens and Mum's standing there. I take my headphones off.

'Dad says can you finish up? We can hear the pedal banging downstairs,' Mum says.

I nod and close the piano lid.

Mum gives me a peck on the cheek. 'Night, then.'

In bed, the window open, I listen to the swish of the sea on rocks far below. It lulls me to sleep like always, but just before I drift off properly, it's like the noise of the waves shifts, so that my new song is the last thing I'm thinking about as I fall asleep.

Chapter Three

Gemma

'Have you even checked your phone?' Cal shouts the next day the second he gets on the bus. Next to me, Esi looks up from her book. It's something by someone Russian. Or possibly in Russian, knowing her. I've been doing that thing where you're looking but not really seeing everything flying past and composing lyrics in my head. We were the first ones on the bus, given we live the furthest away. Esi's family moved here from Ghana when she was a baby, and she's been my next-door neighbour since I can remember. We've been walking down the track to the bus stop together for years now.

'Who are you talking to?' Esi says mildly. Cal bounces along the bus, throws himself down behind us and then pops his nose through the space between our seats.

'Gemma of course,' Cal says. He's waving his phone madly in my direction. 'How are you not excited by this?'

'By what?' I grab his waving hand and take his phone. A second later I shriek; I can't stop myself. 'When did you see this?'

'Last night. I messaged you.' Cal shakes his head. 'So? You doing it?'

I stare at the screen, feeling all the blood in my body firing up my face, making my heart pound as I reread:

From Nashville with Love: The search for the UK's best country songwriters

Country music is booming in the UK. More people than ever are falling in love with the sounds of Nashville. Now we're hunting for the nation's most talented country songwriters. Could you be the UK's next country sensation?

My eyes track back down to the prizes. £10,000-worth of promotion, time in a recording studio, the chance to sing in front of all the major record labels and, best of all, a year's mentoring from The Greenwoods.

'Doing what?' Esi says.

I hand the phone wordlessly to her. She reads, then nods. 'Cool. You should enter. It's that band you like, isn't it?'

'The band I like?' I echo faintly. I hear Cal let out a little laugh; he knows what The Greenwoods mean to me.

'What song are you going to do?' he says. Then, 'You are entering, right?'

'Uhhh …'

It's weird. I'm usually so confident in, well, pretty much everything.

'You have to. This is huge.'

'I know,' I say. 'But what if—'

'Oh no. Nopey-nope. No way. Your stuff's too good to

go to waste. What was that one you uploaded on to YouTube the other day?' He sings a few bars, loudly.

'Oi!' comes from the front of the bus. It's Grumpy Sharon driving today. 'Keep it down,' she hollers over her shoulder. I hand Cal his phone and we pull faces at each other behind our hands in case she spots us in the rear-view mirror. Grumpy Sharon has been known to kick people off the bus before. I'm thinking hard, running through possible songs in my head, but all I can muster on repeat are the words, *I want this. This is mine.* Cal is uncharacteristically quiet, sensing I need some space to process. Esi's gone back to her book. A while later, we pass our old school and Cal puts three fingers up to his forehead in a salute. The bus stops at some lights and he says, 'Oh look, a magpie. Singular. On the school roof.' He shakes his head in mock sadness as he looks at the students arriving. 'And just think, that was us trudging in just a few short weeks ago.'

'Do you mind? Some of us are trying to block out the memory of GCSEs,' I say. I got decent results in the end, but the hours of revision and the gut-clenching feeling walking into that exam hall have made me wonder more than once why I'm subjecting myself to more of the same at A level.

I've got a free period first thing, so technically I don't have to be at college until ten, but Mum goes the other way into work and Dad always drives Michael to training. My seventeenth birthday cannot come fast enough. While Esi heads off to Chemistry, I go with Cal into the refectory, get out my laptop and attempt to start my Psychology essay, but I keep getting my phone out to read about the competition again. There are three rounds: auditions, then regional finals, with the winners from the twelve regions going on to a national final. The website says the national final will be televised. Whoa.

Before long, everyone else is pulling out chairs and soon I'm in the middle of a noisy argument about *Queer Eye*. Cal reckons the chemistry between the Fab Five is all faked for the cameras. 'None of them can stand each other. Fact. There'll be public spats before long,' he says.

'Spats?' I say, shaking my head.

'Yes, spats. I'm telling you.' Cal sits back and sips from a gigantic cup of tea, his lips pursed primly. 'And have you noticed how they give them all the exact same set of shirts? It's like a uniform or something. I'm gonna grow this –' he motions at his barely-there stubble – 'into a full-on giant Gandalf beard, like that guy from season one.'

'Nice.' I wrinkle up my nose.

Next to me, Phoebe and her girlfriend, Beth, have their heads together over Beth's phone. Beth's one of the few newcomers to our group; she went to school the other side of town, but she's been going out with Phoebe since the middle of Year 11. I think they met online. They've been super loved-up since Beth wangled coming to college here and they get to spend every day with each other.

I'm still thinking about the songwriting competition. Cal looks over and says, 'So, you've decided which song you're doing, haven't you?' and grins. The annoying thing is, he's almost right. The duet I've been working on, 'Sea Dreams', would be perfect.

Phoebe looks up. 'What's this?' After Cal fills her in, her soft eyes get wide. 'Are you going to enter?' she says.

I take a second and the words come to me again: *This is mine*. And I know, like Cal knew, that I made up my mind a nanosecond after reading the word 'mentoring' in the list of prizes.

'Sure!' I say, all breezy grin. It's like muscle memory; you just have to act confident, that's most of the battle. After a while, it stops being an act, and then it's just you. I think.

'I wish I had the guts. Or the voice,' Phoebe says.

She does have the voice, in this breathy, quiet way. We've done school musicals together before, Phoebe usually playing second to my lead, but it's never got in the way of our friendship.

'You do, on both counts,' I say.

Phoebe smiles, but I can already tell she's talking herself out of it, which is kind of a shame because the more I think about it, the more I'm convinced a duet would be my best shot. I'm about to say this when a crash from the corner distracts me. There's an indoor football table set up there, next to the only settees in the refectory. Since term started a couple of weeks ago, it has been swiftly established as the place the second years hang out – usually a gang of *that* sort of guy. The ones who might be in college but at heart they're still at the flicking-girls'-bra-straps-and-giving-them-marks-out-of-ten stage of emotional development. They're normally accompanied by a couple of girls who are 'allowed' to sit and watch their games. I'm sure when I walked by last week I caught them all smirking over a phone with porn on it, if the noises were anything to go by. *Bleurgh*.

One of the guys is whacking the side of the football table, and when that doesn't work, lifting it up to tilt it; it seems the ball has got stuck somewhere. I'm about to turn away, back to my own group of friends, when I stop short.

Right in the centre, a girl with cascades of blonde hair so close to him she's practically got her boobs pressed against his arm, is the guy from yesterday.

Aaron.

Chapter Four

Gemma

There's about five seconds of stunned surprise, which feels like a lot longer, and then I'm sure his eyes meet mine. Before I can decide what to do, Cal's snapping his fingers in front of my face and saying, 'Wakey-wakey, it's almost ten.'

I stand up, flustered, fumbling with my laptop and shoving it in my bag, before looking over again, but there's no sign of Aaron. Cal links his arm through mine and we walk up to meet Esi in Psychology. We're launched straight into research methods, our tutor telling us we're going to be designing our own mini-projects over the next few weeks. So it's not until we're back at what's becoming our usual table, when we can grab it, at lunchtime, that I get the chance to mention my Aaron sighting to Esi.

'He was with the knoboons,' I say.

The knoboons is what Esi christened the table-football lot on our second day, after we'd been having an in-depth conversation about what different groups of animals were called. This was because she'd slipped us the conversational nugget that a group of giraffes is called a 'tower', which had me in hysterics. I also bet her it wasn't true, which was a mistake because she immediately whipped out her phone.

'What are you betting, exactly?'

'I'll do all the floor mopping and toilet cleaning at the cafe for the next three weeks,' I said, which was a tad over-confident of me, in retrospect.

Cal gave a sad shake of his head. 'Hope you've got marigolds.'

They were right. Google confirmed that a 'tower' was indeed what a group of giraffes were called.

'Oh,' I said. 'I thought it'd be a herd, or something.' Then I got the giggles again. 'Go on, what are some others?'

Esi read them out while we tried to guess. 'Lions.'

Cal rolled his eyes. 'Pride. Give us something harder.'

'OK.' She looked over at the lads in the corner, then gave a wicked grin. 'Baboons.'

'Er, troop?' Cal said.

One of the table lot was playing obnoxiously loud music, with lyrics to match. Esi wrinkled her nose. 'Yep, a troop of baboons. Or –' she got this inspired look in her eyes – 'knoboons.' We all collapsed in laughter, apart from Beth and Phoebe, who were busy gazing at each other.

Now Esi raises her eyebrows and says, 'You sure it was him? He seemed older than that the other day.'

'Yep.' I look around, as if he's going to materialise in the refectory right in front of me. 'That's the third time I've bumped into him, how weird is that? It must mean something.'

Esi opens her mouth, probably to tell me for the millionth

time there's no such thing as the universe intervening, or fate or whatever, but at that moment, Rachael comes up. She gets the late bus in on a Monday, because she hasn't got any lessons until after lunch, which everyone else is deeply jealous of.

'What's up then?' she says, flopping down next to Cal and flipping her gorgeous-as-always hair back over her shoulders. I wish my hair would go that shiny but it has a tendency to frizz. Rachael's is so smooth, I want to reach out and touch it, and judging by the way Cal's looking at her, he's having similar thoughts. He clears his throat and says loudly, 'Gemma's got a Mystery Man.'

Rachael's eyes light up. 'Oh yeah?'

'Not exactly …' I say.

At that moment, my phone buzzes with a notification from my YouTube channel.

'Hold that thought,' I say, one finger in the air. The next moment, my jaw drops. The comment is on my latest video, the one I uploaded the other week:

Love this. You have an amazing voice.

This isn't what's got my heart going extra fast, though – I get comments like that all the time. Nope, it's the name of the person making the comment that I can't seem to stop looking at.

Aaron Weaver.

Esi looks over my shoulder. 'Wait, is that …?' She squints at the thumbnail. 'It's him!'

'Who? What?' Rachael says, looking from one face to another like a meerkat, which makes me smile. I bring her up to speed with the football match and the cafe and seeing

28

Aaron earlier. She sighs happily. 'That's so romantic. How did he find your channel?'

I shrug.

'He must've asked around, found out your name,' Cal says reasonably, without looking up from madly swiping at his phone. (He's on his millionth attempt to get top run on Subway Surfers. It's never going to happen, but we indulge him anyway.) It's not like I'm particularly anonymous; I use my full name on YouTube because, well, you never know. A scout from Decca Records might be browsing one day and … OK, that's probably also never going to happen, but still.

'Yep, that's definitely romantic. He's well into you …' Rachael says. I dart her a quick look – she can sometimes be a bit cynical – but she only seems wistful. Then her face clears and she says in her normal voice, '*Anyway*,' and a moment later she's inviting everyone to a party some girl in her Geography class is having on Saturday night.

The conversation moves on to who's going, but I sit back while I consider what to say in response to Aaron. I settle on … nothing. Let him do the chasing. Still, I can't stop myself scanning the refectory for a sign of him, or from feeling a teensy bit disappointed when he doesn't appear. But by the time I've emerged from double Biology (why, *why* did I think this was a good idea?) the thoughts have been driven out altogether. It would seem the teachers at school were right when they warned about the leap up to A level; my head's spinning.

I set off for the bus home. As I'm coming out of the main entrance, I sense someone walking up fast beside me. A moment later, I'm overtaken by a cloud of perfume. It's the blonde girl I saw body-checking Aaron in the refectory earlier. I register this just as someone leans on a horn. It's coming from a pretty nice-looking car – I can't see the make, but it's dark and way sleeker than a lot of the buckets people rock up to college in – which is pulled up at the edge of the car park. Blonde Girl immediately pivots and snakes her way over, then leans so far down she's in danger of falling through the open window on the passenger side, boobs first. I carry on walking, but out of the corner of my eye catch the girl straighten abruptly. She turns and gives me the sort of stare that's designed to inflict mortal injury. Luckily for me, that sort of thing only makes me laugh, though I'm curious now as to exactly why she's exiting stage left in a storm of heels. Then a voice floats out of the car: 'Gem!'

It's him. Of course it is.

I pause for a second, then tip my chin up and take my time walking over. I stand, arms folded like I have about three minutes – which incidentally is totally true if I'm going to catch my bus – and I'm prepared to give him 0.5 of those.

Oh, and I am not about to go leaning down into his car. I don't need to though, because Aaron's already leaping out, striding around the bonnet end and coming to stand next to me. He's tall, but I'm wearing heels – and I'm five nine barefoot – so we're pretty much level-pegging it in the height stakes.

I wait for him to speak first. And suddenly he seems less confident, now we're actually face to face again, lifting his hand to run it through his carefully styled hair. I don't want to, but part of me can't help finding this cute, especially when he says the next thing, which is, 'You saw my comment?'

I raise my eyebrows to indicate yes.

There's a pause.

'I loved your video.'

'Thank you.' I shift my bag, conscious the bus will soon be leaving without me on it.

'You want a lift home?' Aaron says.

'Do I seem like the sort of person who gets into strange boys' cars?'

He inclines his head as if to say this is a fair point, but then says, 'Ah, but I'm not a stranger now we're internet buddies.' Then he deploys *that* smile. And it totally works. A charge goes right through me, like it's leaped straight from his mouth, his eyes, into my skin. All of a sudden, I want to laugh. Instead I say, deadpan, 'I don't know, has the dog been sitting there?' I nod to the passenger seat.

Aaron's smile widens. 'One hundred per cent dog-hair free, I swear it.'

He holds my eyes. Neither of us moves. I'm so close to leaping into that car, but instead I pull my gaze away, say, 'No thanks, not today!' with a laugh, and the next moment I'm dashing away from him, down the slope towards the bus.

I just manage to swing myself on before Grumpy Sharon shuts the doors. The bus pulls off and I slide into a seat next to Esi in time to see Aaron slouching back against his car. He raises a lazy hand to wave at me as we pass.

He's smiling too.

31

Five minutes later, my phone goes, like I knew it would. A private message request on my Instagram. He must have followed the link from my YouTube channel. I hit Allow.

Tomorrow then? Come on a date with me. A

A few minutes later: **Go on ...**

Then: **At least talk to me.**

Please????

I look at Esi, nose buried in her Russian book, and the trees outside the window, framed against a blue September sky, and I sit back in my seat and start typing.

All right then. What do you want to chat about?

Chapter Five

Gemma

The conversation lasts until midnight. I definitely didn't plan it that way, but Aaron's actually super easy to talk to. And persistent. It takes me three goes to end the chat and he only stops after I say it's getting to a 'No, you put the phone down' place, which is deeply tragic.

I'm knackered but smiling when I finally put my phone on my bedside cabinet and turn out the lamp. I seem to have told Aaron a million things about myself. He's really interested in the singing and seems to have watched all my videos, but says the songs I write are the best. He talked a little about himself too, though. The facts I've gathered about him in our marathon chat are, in no particular order:

- He moved here in August from London (glamorous).
- He's repeating a year of college, but I don't know why (mysterious).
- He misses his mum, specifically her epic shepherd's pie (too cute).

- He says he's planned 'something spectacular' for our date tomorrow (eeeee!).

Well, OK, I saved the best fact for last.

I set the alarm for 6.30 so I've got time to get ready the next morning. I beat Michael into the shower for once and pad downstairs with my hair wrapped up in a towel to search out coffee. Mum's up already, poaching some haddock for Michael's breakfast. I flick on the kettle, breathing through my mouth. I can't stand the smell of fish.

'You're up early,' Mum says, going to the fridge for some eggs. She cracks one into the poacher on top of the hob while I try not to shudder. I also hate everything about eggs: the gloopy yolks, the fact they might have become little fluff balls of cuteness in time. Esi has pointed out on multiple occasions that this is entirely hypocritical of me, given I'm not adverse to the odd KFC, and that an unfertilised egg is not in fact a baby chicken, but I can live with the contradiction.

I glance at the cereal boxes, but the fish smell is making my stomach churn and anyway, there's only porridge and muesli and other nutritious-yet-boring stuff.

'I miss Coco Pops,' I say, but Mum's distracted and doesn't answer. She's poking the edge of a knife into the eggs, which are still wobbly. Vile. I put the bowl back in the cupboard; I'll buy something at college.

I pass Michael coming down the stairs with his training bag in one hand.

'Morning!' he says with a big smile. Urgh, why is he so cheerful in the mornings?

'You have too much energy,' I say, but it's hard to get irritated with Michael. 'You also have fish and poached eggs for breakfast.' I make a retching noise.

Michael leans in close and whispers, 'I hate fish.'

'Oh my God, do us all a favour and tell Mum, then. You'll be saving me from death by fish-vom smell anyway.'

'Can't. Dad read an article.' Michael grins at me again, then does his puppy-bounding down the rest of the stairs. I watch him for a second; I can never 100 per cent tell whether Michael loves or tolerates Dad's, erm, *contributions* to his football career. He always eats the gross food so he can't mind that much. Definitely different to the days when he was little. He'd only sit by me, and if I wouldn't eat something, neither would he. He even had to have juice in the same-coloured cup as me or he just wouldn't drink at all. Never in a tantrumy way, more of a sweet but about-as-mobile-as-a-mountain way. Michael's always been pretty determined underneath his easy-going surface.

I shake my head and run up the rest of the stairs to make a start on my hair and make-up. When I'm finally happy, I search for my navy jeans that I know make my butt look awesome, but can't see them. I think back; I'm sure I put them in the wash over a week ago. I go to the top of the stairs and holler, 'Muuum? Where's my blue jeans?'

She doesn't answer so I run back downstairs. Michael's at the table, while Mum's getting stuff out of the dryer. He meets my eyes, flicks his own down to the fish and takes a final stoical bite.

I mime puking to Michael, then say to Mum, 'Are my jeans in there?' I can tell already they won't be; Mum's arms

35

are full of Michael's football kit – a jumble of socks and shirts and shorts.

'Did you put a load on?' Mum says.

Dammit. I was going to the other day, but then the machine was already on and I forgot …

Mum hands Michael a clean set of kit. He grabs it, says, 'Thanks, Mum,' and shoves everything in his bag. Then he takes off up the stairs. Mum picks up his plate and goes to the sink to rinse it. I leave her to it and go back to my room. My black skinnies will have to do, even though they're a bit on the tight side.

I dress and look at myself in the mirror. Not bad. A quick spritz of perfume and I'm all done.

Well, apart from the nervous churning in the pit of my stomach. Something tells me that's going to be there all day.

College trickles by. Cal whistles when he sees me at lunchtime. 'You got a hot date or something?'

'Well as a matter of fact …' I grin.

Every head at the table turns my way. Aaron doesn't seem to be in here, despite a gaggle of knoboons in their usual spot. I'll have to ask him what he sees in them. I fill the gang in – well, everyone apart from Esi, who's in the library.

'So where's he taking you?' Rachael says.

I have to admit I don't know. 'Apparently it's a surprise.'

Rachael snorts.

Beth gives me an encouraging smile. 'We'll want all the details later.'

'Oh, we'll get them,' Rachael says, one eyebrow raised, but then she softens it with a smile.

Leaving college is almost an exact replay of yesterday, except it's me who's clipping down the stairs towards the black car. And this time Aaron's standing next to it. 'Hi!' he says with a grin.

'Hi yourself. Where've you been, then? I didn't see you at college.'

'Skipped it. I wanted to get some stuff ready.'

'Oh yeah?' I peer over his shoulder, trying to see into the car, but the windows are tinted.

'Curiosity will get you nowhere.' He wags his finger, then opens the door and gives a mock bow.

I slide in and he closes the door behind me. His car is neat, smelling of air freshener and faint aftershave. Aaron gets into the driver's side and then we're pulling out of college, driving through narrow lanes. One of the things I love about living here is how you can drive for a while and almost forget you're by the sea, then suddenly you turn a corner or climb a hill and there it is, laid out like a secret. When we get out on to the main road, I say, 'So where are we going then?'

'It's a surprise,' he says, taking his eyes off the road to grin at me. Annoyingly, I can't help but smile back, then realise we're approaching a red light.

'Shouldn't you be watching the road?' I say.

Aaron hits the brakes hard and I feel the seatbelt jerk tight against me.

I huff out a breath. 'Surprises are overrated. Tell me where, or I'm getting out.' I'm only partly joking; I've got one hand on the door handle.

Aaron turns his head to look at me, his eyes wide. I raise my eyebrows in an 'I mean it' way.

'Sorry,' he says. He seems flustered suddenly. 'I just thought … we're going to the beach. For a picnic,' he adds.

I start laughing at this and once I do, it's hard to stop. Must've been more nervous than I thought. But underneath the laughter is something pleased and warm; picnics on the beach are classically romantic for a reason. Aaron's looking at me, an expression I can't quite pin down on his face. My laugh fades and we're just staring at each other in this pretty intense way. Then a car horn blares out behind us.

Without taking his eyes from mine, Aaron leans one hand out of the window and slowly extends his middle finger. This makes me laugh again and this time he's joining in with me as the car overtakes us, the guy behind the wheel shouting out expletives about the light being green and Aaron's mental capacity.

Aaron puts the car in gear like he has all the time in the world and pulls away, raising a lazy hand in a sort-of apology to the other cars behind us.

When we finally get there, I'm actually pretty hungry. Aaron's driven us along the coast and down to a beach I think I last went to when I was about seven, back in the days of Coco Pops, before Michael got scouted. It's out of the way, but it does have sand. You also need to scramble down a massively steep path to get there. We park up in a tiny gravel car park, scooped out on top of a cliff. The second I get out of the car, the familiar beach smell rushes on the wind to meet me, a fresh tang of seaweed and space that always tells me I'm home.

I step up to the fence at the edge of the car park and look

38

down, into the curve of the tiny bay. Sea-carved rocks to one side like long fingers meet at the top in a natural archway, waves pushing over them in a fine white spray. We used to go rock-pooling down here, me and Michael, slipping over the trailing brown-greens of seaweed-encrusted rocks, our fingers catching on the rough edges of barnacles, searching for tiny white crabs and, once, a group of peachy starfish. It was like our own little world.

Aaron's dragging this huge bag out of the boot of his car. He heaves it on to his shoulders and says, 'Shall we go?'

We wind our way down the cliff path, past long grasses threaded through with little purple flowers. I'm not exactly wearing the right sort of shoes for this and a couple of times my feet skid, so that Aaron has to put a hand out to steady me. After the second time, he loops his arm through mine.

It's not until we get out on to the sand that I remember how isolated the beach is, ringed in with rocks. We've got the entire place to ourselves. As Aaron dumps his bag down, I take out my phone, but of course there's no reception out here. I guess this should make me nervy or something; I mean, I don't know Aaron really, do I? I didn't actually tell anyone where I was going, given I didn't know myself. I imagine telling my parents I'm on a date and almost laugh; I'd only get a million questions, plus a load of jokes-that-aren't-really-jokes from Dad about whether he needs to get a shotgun.

But looking at Aaron bent over his rucksack, at the quick, almost shy look he directs up at me, I'm not worried.

'What exactly have you got in there?' I say, because seriously, the rucksack's about the size of a small house.

Aaron grins and starts producing stuff, like a magician with one of those strings of coloured flags. Bottles, a rug, packets of food, even plates and cutlery. Then he pulls out a disposable barbecue and I start to laugh. He looks up again, from where he's smoothing a patch of sand with his palms, and says, 'What?'

I gesture to where the wind has caught one edge of the rug and is lifting it up. 'Not sure it's totally barbecue weather. That rug's going to take off.'

It's like that around here. The wind keeps you company nine days out of ten. I feel it now, whipping the side of my face, bringing the sticky taste of salt spray with it.

'We just need some ballast,' Aaron says, and there's a sudden glint in his eyes. Then he takes one long stride over and in a smooth movement lifts me easily. I register the feeling of his hands spread on either side of my ribcage, just above my waist, and let out a screech of indignation as he plonks me down on top of the rug. Then he gives me a wicked grin, dancing back as I try to swat him with my hands. 'Stay there.'

I can still feel the sensation of his fingers imprinted on to my sides, the rushing feeling of being swung into the air as I sit on the blanket, watching as he tries to light the barbecue. Aaron's flicking a lighter, but every time he gets it near the foil tray, the wind blows it out again. It finally catches on the fourth try and he turns to me with this ridiculously pleased look on his face. Then he pulls out a couple of candles from the rucksack.

'Seriously?' I say.

He makes a *pah* noise. 'This? It's just a light breeze. I will not let it best me.' He puts on a fake accent for the last part, like some guy in a costume drama. But even Aaron has to give up on the candles eventually. Instead, he goes back into his bag and pulls out a portable speaker. I lean forward. 'Is that a Bose?'

'Yeah, it is actually.' He sounds surprised.

'What? Shocked a girl knows her speakers?'

'No,' he says, but he gives this little smirk, like he's trying to wind me up. I resist the urge to lob something at him; there isn't anything in reach except for sand. He slaps the burgers on to the barbecue. I'm about to get my phone out to check out how my make-up's holding out, when Aaron fiddles with the speaker, then bounds over again and drops on to the blanket beside me.

Suddenly, the wind seems to cradle us. There's around six inches between his leg and mine; his stretched out in front of him, while he leans back on his elbows. I'm sitting cross-legged and I turn so one knee is pointing towards him, one out to sea. A familiar chord drifts across my consciousness. 'Wait … is that Bowie?'

'"Starman",' Aaron confirms, still looking at the waves.

'Cool. Gotta love a bit of Bowie.'

Aaron turns to me, again with that super-pleased look on his face. 'I knew you'd be into him.'

'Oh yeah, why's that?'

'Because you have excellent taste,' he says, all teasing now, and I'm irritated to realise I'm blushing. To deflect attention away from my red cheeks, I say, 'Well, a picnic on the beach isn't the most original idea, but you get points for this.' I point to the barbecue, which is starting to smoke, 'And this.'

41

I wave my hand to indicate the whole beach. 'I haven't been here since I was a kid. I forgot how beautiful it is.'

'You're so lucky, growing up here. I love the sea.'

'What, even when it's gale force ten, which it is pretty much all the time around here by the way?'

Aaron leans back again. 'But you get so much space. Enough to really breathe, you know?' He gestures out to the waves. 'It's like this e.e. cummings poem says, "We always find ourselves in the sea."' He holds my gaze for a moment, then he grins. 'Plus, it's not dirty like in London. You don't get goth snot out here.'

I blink, then laugh again. I'm finding it hard to keep up with him. 'Wow, poetry and bogies in the space of thirty seconds. Is this your usual approach with the girls?' I'm definitely buzzing now. Aaron is by far the most interesting person I've spoken to in just about forever. Not to mention the best-looking …

We listen to the music for a little while, staring out to where the sea is a deep green-grey, the waves near the shore white-tipped. 'Starman' finishes, and 'Life on Mars' begins. I sigh. 'I still can't believe he died.'

Aaron nods. 'Yeah, Bowie was a proper original. He said this thing once, about how he was only the person the greatest number of people believed him to be. It always makes me wonder whether that's true.'

There's a pause as I turn the quote over in my mind. 'Hmm. I guess it's like you have to be one way at school, right? And with your parents or whatever. But then when you're with other people …' I trail off, not sure where I'm going with this.

But Aaron leans forward and nods, his hair sticking up in the wind. 'I know, right? It's like, who can you be the real you with?'

I feel out of sync suddenly, like the easy banter we've had up until now has just been replaced with something else altogether.

'Sounds a bit dramatic,' I say in the end, on a light laugh.

For a moment I think Aaron seems disappointed, but before I can decide, another song comes on. I whip my head towards him. 'You like The Greenwoods?'

He holds my eyes. 'Love them. I mean, "Dark Sun Sky" is basically a perfect song, isn't it?'

Wow.

Wow wow wow.

'Yes!' I can't help myself; it's one of my favourites too. I can't believe it. 'You like country?' I say.

'Sure. I mean, maybe not so much the older stuff – I can take or leave trucks and whiskey, but Kacey Musgraves or Blake Shelton ... what?'

I must be really staring at him. I cough, embarrassed. 'Sorry, it's just you must be the first person I've ever met in real life who likes country music.'

He smiles. 'Well what's not to like? It's all about being real, isn't it? Real stories, you know?'

'Yes.' And I do know. How a good country song can crack open your heart, tell you a story that's totally true. I can't believe he gets it.

He really gets it.

We listen in silence. On the second chorus I feel his

43

fingers covering mine and it's like the music is running through our linked hands, pulling us together.

He doesn't let go until there's a flare and sizzle from the barbecue, and then he leaps back up to flip the burgers over. I've got to admit, they smell pretty amazing, especially with the sea air sharpening my appetite. My stomach growls.

'Oh my God, are they done yet?' I call.

'Nearly.' That smile again. It sets off something in me, this shivery, swooping feeling. I've never felt this with any boy before.

Finally Aaron comes over with plates loaded up with burgers in buns, salad, crisps. He's even brought napkins. We spread it all out in front of us, Aaron jumping up to grab a bottle of something fizzing and sparkly. He balances two plastic glasses on top of the mini-coolbox and pours, then hands one to me.

As I take it, his fingertips overlap mine, and now the electric feeling intensifies, runs up my arm. He taps his glass against the one in my hand. 'To the girl with the beautiful songs,' he says.

His voice is light, that half-smile on his face again, but I'm sure I'm not imagining the tiny pause between 'beautiful' and 'songs'. I take a sip of the drink, which turns out to be some sort of fizzy flavoured water, feeling the bubbles on my tongue. I gesture to the picnic, the blanket. 'This is amazing, by the way. Thank you.'

His eyes are saying he wanted to impress me, and I get a surge then, confident and happy, a taste of something completely new that chases the bubbles right down to my stomach.

44

It lasts for about five seconds, enough time to take a bite of burger and realise that it is raw in the middle and sand has worked its way into the bun. I grab the nearest napkin and spit it out. 'Uhhh …' I begin, but a second later, Aaron does the same too, though he just gobs his straight on to the sand.

'Crap,' he says. Then he does a sort of shrug, giving me those eyes that remind me suddenly of Moonshine the dog. 'Guess they needed a bit longer.'

I start laughing again and he joins in. 'And I thought I had everything covered,' he says.

'Shame,' I say, trying to keep my face straight, but I'm overcome by the total ridiculousness of the situation.

We're being buffeted by the wind, sand whipping across the plates. The barbecue is smoking hard in our direction, making my eyes sting. And what sun there was has totally gone in. It makes me laugh more. And now we're both helpless, Aaron practically rolling on the rug.

'Sorry … but this was … kind of …' I get out.

'A crap date?' Aaron says.

'Actually, no. Ten points for effort,' I say.

'Well, that's something.'

'It is.' And suddenly I'm not smiling any more. Because it's properly hit me how much thought he's put into this, all for a girl he's just met.

'I had visions of us having this amazing meal, candles … maybe a walk along the shoreline at sunset …' Aaron says, and there's just enough cockiness about him as he says it for me to laugh again.

'Well, it's fair to say you arsed that one up then,' I say, but

I'm touched, truth be told. I reckon Aaron knows it too, because his embarrassed look has now completely disappeared.

All of a sudden, I want him to kiss me. I know it's only a first date, but who cares?

I lean forward. He's moving towards me and my vision narrows right down to his lips. I can practically feel them on mine.

He reaches forward and brushes my hair back with one hand.

I start to close my eyes …

Then he lets go and pulls away.

I open my eyes, see he's already getting up, packing everything away. I take a few breaths, trying to steady myself. The wind is still as strong as ever. I hook my hair behind my ears; I'm going to have a hell of a time brushing it out later because the wind has heaped it into one tangled mess. Which kind of goes for my feelings too. Why didn't he kiss me? I really thought he was about to. I'm not about to show I'm disappointed though, so I jump up and help him pack away.

When we're done, Aaron hoists the rucksack on his shoulders and then reaches his hand out for mine slowly, like he's not quite sure I'll hold his back. I take it, feeling that shock of his warm fingers again, and suddenly I'm glad we haven't kissed yet. I reckon he's shy, despite the apparent confidence, and it's cute.

We stop right at the edge of the beach, Aaron turning back to take one last look at the waves. The sun's dipping down low, so there's the faintest hint of pink in the sky.

'See, we kind of got the sunset,' I say with a smile.

'Next time we come here, we will,' Aaron says.

'Huh. Someone's sure there will be a next time.'

He tightens his hand around mine. 'There will be. This place is special. And so ...' He breaks off and runs his free hand through his hair.

Are you. I know that's what he was about to say. Then Aaron's gaze shifts from mine to where a circling seagull has swooped on to the remains of the burger he left on the sand.

'Well at least someone appreciates my efforts,' Aaron says with a grin, and the moment passes again.

Still, I can't help the huge beam breaking out on my face as we start up the cliff path together.

Chapter Six

Aaron

'Oi, Weaver.'

That accent on the end of my name, a staccato 'Ah' sound, almost makes me fumble a step. I turn, car keys jangling in my hand. It's only Jonathan aka 'Jonny' Taylor, lengthening his strides to reach me across the college car park. I wait, casually waving my fob to lock the car doors as Jonny gets to me. He gives me and the car an appraising look.

'This year's plates? Nice. Got some guts, that has.'

I give a nod of acknowledgment, but don't say anything. I've only known him a couple of weeks, but I'm pretty sure Jonny knows not-a-lot about cars. He falls into step beside me as we make for the refectory. At the entrance, he turns to me and says, 'So you took out Gemma Belfine?'

I stop. Jesus, guess that's what they mean when they say small town. There's something in Jonny's tone I know well. For a split second I'm back to two-years-ago Aaron. The Aaron who'd jump when his name got hurled at him the way Jonny just did. Two-years-ago Aaron would've scurried away with his head hanging.

But that was then, in the days before I slimmed down and started lifting, made some money designing apps. Before I met Cherine. I'm not that guy any more.

I grin. 'Yeah,' I say, and there's enough meaning packed into that word for Jonny to snigger and say, 'She is definitely *fine* …', which I decide to ignore.

We go into the refectory and I spot her straight away, sitting at a table surrounded by her mates. I recognise some of them from the stuff she's already told me. Esi's easy to spot; small seaside towns aren't oversupplied with racial diversity. The lanky one must be Cal. He leans in to say something to Gem and she throws her head back and laughs.

Jonny's saying something else, but my eyes keep sliding back to where Gem's sitting. She spots me and waves, giving that whole-room smile, but she doesn't come over. It's been two days since our date and we've texted tons, but at college she's always busy with her friends. I think back to all the forums two-years-ago Aaron studied, the whole PUA routine. To Cherine, and the word 'clingy'. I've got to wait for her to come to me.

The beach was a bad idea, the old Aaron frets. I shut the voice down; give another casual glance over to where Gem's sitting.

'Weave's got it bad.' Jonny's voice cuts across my thoughts.

'Piss off,' I say, though I try and make it good-humoured, laughing along when what I actually want to do is introduce his teeth to the back of his throat.

I turn to the football table and flick a pound coin up in the air, then catch it again. 'Who's playing?' I plant my feet square. Jonny takes his place on the other side of the table and Selina leans up against the far end to watch. For a few minutes, my whole attention's taken up with how much I'm trying to win, and how hard I'm trying not to show it. He gets the first point, but it's only to lull him into a false sense of security; I beat him easily. I smash the last ball past his poorly defended goal amid cheers and whoops.

'And *that* is the sweet sound of you getting your ass handed to you.' Selina smirks at Jonny, before stretching her arms up over her blonde head and smiling at me expectantly. But I've spotted a movement out of the corner of my eye.

Gem's leaving with that Cal guy.

I make a show of swiping the pound off the side of the table with a flourish, then say, 'Got to get to the library. See you later.'

Gem has Music first lesson; I got hold of her timetable yesterday. As soon as I'm out of the refectory I do a U-turn and speed up. If I time it right, I'll catch her before she goes in.

Chapter Seven

Gemma

'So I've got an idea,' Cal says as we walk up to Music. 'You know the songwriting competition?'

I give him a look. 'I do.'

'And how you still haven't decided what song to enter?'

I sigh. 'Thanks for reminding me …'

It's not that I don't want to do it. I'm desperate to. But it has to be the perfect song and so far, none of my solo songs seem quite right.

'Well, what about a duet? I could enter with you? Just as a vocalist, I mean. It'd be your song, your entry. But I could come to the audition with you.'

I stare at him, then start to nod slowly. That could work. More than work. 'Sea Dreams' feels like the best thing I've written and it's really meant for two voices, not one.

'That would be amazing. But are you sure? You won't be too busy?' Cal has his own music too, plus, since his dad moved out, his mum's been really depressed. She's always wanting him home, so these days he doesn't come out much, otherwise I would've asked him before.

'I want to do this. I want to help.'

'Then yes! Thank you.' I give him a quick hug. 'You are officially the best.'

'I know.' He smiles. 'Let's start the application at lunch.'

'Definitely. That'll be—'

I break off, because I've suddenly spotted Aaron saunter-ing towards us. I feel my heart do this massive jump in my chest; I practically grab hold of Cal again, but stop myself at the last minute. He's finally come over. Well, all right then, 'finally' might be a bit melodramatic, but we've been texting for two days and he's not even asked me out again so I've been starting to wonder if the date was a bust after all, if that non-kiss meant he'd changed his mind. Which obviously would be his loss, but still …

I remind myself I'm Confident Gemma. I do not go around losing my shizzle over a boy, even one with Aaron levels of hotness and a love of country music. Except, as soon as he smiles, I'm all swooping electricity again and I can't help the hand that flies to my hair. Cal rolls his eyes, nods to Aaron, who nods back in that way guys do, and ducks into the classroom.

I push my hair back and take another step towards Aaron. Then I do a slow smile I may have practised once or twice in the mirror.

'Aren't you late for lessons?' I say.

He shrugs, one side of his mouth twisting up, eyes warm. He smells so good. 'So, what are you doing at lunch?' he says.

I'm about to say, 'Nothing,' then remember I just told Cal I'd do the application with him. I open my mouth, but Aaron gets in first.

'Come for a drive with me.'

I start to answer, but just then Mr Higgins pokes his curly head out of the door. 'Are you joining us today?'

'Uh, yeah, sorry,' I say. Irritatingly, I'm flushing as I turn back to Aaron, all my fake casualness stripped away.

Aaron smiles, then says, 'See you outside the entrance at one,' and before I can confirm or not, he's walking away, hands in his pockets.

As the lesson finishes and we pack up our stuff, I say to Cal, 'Can we rain-check on the application? Just until tomorrow.'

'This doesn't have anything to do with a certain Mr Cheekbones, does it?'

'Well …' I say.

'Go on then. But, you know, try to play it cool.'

I give his shoulder a push, possibly a bit harder than I intended and he lets out an '*Ow!*'

'Oops,' I say in a sorry-not-sorry voice. Then I leg it to the toilets to sort my make-up out before I meet Aaron.

He drives fast, taking the bends with his palm flat against the wheel. We're heading out towards the sea again, mainly because it's about the only place to go around here, but also I can't help thinking it might have something to do with the almost-kiss at the beach the other day. We put the windows down and blast out The Greenwoods. The wind whipping my hair around my face gives me this wild, exhilarating feeling. I start singing along as the next song comes on. When we park up near a cliff path a few miles down from my house, I carry on singing even after Aaron has turned the engine off and the music's cut out.

53

He listens, that half-smile on his face until I finish. 'Your voice is even better in person,' he says, and it's so sincere I know it's not a line.

'I think it's the thing that makes me feel the most alive, you know?' I say.

Aaron nods. 'I can see it on your face.'

And I'm so grateful for the serious way he looks at me, how he gets it.

Gets me.

'Come on,' he says.

As soon as we're walking, he takes my hand and it feels totally natural; safe and warm. The long grasses to one side make a whispering noise, like a counterpart to the sea's song. We amble up to the peak and sit on a clifftop bench looking out at the light glancing off the waves in tiny sparkles.

'So you're definitely going to apply?' Aaron says. I might have been going on about the songwriting competition a bit in the car on the way up.

'Yeah, me and Cal. He's got a great voice.'

Aaron watches the smudged speck of a boat against the horizon. He's still holding on to my hand. 'How long have you known him?'

'Cal? Pretty much forever. Most of us have known each other forever, around here.'

'I like that. People were always coming and going in London. I always wondered what it's like, to feel the ground under your feet and know it's not going to shift.'

I look into Aaron's thoughtful eyes. They're a light hazel colour, with flecks of green. Gorgeous eyes. I totally need to get a grip. I remember how he told me his parents split up and I think I can see the shadow of old pain in his expression. I think about Cal's mum, how he told us he comes home to find her crying. But before I can think what to say, Aaron's hand has tightened on mine, and he's turning in towards me and this time I don't have any doubts what's going to happen.

His kiss is light, gentle. One hand goes up to the side of my face, and then after a few moments, his other hand moves from mine to slide around my back, pulling me in closer to him. He kisses me harder, his fingers at the back of my head now, drawing me into him and holding me there.

I'm dimly aware of the rushing of the waves breaking on rocks below. Of the wind surrounding us, the gentle September sun overhead. Every part of me feels like it's exploding with energy as he draws me even closer, so that one of my legs overlaps his thigh.

Then, just as one of his hands is sliding from my waist towards my chest, I pull back, breathless and smiling. For a second I see that same flash on his face – some old hurt, or uncertainty – then he says quietly, 'God, you're beautiful,' in a way that makes my heart sing. He gives this smile that mirrors my own, before interlacing his fingers with mine again.

We chat about nothing much, watching the waves together, and it feels so comfortable, so right. Like I've known him for years. He tells me about his dad's girlfriend, Jaquie-with-a-'q' and inexplicably no 'c'. 'I call her C-minus Jack,' he says and I start to laugh.

'To her face?'

'In front of my dad? Not if I still want to be alive on my

nineteenth birthday,' Aaron says, and I can definitely read the hurt under his words this time. I get that surge of knowing that comes when you're tuned in to someone, like that feeling when you hit the right note. I give his hand a squeeze and he runs his thumb lightly across the back of my knuckles.

I think suddenly how you could write a whole song telling the story of one hand touching another.

A little while later, my phone goes with a text. It's Esi.

Where are you?

I spot the time on the text and shriek. 'Oh crap!' I wave my phone under Aaron's nose, and he does a double take, then follows it up with his Aaron smile.

'Oops,' he says.

'I'm going to be so late for Psychology,' I say, pulling a face.

'Sack it off. Stay here with me.'

I've already started to stand, but Aaron's still got hold of my hand. I give it a playful tug and for a moment he holds on, then I say, 'No, seriously,' and his expression changes as he realises I'm worried. He leaps to his feet suddenly, pulling me up, and puts on that mock costume-drama voice, like he's Mr Darcy or something.

'I will get you there, fair lady, but we must make haste.'

'You're a doughnut,' I say, but the next moment he's taken off running, hauling me with him, laughing and shrieking as we fly back towards the car.

He's so fast, it feels like my feet barely touch the floor.

★

It's fair to say that after I finally rock up at Psychology only ten minutes late, due to some driving from Aaron that in other circumstances might have been just the teensiest bit questionable – he definitely shouldn't have overtaken on that blind bend – I still have trouble concentrating, because every time I blink, I can feel Aaron's mouth against mine, the way he gathered me up so close to his body I could feel the muscles of his chest.

The way I wanted to see them, and more …

I try and snap myself out of it, but I'm glad when the bell goes. I hurry to get my things together but I'm not fast enough to avoid the disapproving eyebrows of Ms Hines, my Psychology tutor.

'I'm sorry I was late,' I say again.

She purses her lips. 'From what I've seen of you, you've got ability, but there's no point in being here if you don't want to commit, and that means arriving on time,' she says.

I bristle at this. Seriously. I was ten minutes late, once. But I give another apologetic look and tell her it won't happen again.

'So what were you actually doing?' Esi's waiting in the corridor for me.

'Not what: who,' I say, and start to smile, before realising the implications of that sentence. 'Er, I mean, I went for a drive with Aaron. Lost track of time.'

Esi has her eyebrows up near her hairline while she waits for details.

'… and we kissed!' I say. It bursts out of me. Esi opens her mouth to say something, but Rachael's voice cuts across us.

'Who kissed? What have you been up to? Ohmigod, you kissed Aaron Weaver? He's so fit.' She gives a 'You're-so-lucky' kind of sigh. And the next moment we're all piling along the corridor towards the exit, as I give Rachael all the details. Twice.

Chapter Eight

Gemma

'You ready yet?' Esi's tapping her foot in the entrance to my room; I think Michael let her in. It's Saturday night and we're going to this party Rachael's been talking about all week. Esi's still wearing the same jeans she had on at the cafe earlier, though she's swapped out her top for a deep red one with three-quarter-length sleeves and a few bracelets on each wrist. Her twists are piled up on top of her head, held in place with a fabric hairband that totally goes with her top. How does Esi manage to create a look that's effortlessly awesome in five minutes? While I've been getting ready for, ooh, about two hours now, if you count shower time?

It was touch-and-go if I was even coming to the party tonight; I was kind of holding back in case Aaron had plans, but he already had some drinks night on the go with Jonny and co.

'I'd rather spend it with you,' Aaron said on the phone last night.

'It's fine, I don't mind,' I said, Cal's joke about playing it cool sounding in my head. Plus, Rachael would probably kill me if I ran off with some guy, even an Aaron-shaped guy, and missed the first big party of college.

'Come on, or Mum's not going to take us,' Esi says. Esi's mum, Baaba, said she'd give us a lift which is just as well because Dad and Michael are already settled in front of a UEFA Nations League match – Denmark v. someone-or-other – before switching over to *MOTD*, and Mum doesn't like driving after dark. I give myself a last once-over in the mirror, decide that'll have to do, and follow Esi downstairs.

Her mum's already waiting in the lane, engine running. She greets us with a smile as we pile in.

'That's nice,' she says, nodding at my new cross-body bag. That's the thing about Esi's mum; she always has something lovely to say and she notices stuff.

'Thanks,' I say.

The drive only takes twenty minutes and then Baaba is pulling up outside a terraced house not far from the town centre. 'I'll be back at ten,' she says, and leans over to give first Esi, then me, a kiss on the cheek. 'Remember—'

'I know, Mum,' Esi interrupts, but gently, for her. Esi's parents don't mind her going to parties, but only if she's with someone they trust – like me, more fool them – and as long as she definitely doesn't drink. We thank her and pile out towards the noise of bass pouring from an open window into the street. It sets off something low and buzzy in me. There's not much point knocking, so I hitch my bag up higher on my shoulder and we go in.

Through the open door at the end of a short hallway I see a few people gathered in the kitchen, drinks in hand,

and to my left another handful scattered around the living room. Rachael's perched on the arm of a sofa chatting to Beth and Phoebe. Esi goes over to say hi, but I give them a quick wave, mime drinking and wander into the kitchen to see what's on offer. I've brought a big bottle of cider, because I'm cheap like that, but if there's anything better going I'll have it: In the kitchen people are gathered around a big bowl of sludge-coloured liquid. One of the lads, whose name I don't catch, hands a cup of it to me, his eyes only straying upwards from my boobs for a nanosecond. I take a small sip, then nearly gag. It tastes like six different spirits all at once, including Baileys and MD 20/20, which believe me is not a combination you ever want to try. It's as though we're still nicking drinks from the backs of our parents' cupboards – or drinks cabinet, in the case of Rach, who lives in a big four-bed detached house in the best bit of town, unlike our ramshackle cliff houses.

I'm too slow to stop someone grabbing the cider and pouring that into the mix, so I take my rank drink and wander off.

In the living room Rachael's eyeing me from under her heavy fringe.

'Hey,' I say. 'Have you tried this stuff?'

'I'm not insane.' She makes an airy motion to a bottle at her feet. 'I brought my own, anyway. Here, chuck that and have some of mine.' She fills up her cup, takes a swig from it and offers the other side to me.

It's fifty-fifty vodka and Coke. I feel it catch the back of my throat as it goes down and give a small cough. When I hand the cup back to Rachael she's grinning.

'Like the old days,' she says.

I know what she means. We both had our first taste of alcohol at sleepovers.

The music's been cranked way up, a blur of beats. A couple of people are attempting to dance, badly. Robbie Wellings is, astonishingly, getting off with a girl on one settee. I can't really see what she's like because he's basically attempting to swallow her whole, while his mates look on and give the odd whoop, which is about as close to any action as they'll ever see unless things have seriously changed since school. The girl doesn't seem to care.

Rachael offers me another sip of the vodka and I take it, chasing that buzz you usually get from parties. The free feeling of alcohol and music and possibility. But it isn't until my phone goes in my pocket with a text from Aaron that I really perk up.

Having a good night? x
Just getting started! G x

I swig back more vodka, listening as Esi and Beth start a debate about which is the better film: *Wonder Woman* or *Black Panther*. I'm tempted to throw *A Star is Born* into the mix, just to provoke Esi, but realise I can't be bothered. I tap my foot along to the music and think about Aaron instead. A couple of people stumble past and from where I'm sitting I've got a straight view of someone vomming on the front doorstep. I look at Rachael and see the same disappointment mirrored in her eyes.

It's not like the party's terrible. It's just a bit … more of the same as school, I guess. Not sure what I was expecting from my first college party, but I don't think it was this. I'm

62

seriously thinking about asking Esi what the odds are her mum will come and get us early, when Rachael suddenly says in my ear, 'Well this is a pile of wank. Want to come to Fimo's?'

Fimo's is a bar in town, about the only one in a fifty-mile radius that stays open until 2 a.m.

I glance at a girl who looks like she's well on her way through the cycle of get drunk, throw up, cry about some boy who probably doesn't deserve it, then pass out before waking up with serious regret. Robbie Wellings is now shouting something about playing Spin the Bottle.

I shout over to the others. 'What do you reckon? Fancy going to Fimo's?' Esi's deep in conversation with Beth and frowns slightly before turning to me.

'Seriously? That'd be a no.' She laughs. Her parents might be fine with her going to parties, but they are not going to be down with her sneaking into a club underage.

Nor, when I come to think of it, are mine.

But I'm nearly seventeen now. And I'm in college. With – maybe, possibly – a serious potential-boyfriend-shaped guy on the horizon. Who is used to clubs in London and all sorts of cool stuff. Isn't it about time I lived a little?

'I want to go!' I say.

'And how're you getting home?' Esi says. She sounds just like her mum.

'We'll get a taxi,' Rachael shouts, waving a couple of twenty-pound notes under Esi's nose.

'And I'm telling Mum what, exactly?' Esi says.

I think for a moment. 'That I'm staying at Rachael's?'

Esi raises her eyes to the ceiling for a moment, then looks at me. 'Fine.' She grins. 'Don't do anything I wouldn't do.'

It's a well-worn routine with us. I think it started when we were about ten. Esi was always ten-going-on-fifty anyway, and she'd pick up all these grown-up expressions. This one stuck, probably because I'm basically always doing stuff she wouldn't. I smile back and say what I always do.

'As if I would.'

Aaron

The bar's tight-packed, close with twenty- and thirty-somethings sporting haircuts at least five years behind the ones back home. Jonny's got in pitchers and has made up a game with arbitrary rules so that every five seconds someone else is downing a pint to chants of '*Chug* it!' When it's my turn, I slug mine down in less than five seconds, enjoying the whoops from the lads.

'Christ, Weaver, you got that down your neck fast enough.' It's Binners – real name Mark Binney – hollering from his spot to my left. His voice is nasal and admiring, his eyes foggy with alcohol. I give him a shrug and a cocky smile, then throw back another pint for good measure.

As I thud the triumphant glass down on the table, Binners shakes his head, grinning. 'Dayum,' he says, in a crap imitation of someone, anyone, with more cool than him. I feel myself bristling and realise why he bugs me: that need to please, his overeagerness. That used to be me.

'So, have you shagged her yet?' Jonny's voice intrudes on my thoughts. It takes a moment to work out he's talking to me. For a split second I don't know how to react, then I laugh. 'Eff off, Jonny boy.'

Jonny gives a derisive sniff. 'That'd be a no, then,' he says, to loud laughs from everyone, including Mark Judas Binners.

'Would you really want to go there though mate, that's the question,' Binners says, weaselling in Jonny's direction now.

'What's that supposed to mean?' My voice comes out sharp, which gets me a round of *Ooohs*, their voices lilting up and down.

Jonny leans forward, pint in hand. 'Just, you don't know where's she's been, if you catch my drift.' He looks around the table.

Binney yells, 'More like who she's been under,' at which Jonny grimaces, as though he's suddenly developed delicate sensibilities. 'Callum Smith, most likely,' Binney adds, to more shouts of laughter.

I sit back, smiling like I don't give one, but inside, my stomach's knotted hard as I try to work out if it's true. Jonny mouths off about pretty much every girl he sees: to him they're all sluts, bitches, or worse. Right now, he's pulling a face and miming the word 'gay' in Binney's direction.

'Just cos the only action you'll ever see is this, Binney,' Jonny says, pumping his hand up and down. Everyone howls as Binney goes red. I sense he's about to ignite. Jonny does too, but instead of backing off, he starts humming a song under his breath.

'Shut up!' Binney says, voice streaked with desperation.

I look from one laughing face to another. Clearly the song means something, but I'm not about to ask. Binney's mouth wobbles so I pour the last of the pitcher into his glass and shove it at him, which everyone seems to take as their cue to move on.

Then Jonny looks at me. 'Don't listen to the Binster. She's all right, that Gemma.' And for a moment he seems to be offering me that rare thing in this sort of circumstance – an olive branch, or at least a sliver of one.

'I wasn't,' I say briefly, then raising my voice, 'Same again?'

There's a general cheer of agreement at this and I take myself to the bar. While I wait to be served I think about what I'm even doing here. Why this group, why now? Why this town? The last one's easy enough: I had to get out of London, and living with Dad, who's not going to win any hands-on father medals any time soon, means I get plenty of space. But getting in with this crowd doesn't have to be top of my to-do list. I don't even like them half the time. So why am I here?

The answer comes at the same time as three new pitchers of lager: because I can be. Unlike the old Aaron, I can make these guys like me or, more importantly, respect me. A big part of me needs that, after everything that happened in London. To prove it hasn't turned me into the old Aaron again, friendless and pathetic. Besides, the alternative is sitting in an empty flat that's not my home, thinking – and Christ only knows, I've had enough of that.

As I hand over a note, my phone goes. For one wild moment, I'm expecting it to be her.

Cherine.

It's the lager that does this: lowers the barriers I've scaffolded around myself, puts me back into the old habit of checking, waiting, checking. Where is she? What's she doing? Is she thinking about me? Thoughts I'd never let anyone in on.

Then I realise the image of Cherine's long hair, her dark eyelashes, that turned-up top lip, are morphing somehow, being overlaid with another girl's smile. Gem.

Because Gem isn't like Cherine. She's worth ten of Cherine. I know it.

I take two pitchers to the table, go back for the third. But before I grab it, I look at my phone. I scroll back through the last few messages from Gem, full of smiley faces and emojis, and suddenly I want to speak to her. I wonder how she's getting on at that party and who else is there. Like Callum Smith, just for example. I replay what Binners said about him. Then I notice a status update on her Facebook: she's checked in to a bar called Fimo's. I click on the website. It looks like a dive. Why would she go there?

I push my phone down deep into my pocket and take the other pitcher back to the table, ignoring Jonny's needling about how long it took. But as the next round begins, I can't help taking my phone out again, wondering.

Ten minutes later, I've made up my mind.

Gemma

In the taxi things start to look up. We drink more of the vodka and I introduce my new favourite topic: Aaron. 'He runs his own business,' I say, and I can't deny there's just the teensiest hint of bragging in my voice.

67

'Doing what?' Rachael says.

'He makes apps. How cool is that? And he says he's getting his own flat soon.'

To be fair, he only mentioned getting his own flat as a vague aspiration the other day by the beach, but it's worth it because she gives an impressed nod and hands me the bottle of drink. 'I wish I—'

'Did I tell you he likes country too? And he's an amazing kisser.' I can't help talking over her. Maybe it's the alcohol.

Rachael puts her head on one side. 'All right, stop before I chuck you out, you lucky cow.'

A little while later we spill out of the taxi at the bottom end of town and drunk-walk under the Christmas lights already strung between discount shops. Fimo's might not be a London club, but everyone knows they never ask for ID. We duck in out of the cold and push our way through to the bar. All the side tables are full, music pumping out from the glass-topped DJ booth at one end of the dance floor. Rachael manages to shimmy into a narrow gap as someone turns from the bar, leaving me stranded three people back. She flashes a winning smile at the guy she's just queue jumped. I watch as he makes a gesture to his mates, his hands squeezing thin air just behind her butt and they all laugh. Rachael shouts her order to the girl behind the bar all oblivious, but I see him cop a handful on the way back through. She turns, but faced with six of them all laughing, simply shrugs and pushes on back to me. We exchange eye rolls.

'You're getting the next lot,' she yells in my ear.

We find a pocket of space on the edge of the dance floor.

It's too loud to talk much in here, and anyway, Rachael seems more intent on scanning the crowd. Her eyes come to rest on a boy not much older than us. He's dancing with what I guess you'd call more enthusiasm than skill, but when he meets her eyes she juts her chin up. He starts snaking towards us and a moment later, she's thrust her drink in my hand and soon she's dancing up close with him, his arms around her waist, their crotches brushing together in this tragic way. I finish my drink, then start on hers while I run through my options. I watch drunk faces under the lights, trying to pretend I'm not starting to stress. After three more songs watching Rachael and the boy kissing in the purplish light, I grab her arm and yell, 'Toilet break?' in her ear. I have to yell another two times, but she finally follows me into the Ladies.

I sit down more heavily than I meant to on the toilet and when I come out, the floor seems to be coming up to meet my feet faster than it usually does. Rachael's putting more lipstick on.

'He's hot?' She says it like a question.

I turn my 'Meh' into an '*Mmm*'. Then add, 'What's his name?'

'Who cares? Look, you don't have to hang around. I'll probably go home with him anyway,' Rachael says airily, but there's a flicker of doubt chasing her eyeliner as she touches up her eyes.

I consider telling her this is a monumentally bad idea. I know before I've even opened my mouth she's not going to listen. 'Rach, maybe grab a taxi home with me? You don't know anything about him, you—'

She zips up her bag and marches out. I follow, hoping he's lost interest, but nope, he's taken the opportunity to get shots in. She takes the two he's offering her and drinks them one after another. Then, with a sinking feeling, I realise the guy's not alone. Looks like he's with the gropey boys from the bar.

'Awesome,' I mutter to myself. Because Rachael might be a pain in the arse when she's drinking, but I'm not going to leave her here to do who knows what. Or have who knows what done to her, seeing as she's now dancing right in the middle of the group and one of the other lads has come up behind her and is pretty much trying to dry-hump her.

Before I can do anything, Rachael turns, her face flushed, and shoves him away. Dry Hump Guy staggers a step back, then as I move forward, figuring now would be a good time to drag her away, he starts spitting swear words at her. I catch the word 'slut' more from the shape his mouth is making. Oh, actually, make that 'sluts' as he seems to be including me. Rachael's shouting back, while I've got hold of one of her arms, trying to pull her away. The rest of the guys are either looking hostile or laughing. I glance around. No one seems to care. I feel the first flickers of panic. Rachael's still shouting at the guy, one of her boobs danger-ously close to escaping from her top as she pulls against my arm. Then, just as I see a bouncer ploughing a path through the crowd towards us, an arm inserts itself between Rachael and gropey boy. It happens so fast; one minute he's yelling the C-word at us, the next he's on the ground, looking as surprised as we are to find himself there.

I whip my head around to see who our rescuer is, and my legs nearly go from under me.

It's Aaron, standing over the gropey guy like some avenging hero from a movie.

Oh. My. *God*.

Rachael yells for us to stop the taxi twice so she can heave at the side of the road. I hold her hair, keeping my face turned from the sick smell. After the second time, Aaron has to sweet-talk the driver into not kicking us out to walk the rest of the way. He doesn't say much, apart from asking Rachael her address, which I have to give while she leans on my shoulder, face pale, emitting wafts of sick-scented vodka breath as she groans. I sneak a look at Aaron every so often, but his expression is so serious and closed I soon give up trying to make conversation.

When we get to Rachael's house, Aaron helps me extract her from the back of the taxi and I use her key to open her front door. 'I'll take her up if you could wait?' I whisper. He gives a short nod and gets back in the taxi while I drag her inside and try to sneak her upstairs. We're met at the top by her mum wearing a satiny dressing gown and a less than ecstatic expression.

'Uh … hi, Mrs …' I've totally forgotten Rachael's surname under her mum's steely gaze.

'Hello, Gemma. I'll take her. Thank you for bringing her home,' she says in a quiet voice that manages to pack way more of a punch than shouting would. She takes Rachael's arm and gives her a look that contains exasperation, worry and a smidge of disgust as Rachael blasts her with her puke breath. 'Stop fussing! I'm fiiiine,' Rachael wails.

She completely isn't; her dad's also emerging from a bedroom, and I suspect from the way her parents are now exchanging looks that Rachael's in reasonably deep shit. Time for me to scarper before they call my parents too.

Back in the taxi, Aaron gives the driver my address. As we pull off, I turn to him. 'Sorry about all that. Rachael can get a bit … Thanks for rescuing us. It was lucky you were there.'

'I just want to make sure you're OK.' He says it gently, but there's a look in his eyes I'm not sure how to read. Is he worried? Annoyed? Can't tell.

'I'm fine.' I twist in my seat to face him. 'Seriously. I was handling it. But I was glad of the backup.'

'You should be more careful …' Aaron begins, but we're pulling up outside my house. Aaron leans over me to open the taxi door. He smells amazing. I, on the other hand, probably reek. 'Somewhere like Fimo's isn't the place for you. You're better than that,' he says and there's that smile, like driving out of a heavy rain shower into bright light. It totally works. He calls softly after me, 'I'll wait to make sure you get in safely.'

I attempt a normal walk up the path, but I'm not entirely sure I manage a straight line. Still, it only takes one attempt to get my key in. I turn and wave, a big smile plastered on my face, before I shut the door.

Well, that could've gone worse.

I *could* choose to see Aaron having to rescue us as deeply humiliating, but as I gulp down a glass of water then go for a wee, my brain's furiously putting a positive spin on things.

72

It was sweet of him to intervene and his mini-lecture in the taxi was only because we'd worried him. We probably cut his night short too; he must've had to ditch Jonny and the college dudebros. I wonder how I missed them in Fimo's. Maybe they'd only just arrived … Hang on – *what the hell is that?*

I've just caught sight of myself in the mirror and it is not pretty. My make-up is a disaster, hair not much better. The concealer's come off all my spots and there's a big stain of something down my top. I have no idea how it got there. Plus, there's a definite waft of sick lingering around me and I don't think it's just smell hangover either. I reckon Rachael's splashed my shoes. And if my bloodshot eyes and eerie pallor are anything to go by, there's every chance I might be puking too in the not too distant future.

I look the exact opposite of hot.

Aaron's never going to want to see me again.

Chapter Nine

Gemma

It's fair to say hauling myself into the cafe the next morning is painful. But I've told Cal I'll meet him there to do the application. He never wants people over to his house, because his mum finds visitors hard to handle.

He's already waiting with an oversized chocolate milkshake at one of the tables when I get there and bounds to his feet when he sees me. 'Hi!'

I groan, and slump at the table, sunglasses still on.

'Fimo's was good last night then?' he says.

I give another moan in response, fold my arms on the table and rest my head sideways on them. I still have The Fear from last night. Why did I let Rachael get so drunk? And what must Aaron have been thinking when he had to ditch his mates to sort us out? We must have looked a right state.

'Coffee,' Cal says, and goes up to the counter. A few moments later, he slides a cup along the table, until it's resting a couple of millimetres from my nose.

'Thank you,' I say. I raise my head a few inches. 'I am

never drinking again. Why did I think Fimo's was a reason-able plan?'

'Don't give her any sympathy. Silly girl.' It's Dora, wield-ing a cloth, which she splats down on to the next table along and begins scrubbing at the coffee rings left by the last two customers.

I lift my head higher. 'What?' I say, trying to sound innocent.

'You think I don't know a hangover when I see one? Best thing for it is a good fry-up. I could do you one, if you like.'

This immediately conjures images of fried eggs glisten-ing with fat, and for a second I'm in serious danger of finally puking. It might be a relief at this stage. I give a weak 'No thanks' and an even weaker smile, and Dora clicks her tongue.

'Well, don't do it again. Oh, and I need someone to cover Sunday's shift next week, if you're interested?'

'Michael's got a home game.' I say. 'Esi might be able to come after church, but I guess she'd be a bit late. I can ask her anyway if you like?'

Dora nods, then gives me a pat on the shoulder that manages to be disapproving and comforting all at the same time, before disappearing back behind the counter.

Saying Esi's name has made me realise I haven't actually texted her since the one I sent very late last night. Or more accurately, in the early hours of this morning, updating her on the whole Aaron-rescuing-us thing and what a mess I looked. Her response wasn't massively reassuring – some-thing along the lines of **Who cares if he's that shallow?**

Rachael's text, when it finally came through at about ten, was better:

OMG I am sooo ill :(:(although A was AWESOME last night. Like something out of a film. xxx PS hope you are in as much trouble as I am.

I totally am not, because unlike Rachael, I am capable of sneaking in quietly. Plus, Mum and Dad were way too focused on getting Michael on the bus for his away match today to notice the state of me, thank God.

'Sooo, we doing this or what?' Cal says. I push my sunglasses on top of my head and take a proper look at him. He's so good-natured, not even giving it out to me for cancelling on him the other day and then disappearing last night.

'Oh God, I'm sorry. Yeah, come on.'

'Excellent.' He whips his laptop out of his rucksack. A moment later he's logged on to the cafe Wi-Fi and got up the application page. 'Right, here we go.'

I squint at the form. My head is thundering as loud as the music Dora has on; I'm not in the mood for 'Rhinestone Cowboy' today.

We go through the form, then I see we have to book an audition date.

'The Bristol one's in a couple of weeks. Do you think that'll give us time to rehearse?' Cal says.

My head hurts too bad to decide. 'Let's just go for it,' I say. *Aaron's probably going to ditch me.*

'OK!' His fingers fly over the keys. As I watch his details go in, then mine, my mood starts to pick up, and by the time we're ready to press Send I'm definitely feeling perkier.

'This is pretty exciting,' I say as Cal's hand hovers over the Return key.

'Do you want to do it or shall I?' he says with a grin.

'Together,' I say, putting my hand over his. 'On the count of three? One, two, three!' We press down and the box disappears. A second later an acknowledgement message appears on the screen and now I am really bouncing on my seat. 'Yessss!' I say.

Cal holds his hand up for a high five and I smack my palm against his. 'To the greatest country song ever written,' he says, and we're grinning at each other like little kids about to see Santa.

Which is the moment a voice from behind us says, 'Hey, Gem.'

Chapter Ten

Aaron

It's getting light by the time I get home. I can't stop running through everything in my head. What was she doing at Fimo's – why there? The same questions circling, refusing to land. I think I know the answer to the last one: she was looking out for that girl … I think for a minute. Rachael. She really is the sort of girl Jonny has a point about.

When it's obvious I'm not getting any more sleep even if I wanted to – the seagulls making their harsh-croaked racket on the roof say otherwise – I go downstairs. The flat has a damp, sticky feel that comes from its proximity to the sea, at a guess. I bet it's a bitch here in winter. No one's about except Moonshine, who greets me with a short whine, then sits, wagging her tail, waiting to be fed. I wonder how long she's been on her own for; there was no sign of Dad last night. I've got her trained up since I moved here, though; no more barking at me to get up. I fill her bowl, tell her to sit while I put it down. Her fur quivers as she catches the scent of food, but she knows now I'll whip it away if she doesn't wait nicely.

'Good girl, OK then,' I say after a minute, and she dives forward, burying her face in the bowl.

I look around the empty flat. It's not like I was expecting anyone to be in; Dad spends more or less all his time at Jaquie's and he's made it pretty clear he's not about to change just because his son's shown up on his doorstep. Suits me. I can do my own thing. What would we talk about anyway after all this time … other than the dog, which Dad's already admitted he only bought 'to pull' – disgusting thought, given he's the wrong side of forty. He can't even look after Moonshine properly, so it's tough to picture him cooking my eggs the way I like them and sitting at the table with me like Mum used to. What's he going to say? 'Sorry about legging it off with Tania and leaving you and your mum to it, mate'?

Love-of-his-life Tania who lasted about two months after he disappeared. C-minus Jack's the latest in a pretty long line.

I fix myself some of those pancakes that go in the toaster and check my bank account. I could afford a deposit on my own place now if I wanted to; I wasn't bullshitting Gem about it, even if I got the sense she couldn't tell whether or not I was. I could see it in that cute little furrow between her eyes she gets when she's puzzling stuff out. But why waste the cash if I'm not getting bothered here? I've got bigger plans than making a few grand online developing mobile gaming apps, unless one hits it big. I look at Moonshine. I could do a dog-training app. But I want more. I read that investing is where the real money gets made. The place the winners hang out. And if the last few months have

79

taught me anything, it's that you have to be a winner or there's no point even being here.

I take my pancakes to the breakfast bar and perch on a stool, imagining my name reading 'Aaron Weaver, CEO'. That cheers me up.

A shower later and I'm humming under my breath, thinking about Gem. I pull up one of her videos to listen to as I get dressed. I should meet up with her. I have a look at the app I downloaded on my phone once I'd dropped her off safely; I figured she could do with someone looking out for her after last night. All I needed to do was put in her number.

She's at the Beach Cafe. I think for a minute, then grab the lead and a moment later I'm walking an ecstatic Moonshine down towards the seafront.

I tie Moonshine outside and she lies down obediently, her face between her front paws. 'Good girl,' I say, then push open the door.

At once, my smile fades. She's sitting with ginger, lanky Cal, and as I walk towards them I see her hand on his. A minute later they're high-fiving and he's grinning into her face in a way that reminds me of the dog. For an instant, I'm back to Cherine laughing, Cherine gazing into that guy's eyes …

'Hey, Gem,' I say.

She lets out a shriek, one hand going up to her hair, and then she smiles in this totally different way to the one she was giving Cal.

See, nothing to worry about.

'Oh my God, Aaron! Hi!' She jumps up and comes over,

then goes in for a hug, starts to think better of it and smiles again instead, so I lean and pull her into me, smelling the fresh scent of her hair. My eyes meet Cal's briefly over the top of her head. 'It's so good to see you,' she says to my shoulder.

'How're you feeling? You look great,' I say.

Gem laughs. 'I look like hell, but points for saying otherwise. I just need to go to the Ladies – back in a sec.' She grabs her bag on the way, gives me another one of those beautiful smiles and disappears into the toilet at the back of the cafe.

I slide into the seat she's just vacated. 'Hi,' I say, and hold out my hand. 'It's Cal, isn't it?'

Cal's handshake is all kinds of limp-wristed. 'Hi,' he says.

'What have you two been up to?' I say, giving him a full-voltage smile, which seems to relax him.

'We've done our application for Gemma's song. We're going to audition.' He gestures to some kind of confirmation message on the screen.

I read it, then say, 'Bristol? I'll take you guys.'

'That's OK ...' Cal says, sounding uncomfortable.

'You drive?' I say, guessing he doesn't.

'No-o, but my brother—'

'I'll take you. It's no problem. I'd like to support Gem. She's really talented, she deserves to win.'

'Yeah, she's special,' Cal says.

Once, when I was a tubby, blushing loser, I got invited to a birthday party. Which for my mother was not far off the Second Coming: seven-year-old Aaron, like his fifteen-year-old counterpart, didn't get invited to many social

81

events. But this one was an all-class party, and though Jacob Mathis had set a precedent by holding a Laser Quest party for every boy in the class except me, even Tariq Khan couldn't leave me out of a whole-class affair. The invite duly went in my book bag, and my mother got my hair cut and bought a button-down shirt that scratched but was 'flattering – matches your eyes'. And hid the podge, though she didn't say that part.

There's a picture of me at that party next to the entertainer, who was somewhere between a clown and a crap magician. He'd picked me out of the crowd to help him with a magic trick; some lame thing with a pack of cards. And I'm standing there holding an ace with an expression that's a magic trick in itself: cover the eyes and you see my mouth, beaming, the curve of those hamster cheeks, but slide your hand down and my eyes are wary and alert, like I knew I was about to get rumbled for something.

Cal has an air about him like that boy in the picture as I look at him. He reddens and says, 'I mean, she's got this amazing talent when it comes to writing songs. Unique, you know?'

I'm still holding his gaze, searching. 'I know it,' I say, and it's clear we both understand that I know how Cal feels about Gem.

Just then she reappears. She's clearly been doing her make-up and she looks stunning, not that she didn't before, but it's amazing what girls can do with the right amount: not too much, but enough to bring out her lips.

I stand before she gets the chance to sit back down. 'Moonshine's outside. Fancy taking her for a run on the beach?'

'Sure!' She smiles, all sunshine, last night forgotten.

And so is Cal. She turns and starts to walk out with me, before remembering he's there and swivelling back to say, 'See you in college? We'll practise, like, all week, OK?'

'OK,' Cal says, then he does a thumbs-up. I give him a nod, and steer Gem out with one hand on her back, but as she rushes over to untie Moonshine, whose tail is going mental, I can't help glancing back through the closing door at Cal, putting his laptop away. He looks up and meets my eyes before raising one hand in a weak sort of wave. I give him a big smile and let the door close.

Chapter Eleven

Gemma

'That wasn't bad for a first run-through, right?' Cal says.

We're coming out of the music studio at college on Friday morning; we both do Music A level and Cal's got permission for us to practise there when it's free. The whole room is slightly dingy and run-down, but it does have decent acoustics. Sometimes I wish I could've gone to Portsmouth College. They've got recording studios, chances to do live gigs. But it was too far away by bus and no one would've been able to get me there by car, as well as Michael to football so … well, if I can get in to uni to do Music there will be opportunities there. And you've got to make your own, haven't you? Like this competition.

'Yeah,' I say, though I know we've got a long way to go to get it right.

My phone goes off with a text and I whip it out of my pocket, then smile. Aaron's been busy with his app-developing, but he's been texting all week. This is his third message of the morning.

At lunchtime, I get to the refectory and hover, looking

for Aaron. He comes in just as Phoebe's waving me over to where most of the gang are sitting at our usual table. I can't see Esi; she's probably in the library, but everyone else is there.

'Do you want to sit with your friends?' he says.

'I don't mind,' I hedge.

'Shall I come?'

I smile. 'Yeah, let me show you off.'

Aaron does a fast double-raise of his eyebrows that makes me laugh and we sit down.

He's met Cal and Rachael, of course – 'Hopefully I don't puke near you this time,' she says easily – and I introduce him to Beth and Phoebe. Aaron gives them a wave, then says to Phoebe, 'Nice earrings.'

'Thanks!' She's got these sweet little parrots with tiny feathers in them.

Cal gets out his phone and starts to jab away at some game. Aaron looks over his shoulder and says, 'Hey, you want a cheat for that?' He takes the phone and fiddles with it, then gives it back. Cal lets out a shout.

'How did you do that? I can't die!' He looks around the table in amazement. 'I can't die, people!' We all smile as he redoubles the jabbing.

'Aaron develops apps,' I tell them.

'Really?' Beth's leaning forward. 'I've been getting into coding.'

The next thing I know, Aaron and Beth are deep in conversation about the merits of different building platforms.

I watch, a warm feeling in my chest seeing Aaron getting on so well with my friends. He's swapping email addresses with Beth now, promising to send her some useful links.

'He's so gorgeous,' Rachael whispers in my ear. 'And sweet. Seriously, Gemma, he's like the full package.'

'I know,' I sigh happily.

As if he's got some sixth sense, Aaron looks up. 'What?'

'We were talking about, uh, periods,' Rachael says, and I nudge her. 'What?' she says loudly, 'I thought you wanted to talk about that flooding incident when—'

I push my chair back. 'Anyway, shall we go?' I say to Aaron. He looks between me and Rachael, an adorable, confused expression on his face.

'Um, sure. It was great meeting you all properly,' he says. Everyone smiles and choruses byes back while I drag him away.

'My friends really like you, I can tell,' I say as the bell goes.

'Really?'

'Really really.'

He looks so pleased for a minute, it's like he's twelve years old. Then it's like he shakes himself or something and the pleased look is replaced by a cocky smile. 'Just call me Mr Incredible,' he says.

'Idiot,' I say, jabbing him in the ribs.

Later, after college has finished, we get into Aaron's car; he's said he'll drive me home.

He has one hand on the rest thing between the seats – about *two millimetres* from my thigh. 'Shall we drive out somewhere first?'

'Sure!' I say, although most of my brain is taken up with thinking how close his hand is to my leg.

'Where shall we go?' Aaron says.

The beach is kind of becoming our thing, and he nods when I suggest it. We head out of town and towards the coast road and I realise I've suddenly stopped thinking about the sea as the vague backdrop to my normal life and instead as something special belonging to Aaron and me. Then I have an idea.

'Why don't we go to Lullsmouth? It's only ten miles along. There's this beach with an amazing cave. You can walk right to the back.'

'Okey-dokey-do.' Aaron says it without thinking and I laugh at the unexpectedness of this. In response, he leans down and flicks on some music, which swallows up my laughs. It's not country this time, but rock, the thud of bass going through the back of my seat.

When Aaron takes a sharp bend, I fling out both hands to steady myself. 'Uh, I think this road gets quite narrow here,' I shout over the noise of the music, but I don't think Aaron hears me. The next moment, something comes around the corner at the same time as us and Aaron slams the brakes on so hard my head swings forward, then back against the headrest, my seatbelt locking tightly against my chest.

'Whoa …' I start, in what I hope is a jokey voice, but Aaron's too busy beeping, then exchanging the finger with the other guy, to hear. We manage to wriggle past, but now my excitement's been swallowed whole by a knot in my stomach. What is it with guys and cars? Dad's the same.

I'm about to yell 'Slow down!' but Aaron has that same set look in his eyes Dad gets when he's in one of his driving moods, so I settle back again without commenting until we get to the little parking bay at Lullsmouth, when I say, 'Here's good.'

I have to repeat myself, then Aaron finally seems to notice I'm still in the car and turns in sharply at the last minute. He parks up, switches off the engine and suddenly there's quiet. I glance at him, see he's still got that pale look of anger about him, so I say, 'Wow, that guy was an arsehole.'

Aaron smiles at this, then hops out to get a ticket. By the time he returns, he's got his usual bounce back and it gives me this rush of relief. He puts the ticket on the dashboard, then comes around to where I'm oh-so-casually leaning against the car. I'm not about to say anything about the driving: years of watching Mum bite her tongue have taught me it's the best plan, but to my surprise Aaron takes one of my hands and says, 'Sorry if I scared you earlier. I was probably going a bit fast. It just winds me up, because that other guy was, too, but he reckons he can pin it on me because I'm younger …'

I'm so surprised at the way that, unlike Dad, Aaron can stop and apologise, that I don't reply for a second, and by the time I've decided what to say, Aaron's mouth is already heading for mine.

We fold into the kiss, Aaron up close to me, the car at my back. My heart's flying and this time it's with a mixture of all the feelings: nerves, excitement and, to be totally honest, I'm massively turned on. Especially when he pushes even closer so he's pressed right against me and runs one hand down my side so it's resting just above my butt. The whole thing's so hot I think I'm actually getting the weak legs they go on about in songs, but then he kind of pushes his tongue in further and it goes from hot to vaguely gag-making. It takes a few seconds to move my head to one side.

'You OK?' Aaron says between a couple of breaths so heavy they're like sighs.

'Yeah, just coming up for air!' I say, and sidestep a little. Aaron pulls back and for a tiny moment I think I see the same road-ragey look on his face as in the car, but then I realise I'm mistaken because he takes my hand and gives it a gentle stroke, his eyes soft.

'I'm sorry, I can't help it. I could kiss you all day.' Then, seeming to sense the moment's become pretty intense, he gives another grin and pulls me away from the car towards the beach. 'So let's have a look at this cave then.'

We walk along, carrying our shoes and socks. Good job I remembered to remove all the chipped varnish and repaint my toenails yesterday, otherwise this would've been a disaster. The beach is this empty expanse of fresh sand, cool and soft underneath my feet. We're not talking much, but in that comfortable way you get when you've known someone a long time. I think.

'Here it is,' I say as we get to the cave, doing a *ta-da* motion with my hands.

'Wow.' Aaron peers in. 'How far back does it go?'

'Pretty far.'

We go in. At once, everything's much cooler, the smell of sea mingling with rock. I'm not entirely sure rock has a smell, but caves do. I put one hand out to touch damp smoothness. At the very back of the cave, where it's gloomier, Aaron looks up to where light seeps through a small gap in the rocks above our heads.

'Do you reckon a person could get through that?' he says.

'Only if they were really skinny.'

'You should give it a try,' Aaron says.

I'm so pleased he thinks I'm skinny that I'm standing there just savouring it for a minute, when he lifts me as though to boost me up. I let out a shriek and clutch at him as my head looms closer and closer to the ceiling. 'I'll get stuck!'

He lets me drop, catching me around the waist so I don't fall over as my feet hit the floor. Then he pulls me in against him again and we start kissing. This time his hand moves straight to my breasts over my top; first one, then the other, and it feels OK here in the dim light, the sound of the sea hushed and far away, like we're not quite in a real place. His other hand is basically on my butt, then up to the back of my head, then down my back and towards my butt again.

What feels like a very long time later, I break off. Both of us are breathing hard.

'You are one –' he seems to substitute a word at the last minute – 'amazing girl.'

'I know,' I say. It comes out in a gasp, which wasn't quite what I was going for. Luckily, he probably can't see how much I'm blushing in the gloom. When he tries to kiss me again I duck away, towards the light. Outside, the sun's come out and it takes my eyes a moment to adjust to the glare coming off the sea. I feel weird, I suddenly realise. Like when you've gone over the top on a roller coaster and you're hitting the first big turn, wind whipping your face, everyone screaming. Arms up high.

Aaron's standing next to me, looking out to sea too. After a moment I turn my head and realise he's not; he's actually looking at me.

'Are you OK?' His voice is so gentle, it's hard to hear it above the waves.

I give a bright smile. 'Of course!'

'I wasn't −' he coughs, colours up − 'coming on too strong? It's just,' he adds in a rush, 'you're so sexy. I mean −' he pushes his hand through his hair sheepishly − 'beautiful.'

I start to smile, because he's stumbling over himself and it makes me feel more ... I don't know, in control, I guess. Then he takes one of my hands and the whole world seems to be fading out, so all I can see are his hazel eyes holding mine. 'I really like you,' he continues. 'Like, a lot. I've never met someone like you before. And ... I know this is kind of soon, but I think when you know, you just know. That there's something special here, something as huge as this.' He gestures to the dancing light skimming the waves. The sea goes on forever. I manage a small nod, my heart going fast.

Then he gives an embarrassed laugh and says, 'Hey, do you know how long it's been since I built a sandcastle?'

I blink at the sudden change in his voice, the way he's standing. He's gone from seeming so old, or wise or something, to a teenager like me. Then he's taking off towards the damp sand lower down where the tide's going out, scooping up handfuls. 'Come on,' he yells.

I kneel and we get to work. We don't have a bucket or spade but Aaron does most of the scooping. I'm on the smoothing-it-out-with-my-fingers and finding-shells-and-bits-of-seaweed-to-decorate-it duties. Aaron assumes the role of director, sorting through my pile of shells.

He picks up a chipped one, 'Reject!' he says and flings it to one side, then holds up another, squinting in this exaggerated way like he's pricing up a diamond. 'And as for this sorry excuse for a shell – way too tiddly.' He pitches it after the first.

'How very dare you,' I say, but then I start laughing at the word 'tiddly'. After twenty minutes, we have a pretty decent cone-like structure, with a wig of seaweed dripping down one side and a ring of shells at its base. I stand back to admire it.

'Not bad,' I say.

'Just needs one more thing,' Aaron says. He leans down with a seagull feather he's picked off the beach and scratches our initials into the side of the sandcastle, in an attempt at fancy italic swirly writing.

'I love it! We should add "4 EVA" or something,' I say laughing.

Aaron grins, then sketches it in and comes to stand next to me. He takes my hand and turns me a little towards him. His eyes are suddenly soft.

'Do you believe in that?' he asks.

'In what?'

'Forever? Or fate, at least, like some things are meant to happen? That there's one person out there for you and you're supposed to find them?'

I swallow hard. 'Like soul mates or something?'

'Yes.' Aaron's still holding my eyes and my heart's going so fast I can feel each beat staccato-like in my chest. I see us almost from a distance. This boy, the beach, the way the light is just slanting towards sunset. It makes me think about this country song I've always loved, by Janie Wynell, called 'Holding His Eyes'. It's about how sometimes the most powerful emotions can only be expressed in a look. A knowing without words. And even though it's one of my favourite songs, I don't think I've ever really understood it properly until this moment.

'Yes, I think I do believe that,' I say quietly. It's like we exchange something then, some sort of energy. Aaron nods, then leans towards me and gives me the softest, most gentle kiss. Then we kind of hug for a long time, until Aaron pulls away and takes my hand. We start walking up the beach. For a while we're quiet, like we're both getting used to this new intensity.

'Remember that day you were watching the football match?' Aaron says it like it was in the distant past, and I know how he feels. 'I knew you were special that first time I saw you. And I could see it, even then, the way your parents never once noticed. They don't, do they? Too busy watching your brother.'

'I …' I swallow. It's like Aaron's said something out loud I've never dared to even think before. The feeling is the same as salt water on a cut. I make myself smile, drag up Confident Gemma. 'You just thought I was hot, admit it.'

Aaron leans over to tickle me, and I screech and take off. He chases me all the way up the sand until he catches me and we collapse in a heap, him half on top of me. Then there's a lot more kissing, quite a bit more touching – though I move his hand away when he tries to undo my jeans. He doesn't seem to mind, just whispers, 'Sorry, can't help it, you're just too hot,' in my ear, which makes us both burst out laughing again.

We make it back to the car, finally. It's been hands-down one of the most incredible afternoons of my life. I rest my head back against the seat as we zoom towards my house, smiling, images of our initials on that sandcastle playing in my mind as I think about love at first sight.

Aaron drops me at the bottom of the lane, making me promise to text him when I'm home safely. Then he leans over and gives me another one of those melting kisses. As I'm just stepping out of the car he says, 'Gem?'

I lean back in. 'Yeah?'

'Nothing, just …' He breaks off, but gives me this intense look. He starts to say, 'I…' then shakes his head, grins and says, 'As you wish.'

'What? Wish what?'

He winks. 'You'll figure it out.'

'Umm, OK? See you tomorrow!'

I shut the door on Aaron's laughs and I'm so happy I more or less skim the ground up the lane.

Chapter Twelve

Aaron

Should I have said it to her? Will she figure it out? It's a cult film, the sort I used to watch back home, before. If she does figure it out, what will she think? It's like offering a slice of my heart on a plate, and even though girls say they want sensitive, when they're confronted with it, yeah, that's a different story. That's nice-guy, friendzone, puppy-eyed geek territory, like Callum.

I'm such a dick.

All these thoughts are chasing their tails harder than Shiney (I've dropped the 'Moon': it was too ludicrous for a dog) as I drive back to Dad's place.

What if I've wrecked it, scared her off?

I accelerate, trying to flatten the thoughts with my car. Remembering the feel of her body underneath me, how hard it was to pull back. I speed up a bit more, loving the way the car holds to the bends, how I can get the acceleration out of them just right ... until I fly around the next bend almost on top of some old guy doing about thirty. I hit the brakes and the back end slides out. There's an exhilarating second of the car taking over, no control left, then I lift my foot off the brake and the car corrects itself in time for me to punch my foot down again and just avoid rear-ending him.

I catch one glimpse of the driver's face in his rear-view mirror – glasses, fuzzed white hair – and then I'm past him, accelerating away.

Back at the flat I park up and slam the door shut. For a sudden second, the guy's face flashes in front of my eyes again: his hands gripping the steering wheel, his features squeezed together in … I'm about to say fear – then I jab my key fob at the car and slam into the flat.

Not my fault if he's too old to be on the road. Probably did him a favour if I shook him up a bit.

I do some weights for a while; I brought my set down from London. At least Dad's got a decent-sized flat, not like the tiny space we had back home. Another unwelcome image flitters through my brain: Mum's face, after it all kicked off with Cherine. The things she said. All that shit about how she didn't raise me that way and where she went wrong. Like she wasn't even on my side.

Then rage is here, like an ink stain spreading to blot out words I refuse to read. I push harder and harder with the weights, letting the scream of my muscles take over. After a hundred reps, I'm covered in sweat and panting.

I slide off the bench and fix myself a protein shake, then neck it standing in the kitchen. I must've dropped Gem off at least an hour ago now. Will she have got the reference? Will she have checked? I get out my phone and all the old worries lift off me like flecks of rust.

Because she's texted back:

As you wish. Gem xxxxx

Chapter Thirteen

Gemma

It's an old film called *The Princess Bride*. It's some kind of cult classic, so as soon as I google, there's loads of references to the 'As You Wish' thing, and what those references all say is that the main character uses those words as a substitute for the most important three in the universe:

I.

Love.

You.

I feel like my chest's about to burst with excitement and happiness. No one's ever said 'I love you' to me before. Well, apart from Mum (Dad doesn't 'do' shows of affection, unless it's whacking Mum on the butt or ruffling Michael's hair or something), but it's hardly like she counts, she *has* to say it. No guy's ever said it to me before. And in such a romantic way.

I have to tell someone.

I don't bother to text Esi; it'll be quicker if I just hammer on her door. Baaba opens it.

'Goodness, you look happy!' she says, with that wide

smile of hers. She should know; I've never seen a happier family than hers. I used to want to live here when I was younger, even though Esi's parents are way stricter than mine, especially about things like homework. Well, Esi smiles way less than her parents – I sometimes wonder how they managed to produce someone so self-contained when they're so … what's the word? It starts with an 'e', I remember doing it in English once, but right now I have to settle for 'happy'.

What can I say? I'm not as brainy as Esi.

'Is she in?' I say now.

'She's out, I'm afraid. She had an extra training practice for that tournament. Did she not tell you?' Baaba says.

For a ridiculous second, I'm super annoyed Esi's not here to hear my news. I think back to what everyone was talking about in the refectory earlier, but all I get is images of my phone, which kept pinging with messages from Aaron.

'Oh yeah, she did tell me actually,' I say, then add another 'Yep' for good measure. I mean, she probably did, right?

'I'll tell her you came by,' Baaba says, and though she's smiling, I sense it's not all she wants to say. Which is my cue to go.

Sometimes I think Esi's mum sees me way more clearly than my own parents do.

Still, I can't feel annoyed for long. As soon as I'm back home I text Aaron:

Me: **What's a word for happy, beginning with an 'e'? xxx**

(Yes, I'm up to multiple kisses in routine texts and feeling good about it.)

He types back straight away: **Ecstatic?**

Me: **Nope. Sort of more like joyful, I guess?**

After a pause Aaron types back: **Ebullient?**

Me: **Yes! I knew you'd know.**

I love the way he knows all this stuff, how he doesn't take the mick or tell me to just google it. He's so smart.

We arrange to meet up after I finish at the cafe tomorrow and sign off. For a moment, I wonder what to do with myself. Dad and Michael are watching a match downstairs, but I don't fancy going to join them. I'd only have to listen to them analysing formations and free kicks and talking about Michael's match tomorrow. Or is it training? For once, I think I might have lost track. It feels like everything's suddenly tilted a little to the side with those three words, as though I'm a different person. I go to my mirror and the girl looking back at me seems the same, yet her eyes are full of the best kind of secrets. I'm glad now that Esi wasn't in, because somehow this feels too new, too special to share with anyone except Aaron.

The next day at the cafe, though, I last about thirty minutes before Esi prises it out of me. Rachael's there too. Her parents give her loads of money so she doesn't need to work, but sometimes she comes for cake and chats. Right now, she's sitting at the counter with a huge cup of herbal tea in one hand and her phone in the other. We've had a steady trickle of older customers in. One of them stops at the counter to chat after she's paid, while Esi sorts out the order.

'Lovely for September, isn't it?'

I smile, which is all the encouragement she needs.

'I thought we'd be lucky with the weather. And it's cheaper of course in September, but then you never do know. But I did say to Janice – she's my friend over there, but she's put out, you see, because of the cake …' The lady leans in closer, and half mouths, 'Diabetes. It's a terrible trouble for her. But in any case, I said I could feel it would be a good September and I was right …'

I tune out as she goes on, vaguely nodding and smiling in the right places. Then I realise there's been a bit of a pause.

'Um, sorry, what was that?' I say.

The woman's lips have kind of pulled in on themselves. 'Well, I know you girls must be busy,' she says.

Esi's beside me suddenly, smiling at the lady. She carries the tray out to where the other woman – whatever she was called – is sitting, and stands there for a while, chatting with them both. When Esi gets back to me, her smile's gone.

'What's with you today?' she says. 'You never even bothered to pretend you were listening to what she was saying.'

I'm trying hard to look sorry, but I keep thinking about Aaron and the three words. 'Sorry, I just have, um, stuff on my mind.'

'Like?' Esi's practically tapping her foot, as if she's fifty or something. Then she stares at me hard. 'Is this boy-shaped stuff?'

I can't hold the grin back any more. 'Might be.'

Esi makes a face like she's swallowing back several thousand words. She settles on 'Well, you should be paying attention to the customers. They like to have a chat. Don't ignore them because you've got some … I don't know, crush or something.'

I feel a small flare of annoyance, mixed with guilt, but squash it back down. 'It's not like that … A crush,' I say.

Rachael looks up from her phone. 'Give her a break, Esi.'

I can't hold it any more. 'He said he loves me!' My voice has gone a leeetle bit squeaky. Rachael squeals.

'Really? No way. This is huge!' She leans forward. 'Details, right now.'

Esi's mouth is open like she's the lead in some melodrama. Seriously.

'Well, sort of said it,' I add, realising I don't actually want to explain the *Princess Bride* stuff. It feels private.

'Aww, you two are just too—' Rachael begins.

'Are you for real? You've known him about two weeks!' Esi's voice is loud enough to make a couple of heads turn.

And now I really am annoyed. Why does she get to stand there telling me off for talking to the customers wrong, or deciding how I feel?

'Oh come on, how many boyfriends have *you* had?' Rachael's saying.

Esi snaps her mouth shut, and I feel bad, but Rachael's right. Esi's never even kissed a boy. I mean, I know she's pretty cautious about that sort of thing, but seriously, she never even talks about who she fancies.

'Actually,' I can't help adding, 'there's such a thing as love at first sight. Take my nana,' I start.

Nana used to tell the story all the time of how she met my grandad. 'Moment I set eyes on him, I just knew he'd be

101

the man I married,' she'd say. And it was true. According to Nana, they stayed in love right up until Grandad died. She used to show me all these pictures of him, and get such a happy, faraway look on her face.

Esi rolls her eyes. 'You can't use that as your yardstick. It was a different time back then, and anyway, hindsight's twenty-twenty, isn't it?' Esi says.

Rachael's shaking her head.

'That's not true …' I stop because the door's just opened and in walks Aaron.

Straight away, it's like the air becomes lighter. I watch as he walks towards me, his hair slightly damp and wavy, like he's been walking along the seafront. And I can't explain it, not to Esi, maybe not even to myself, but sometimes the way a person smiles at you is all you need to know.

I'm more positive than I've ever been in my life.

He's the real thing.

Chapter Fourteen

Aaron

Gem's smiling so widely, her face flushed, eyes full of warmth. So I don't wait. I don't even ask. I go right behind the counter, pick her up and twirl her around as she lets out a shriek, then push my lips to her laughing ones.

It's a struggle to break away, even while I'm conscious of the customers watching and her friend making a noise in the background between the click of a tongue and a sigh. After a few moments, Gem wriggles to be let down, and I can't help squeezing her just that bit tighter, hear her say, 'Oof!' before I relax my grip so her feet slide back to the floor.

I keep one arm around Gem's waist as she kind of surveys the cafe, a hint of anxiety on her face. One or two of the old people have pursed lips, but a lady at a table further down is looking fondly in our direction. I fix my gaze on Gem and give her an abashed grin. 'Couldn't help myself. I've missed you.'

'Me too.' Gem sounds breathless.

'Hi, Aaron.' Rachael's smiling broadly at me and I smile back at her.

The friendly woman comes up with her empty cup for a refill. She looks at Gem and says, 'You remind me of when I met my husband. Everyone said to wait, but we knew right away. Married six months later, and together fifty years now.' She nods twice, and both Gem and Rachael turn with a look of triumph to Esi.

'See?' they say in unison, then both start to laugh.

Esi rolls her eyes, looks at me and back at Gem, clearing her throat theatrically.

'Oh! Aaron, this is Esi,' Gem says. 'I don't think you two have officially met.'

Esi sticks out her hand, which I take and for a second I think we're going to get into a whose-grip-is-strongest pissing competition. But she's Gem's friend, so I give her a full-wattage grin and mentally cross my fingers she'll like me.

She gives me a steady look back, intelligence dancing in the depths of her eyes, like she's working out all the pieces to a jigsaw puzzle. I find myself breaking eye contact first; girls like her bring out the old Aaron in me.

'What are you doing here? I don't finish for another hour,' Gem says. 'Not that I'm not pleased to see you!' She gives a swift glance up the cafe, then plants a hasty peck on my cheek.

'Couldn't stay away from you,' I say.

'Gemma.' Esi's voice is firm, holding back irritation. 'You know Dora won't like it if she catches Aaron back here.'

'She's not here though, is she?' Gem says. She's going for teasing, but there's an edge to her voice.

'Just wanted to see Gem,' I say.

'You can see her from the other side of the counter,' Esi says.

Gem glares at Esi, then gives me a sheepish look. 'Actually …' she starts.

'I'm going, I'm going,' I say, hands up. 'Sorry. I don't want to get anyone into trouble,' I say, as nicely as I can, in Esi's direction. Then I look at Gem. 'I'll come back later,' I say as I reach the other side of the counter.

'No! I'll get you a coffee,' Gem says quickly. 'Stay there. I won't be a minute.'

I sit next to Rachael, who starts chatting about college stuff, but I'm only half listening because I'm watching Esi's body language. The way her arms are folded as she glares at Gem's back. I think I'm starting to understand Esi. Cherine had a best friend just like her: jealous, petty, and didn't I know it when things went wrong between us. It's one of the reasons *why* things went wrong between us.

I'm not going to let that happen again, not with Gem.

Chapter Fifteen

Gemma

'Here.' I hand a large mug of coffee over. 'I can't believe she wouldn't let me give it to you for free.'

'Fear not, fair maiden, for I am with money,' Aaron says, then gives me a puzzled look. 'Actually, that sounds slightly dodgy.'

'Well as long as you're not with child,' I say drily. Aaron clutches his stomach in mock concern. 'It's on me, don't worry.' I grin. 'I'll put it through as a small.' I'm trying to pretend I'm totally cool about the whole 'As You Wish' – or AYW as I'm now calling it in my head – thing, but it's kind of tricky because my heart's going so hard.

Rachael coughs and says, 'We-e-e-elll, you two are making me want to puke. I'm off.' She gives Esi a quick hug, then me, and saunters out of the cafe, turning at the last minute to pull a face at me while fanning herself. I giggle.

The next moment Aaron's getting out his wallet, pressing a note into my hand and closing my fingers around it.

'Here. I don't want you spending your money on me. That's my job.'

'Seriously?' I make a show of looking about me, eyes wide. And also because I'm a wee bit nervous of what Esi might say if she overhears that. 'We *are* still in the twenty-first century, right?'

Aaron laughs. 'Keep it. I earn more money than you. Why don't you get some cake? Get some for Esi too.'

I take the money up to the counter and start ringing up the price of Aaron's coffee on the till. I sense Esi a few paces away from the rays of disapproval lasering my back. I don't get it – why can't she just be happy for me?

'You want some cake? Aaron's treat,' I say, turning with the note still in my hand.

Esi glances at Aaron, who smiles at her, then back to me.

'I'll have lemon drizzle,' she says with a sigh, picking up a knife. 'Shall I cut one for you?'

I'm about to say yes when I remember my dress for the audition is a tad on the tight side. I shake my head. 'I'm on a diet,' I say, even though I know full well this is guaranteed to set Esi off into a long rant featuring words like 'patriarchy' and 'beauty standards'. I'm kind of wanting it, right now, because the air feels wrong between us, but she simply moves the knife over and cuts herself a piece big enough for the two of us and starts eating.

I ring up the price of a single slice of cake anyway – I'm calling some waitress/general dogsbody privileges – and grab some change, then take it over to Aaron.

'You're not having cake?' he says.

'I'll have one later,' I say.

'You should have one.'

'Ah, I would, but I need to fit into my audition outfit, so …' I do one of those apologetic half-smiles while I pat my stomach – just like Mum does, I realise with horror.

Aaron laughs. 'You'd look beautiful whatever you wore, and anyway, I like it.'

'Like what?' It's Esi, materialising next to us.

It's so nice to hear Aaron say I'm beautiful. I'm not the sort of girl who goes fishing for compliments, or who thinks her perfectly-in-proportion ears stick out too much or anything like that. I know my good points and I work with what I've got. And I definitely agree with Esi; I'm not dieting for anyone. But I really, really want to wear that dress to the audition. That's another thing I argue with Esi about – yeah, it shouldn't matter what you wear or how you look, but in the music industry, image is everything, right?

I'm thinking all this with only half my mind on the scene in front of me – which is a bad idea as I tune back in to hear Esi say, '… next thing you'll be saying you "like your women with a bit of meat on them". That's a bit on the dinosaur side, isn't it?'

Aaron's mouth is hanging open, just a tiny bit. Then he starts to reply but I cut across him.

'Ohmigod I've just remembered!'

'Remembered what?' Esi says.

'Uhh …' I think fast. 'That dress. It's, um, got a stain. What am I going to do for the audition?' I pull a tragic face, which Esi sees straight through, obviously.

But Aaron puts his arm around me and squeezes. 'Don't worry, I'll take you shopping and buy you a new one,' he says, his lips almost brushing my ear.

'Really?'

Aaron grins.

Esi doesn't.

The rest of our shift is kind of painful. Aaron stays, doing the rounds of the cafe, chatting to the customers, charming all the old ladies who basically want to adopt him and feed him cake and tea forever. He takes cups back up to the counter, pulls more than one tray out of my arms and carries it to the customer's table for me, and when things get quieter, leans up on the right side of the counter and tells jokes or listens while I talk about the audition.

The more he helps, though, the quieter Esi gets, until just before it's time to lock up, she says, 'I can finish this on my own. Why don't you two get out of here?'

'Really? You're a babe, Esi,' Aaron says while I try not to laugh. Calling her a 'babe' is not going to go down well.

To my surprise though, she simply grimaces slightly, then says in about the friendliest voice she's managed all afternoon, 'See you later then.'

As I go to follow Aaron out, she takes my arm. 'Just … slow it up. You don't have to rush into anything you don't want to,' she says quietly. And now her eyes look more worried than annoyed.

It's tempting to ask her what experience this 'go slow' advice is actually based on, but that would be too bitchy so I simply say, 'It's all good.'

I start to leave and suddenly she's calling out, 'Hey!' I turn back and Esi gives me a smile that says she's offering an olive branch. 'Don't do anything I wouldn't do!'

I return her smile. 'As if I would,' I say. Then I'm off

after Aaron, but I feel her gaze on me the whole way up the cafe.

'Do you want to try in here?'

I really should be home by now, but Aaron's driven us along the coast to a very posh harbour, full of silky people who own the yachts moored at the marina and shop in places I could usually only drool at. We're talking all the designer labels. I felt a bit *Pretty Woman* in the first shop, but Aaron kept pulling stuff out for me to try and charming the sales assistants and now we're somehow in the third and I barely feel out of place at all.

Aaron picks up something I'd never usually go for; too short and clingy in the butt area for starters. It's also this unbelievably unflattering shade of green. 'What about this one?'

'You are kidding, right?' I say.

'What? I think it's nice.'

I start to laugh and shake my head, giving him mock-tragic eyes. 'Oh, poor sweet boy. You know so little.'

Aaron puts one hand up to his chest. 'You cut me deep,' he says in an American accent.

'Shrek?' I say.

He grins. 'What about this one then?' He's grabbed another dress at random. This one's day-glo yellow. We collapse, me letting out an accidental and super-unattractive snort. The sales assistant's trying to kill me with her gaze. She also clearly thinks he's way too hot to be with me.

'We're closing in fifteen minutes,' she says, sounding bored.

I'm just about to suggest we try another shop quickly when I spot it. It's this belted black dress which would go amazingly with a pair of ankle boots I've got in my wardrobe, just waiting for a chance to be worn. It reminds me of the dress Tara from The Greenwoods wore on their first album cover. With a cowboy hat and my hair curled it would look almost as good as Tara's outfit. I run my fingers down the fabric.

'Try it on,' Aaron says, making me jump. For a split second, I'd forgotten he was there.

I go into the changing room and wriggle into the dress. It's perfect. I turn around again and again and I just know, this is it. *The* dress. There's no price tag though. I squint at the mirror again. I need another layer of mascara on ... I grab some out of my bag.

'Are you ready?' Aaron calls.

'Almost!'

I need some lipstick too.

'Come on-n-n-n,' Aaron says in a way I think is meant to be teasing. I drop the lipstick into my bag, mash my lips together a couple of times and pull my shoulders back ready for my big entrance.

The sales assistant is standing seriously close to Aaron. He steps away from her as I emerge and says, 'You look stunning.'

I mean to say, 'Hell yeah I do,' or something like that, but Confident Gemma suddenly morphs unexpectedly into Reassure Me Gemma, mainly due to the sales assistant's smirk. 'You think?' I say instead.

Aaron slips into what I'm thinking of as 'Stately Home

111

mode'. 'My lady, thou art the fairest creature I ever beheld.'

It's exactly the right thing to say. All my confidence comes surging back, especially when the sales assistant looks between us, clearly thinking we're mad. I do a little curtsy. 'Why thank you, kind sir,' I say, trying not to giggle. Aaron's eyes are dancing with amusement.

I take the dress back off and hand it over to be wrapped. But when the shop assistant says the price, I nearly fall over.

'That's way too much, Aaron ...' I begin, but he makes this gesture which if I didn't know better could be a 'Shut up' sort of one, giving me a brief frown as he whips out his credit card. A platinum one.

A trickle of unease begins to work its way up the base of my spine, but the next moment he's turning to me with such a sweet smile, I have to wonder if I really saw the look on his face a moment ago. 'This will blow them all away at your audition,' he says.

And I've got to admit, having the wrapped dress in its exclusive bag feels pretty amazing. In the car, Aaron won't stop talking about how beautiful I looked, how he wanted to treat me, how he's just had a big payout on one of his apps. And slowly, any uneasy feelings I might have had melt away into the leather interior of his car.

He's got money, why not let him spend it on me?

Chapter Sixteen

Gemma

Sunday morning it turns colder just in time for Michael's next away game. I was hoping not to go, but Dad's insisted and there's no arguing with him. So I sit on a folding chair with a jacket on, texting Aaron and trying not to think about what he said the other day. How everyone watches Michael, never me.

Gemma: **I think autumn might be here. I'm wearing my coat** 😔 🍁

Aaron: **I could come down there, keep you warm?** 😊 😊

Gemma: 😃

Aaron: **Hey, did you see this?**

I click on the link and find Janie Wynell has just announced she's working on a new album.

I text Aaron back: **YAAAAYYY!**

Aaron: **I'll take you to see her.**

'Yes! Go on!' Dad roars beside me. I look up in time to catch Michael making a run down the left side of the pitch. He shoots, but is off target. Dad lets out a long groan. Mum rubs his arm soothingly as he mutters, 'He needs to have a word with himself. What's he playing at, spooning that?'

'He's doing OK,' Mum says, but she sounds worried. I tune in to the match for a bit and my heart sinks. Michael's not playing well. It happens like this sometimes, as though something gets him rattled and then he starts missing shots, or passing badly.

The coach takes him off with twenty minutes to go. Dad swears, but before he can shout at the coach – another potential banning offence – Mum's there again, talking in his ear, doing that thing she does so well. Like she's *managing* him.

When the whistle goes for full time, Dad stalks off angrily to the car without waiting for us. I fold up my chair, a sudden sense of weariness coming over me. It feels like I've been here so many times before, riding the football roller coaster.

'He got some good passes in?' Mum says it like a question as we get to the car, all timid. I shrug. Dad's already got the engine running. He doesn't get out to help me pack away the chair into the boot and the second I've shut my door, he reverses out so hard the tyres screech. Mum grips the sides of her chair but doesn't say anything.

'But he passed well,' Mum tries again when we've been going for a bit.

'Some of the time,' Dad says, and I can hear the disappointment and frustration in his voice.

'And that shot just before half-time was on target, the goalie did a good job to save it,' Mum says.

'Yeah …' Dad's voice softens a tiny amount. Mum keeps

up the encouragement, then when she runs out of good things to say, turns to me. 'Gemma thought he did well. Didn't you? Gemma?'

'What?' I look up from my phone to meet Dad's eyes in the rear-view mirror. He looks back to the road.

'She was on that bloody thing the whole time. You needn't bother coming if you're not going to support your brother,' he yells.

It makes me jump. Mum doesn't say anything.

'Sorry,' I mutter after a bit. I wonder whether to say it was about the audition, which is now only a week away. It would be better than telling them I was texting my boyfriend …

Is he my boyfriend? I mean, I guess so. We've already said the AYW thing, so I guess he is? Oh God, this is the sort of thing I used to worry about in Year 8.

Anyway, Dad doesn't really care much about singing, so I keep my mouth shut.

Dad's crazy driving back to the training centre means we beat the coach by a good twenty minutes. I text with Aaron the whole time. I'm supposed to be going to meet Cal at his house so we can practise, and Aaron's offered to pick me up from the training centre, but I'm not sure how to work that one so Mum and Dad don't see.

Obviously, I use Esi.

'Oh, I was going to walk down towards town and meet Esi if that's OK?' I say casually as we pull into the car park.

'That's fine,' Mum says absently. Dad's still stewing over the match.

'We want you home for dinner,' he says, a gruff edge to his voice.

Of course. The post-match analysis. Which is basically going to suck tonight. I hesitate, wondering if I can manufacture a homework-related excuse to get out of it, but football trumps, well, pretty much everything, so I just say, 'Yep, be back before six.'

That'll only give us an hour to rehearse, but it's better than nothing.

Once I'm up the road and out of sight, I text Aaron and a moment later he comes roaring down the street and pulls up beside me.

'What's a nice girl like you doin' in a place like this,' he drawls in this Scots accent.

I grin, then straighten my face. 'You're using bad pickup lines on me?'

'Bad lines? It's Sean Connery.'

I look blank.

'*You Only Live Twice*? One of the greatest Bond movies?'

'What, like the spy? I think my Dad watches those,' I deadpan.

'Ouch. You need educating. Badly.'

'Yeah?' I meet his eyes and there's so much electricity between us suddenly it's like my body's crackling. I can tell Aaron feels it too because the look goes intense. I slide into the car and he yanks me towards him immediately, kissing me so hard I'm out of breath. The door's still hanging open.

After an age, I pull back and get the door shut. My mouth feels almost bruised, my body hot in the places his hands touched me. And for the first time, I'm totally sure I'm ready to do more, to take the next step.

Aaron's looking at me, his face tender, his eyes dark and warm. And suddenly everything else goes out of my head: Cal, the audition, football.

'I …' I'm having trouble finding the words.

So's Aaron, it seems. It takes him a long moment of gazing at me, before he puts one hand up to my hair. The other is on my thigh and he's making circles with his thumb on my leg, which is sending shock waves right through me. 'Do you want to come home with me?' he says, and I know what he's asking.

I open my mouth, about to say yes, to say I'm ready, that I know this is right. It feels right.

And then my phone starts ringing.

'Ignore it,' Aaron whispers, but I'm like that dog we studied in Psychology who salivates at the sound of a bell. Can't ignore a ringing phone.

It's Cal.

'Oh crap, I'd better pick this up,' I say. Aaron looks annoyed for a moment, then smiles.

'Go on then.'

I answer, my voice coming out a little breathless still. 'Hey, what's up?'

'Just checking you're still on for tonight?'

'Yeah, we're on our way, be there in ten,' I say.

There's a tiny pause, then, 'We?'

'Oh, Aaron's bringing me. That's all right, isn't it?'

'Course, yeah, no problem. The more the merrier, ha ha,' Cal says in a rush.

'OK then, bye.'

I hang up. 'He sounded weird,' I mutter, half to myself.

Aaron has a look on his face, like he's thinking hard.

'I think we'd better go. Don't want to arse up the audition,' I say. Aaron looks disappointed for a moment, which, well I guess you can't blame him for, seeing as we were basically just about to go back to his and … I start getting hot in the face, which is too ridiculous. I'm nearly seventeen. This is not a huge deal.

'As you wish,' Aaron says, and smiles.

This is so a huge deal.

Cal's made snacks. Lots of snacks. And drinks. There's crisps, cake, dips even, all set out on the dining-room table, next to where Cal's got his guitar out. If Dad didn't get so weird about boys in my room, Cal could've come to mine to practise, but it's good he's started thinking about having people over to his house again.

Esi's sitting by the dips but she jumps up when we walk in and hugs me while the boys shake hands. Boys are so weird. I let go of Esi and give Cal a big hug too. 'Hey! You didn't need to do all this.' I gesture at the food.

He shrugs. His ears have gone super red.

'Where's your mum?' I say.

'Doing a shift.' Cal's mum's a nurse.

'That's good, isn't it? That she's back at work?'

Aaron mutters something about needing the toilet and wanders off and I can't help but think what a sensitive gesture it is, to give Cal some space to talk if he needs to. Aaron knows all about Cal's mum; I told him the other week.

'Yeah, I think she's doing better,' Cal says, his face hopeful, but I can see shadows smudged around his eyes. I pat him on the shoulder.

'You're doing great,' I say. Esi gives him a sympathetic smile.

Aaron comes back in and I pull my hand away from Cal. I'm aware of Esi watching and get a stab of annoyance; I hope she's not going to be weird like in the cafe yesterday. But she just says mildly, 'You getting on with it then?' and opens her book.

Aaron settles at the other end of the table to Esi and pulls out his phone. I pick up my guitar and we begin. There's one or two dodgy notes from me; I've never been able to hit the highest ones with enough power, but Cal sounds amazing.

By the end of the last run-through, I'm fizzing. Our voices go so well together.

'We've got something here, I really think we do,' I say. We both look at Esi.

'Umm, yeah it was … pretty,' she says.

I have to stop myself frowning. I know she doesn't like country, but if she's not got anything more constructive to add I don't even get why she's here.

To support you, a little voice goes off inside my head. It's true, Esi's always been really supportive, even going back to that time I thought it would be a good idea to make homemade lemonade and sell it. I was purely doing it for a profit – think I'd wanted a new Barbie or something – but Esi insisted we should give the money to charity. Neither of us really thought it through though: in mid-summer, people wanted ice creams, not lukewarm stuff that looked a bit like wee from two ten-year-olds. I don't think we even got back what Esi's mum paid for the ingredients, but she said Esi could donate the money we made anyway.

No, Esi's a good person. Way better than me. But sometimes, she needs to live a bit.

'I think it's brilliant,' Aaron says. I smile at him, but I still feel the sense something's not quite right with the song. Then it comes to me.

'It needs more twang,' I say.

Esi laughs. 'What?'

'It's when—' I break off, because I've tried to explain it to her before. 'Never mind.' I bend to fiddle with the amp. 'You need a Tele really,' I say, looking at my guitar. Then I realise, it's also our voices. Both of them together, that is. Cal has a more classical voice and he somehow seems to be pulling me with him.

'OK. We need to get more twang into you,' I say.

Esi sniggers.

'Oh shut up, you know what I mean.'

'I really don't,' she says, still laughing.

I turn to Cal. 'Just more …' I sing a few notes. 'Try and sing like you're a duck.' He copies me and now I have to laugh.

'That just sounds like you're singing through your nose.'

'Oh.' For a second Cal looks crestfallen. I'm taken aback; he's usually so chilled. Then, to my surprise, Esi drops her book and jumps up.

'My favourite sauce is hoisin,' she says, in the worst duck voice ever. We all burst out laughing and then everyone's trying it together, making more and more ridiculous noises until Cal's bent over, wheezing. Even Aaron has a go, kind of. When Cal straightens up and starts to sing again, it totally works. I pick up my guitar and we sing together, Cal picking out the new melody he's added. And this time, something clicks. The song comes alive. I'm so excited I grab one of his hands as we finish. I can feel it; this song is going to be something special.

Esi says, 'You know, that was pretty good. I liked it.' Which is a lot coming from her.

'It was way better than good,' Aaron says from right by my shoulder.

I jump, I almost forgot he was here. Music does that to me, takes me somewhere else. It's one of the things I love about it. Aaron takes my hand out of Cal's and gives it a squeeze.

'We could maybe just switch that bit here,' Cal points to the scribbled-on sheet music. 'You go low?'

'OK, let's try it.' I take a swig of Coke, then we start up again. This time it's even better and by the end of another twenty minutes we're almost perfect. As soon as we finish, I leap over and give Cal a hug. 'That was so great! You're a genius, Callington Cal-Cal.' We both grin. When I was a lot younger, I used to give everyone silly names. For a whole term, Cal was Callington Cal-Cal of Callingsborough. God only knows why. But it was funny.

'And you too, Gem-Gem,' Cal says as he lets go.

Esi rolls her eyes.

'You know what? I think we've got a chance of getting through,' I say.

'You kidding? We're going to crush it.'

A little while later Aaron says he needs to get back so we pack up and say bye to Cal and Esi. 'See you at college tomorrow,' I say to Cal. 'We can have another run through at lunchtime?'

'I'll sort out the music room,' he says.

'Awesome.'

I'm so hyped up with our success I chat most of the way home before realising Aaron is super quiet. And also driving like Dad does when he's in a mood. I trail off as we practically take a corner on two wheels.

There's silence for a minute, then I say, 'Sorry, I was going on a bit, wasn't I?'

Aaron still doesn't say anything.

'I'm just really excited. Thank you for taking me there. Hope it wasn't too boring for you?'

We're nearly at the bottom of the track now. Aaron pulls over and gives me an odd look. 'No, it was very interesting.' I'm not sure what it is about the way he says 'interesting' but I get a sudden sense I've done something wrong. I frown at him, but before I can say anything his face kind of clears and he gives me a quick kiss. 'This is your stop, little lady,' he says in the worst attempt at a Southern drawl I think I've ever heard.

I laugh. 'You know, you really need to reassess your life choices. You should be an actor,' I say, as deadpan as I can manage.

Aaron winks. 'As you wish.'

I give him another kiss, then I go up the track to get ready for yet another football-filled evening.

Chapter Seventeen

Aaron

There's a tsunami of thoughts in my brain, too fast, too strong to push back:

She's not Cherine.

She hugged him. Twice.

It was a friend hug, nothing else.

Was it?

He's clearly got a massive fucking crush on her.

Does she like him?

The way she looked at him when she was singing.

He called her *Gem.* Did she even notice? She didn't, did she? She's just naive. Can't see what's in front of her face. Because she's not Cherine. She's not built like that.

Let him call her Gem, she's still mine.

Is she mine?

She's not Cherine.

She's not Cherine.

She's not—

Chapter Eighteen

Gemma

Esi: **Hey that was great earlier, really.**
    Gemma: **Thanks.**
    Esi: **You at post-match dinner now?**
    Gemma: **Yep.**
    Esi: **I forgot to ask – Did he win?**
    Gemma: **Nope** ☹
    Esi: **Uh-oh.**
    Gemma: **Yeah, Dad's being Dad. I'd better stop texting.**
    Esi: **OK. See you in the morning? Want to tell you something.**

I send a thumbs-up emoji, then put my phone down, but not before catching Dad's frown.

'Do you have to be attached to that thing at all times?' he says.

For a minute, it's on the edge of my tongue to say, 'What, like you and the football results?' because Dad's literally always got the TV or radio on. But I don't want him to confiscate my phone or anything so I say, 'Sorry,' and shut up. Michael gives me a partially sympathetic and partially grateful look;

he's not the sort of person who likes seeing anyone else get into trouble, but then it does shift the flak away from him.

As if he's sensing what I'm thinking, Michael says, 'You all ready for your audition?' which shows at least one member of my family pays attention to something I say.

I chat about it for a bit but before long Dad's turned the conversation back to football so I give Michael a 'Sorry, I tried' look and go back to texting under the table.

The next morning, I knock for Esi and we head down the track together. She's kind of quiet; usually I'm the grumpier one in the mornings, so it takes until we get about halfway down for me to realise she's only giving one-word answers as I talk about guitars. I'd kill for a new one ahead of the audition because mine's pretty rubbish. My dream guitar's a Gibson, not that I'm likely to afford one of those any time this century. I stop and face her. 'You OK?' I ask.

She gazes back, like she's working out how to say something.

'You wanted to chat yesterday?' I say. Then because I can't help myself, 'It's not about Aaron is it?'

'What? Oh for heaven's sake, Gemma. Not everything is about your new boyfriend.'

I take a slow breath, let it trickle out. 'OK. What then?'

'It's …' She looks unsure of herself suddenly. Like I think she might even cry, and the last time I saw Esi cry was when we were about ten. We were building a base in her living room and she swung a blanket up a bit too enthusiastically and smashed the glass light shade. I lied and said it was me, even though Esi told me not to.

'What?' I'm alarmed now.

'I need to tell you … there's something I've been thinking about for a while and I'm pretty sure it's … that I …' She trails off.

The urge to scream 'You're what?' is pretty powerful right now, but I somehow manage to restrain myself.

'It's OK. You can tell me.' I wait for a moment. 'Or like, when you're ready.'

She lets out a laugh. 'I'm not sure I am. The thing is—'

Just at that moment a horn blasts right behind us. We jump in unison.

It's the first time I haven't been totally happy to see Aaron. He leans out of the car, giving us that smile of his. 'You gals want a lift?' Oh God, this is also the first time I've wished he wouldn't do the voices.

Still, I can't help wavering; he looks so cute this morning. Esi's stiffened beside me.

'Oh – I thought I texted we were getting the bus this morning?' I say.

Aaron's face closes down for a moment, then he says, 'Sorry, thought I'd surprise you.' There's a hint of something in his voice I can't quite work out, like I've hurt his feelings maybe.

'You can go if you like,' Esi says, and there's definitely more than a hint of something in *her* voice. Suddenly I feel like one of those rubber stretchy toys, pulled tight. I look between them, hesitating, and see a flash of sadness in Esi's face. Then the bus comes up behind Aaron – who's parked in the bus stop – and beeps.

'You coming?' Aaron says. And seeing as Esi's already walking fast towards the bus I get in his car.

I text her on the way in, but she responds with a brief **It's fine.** Aaron spends ages finding a parking space. Then there's the whole kissing-a-proper-good-morning when we do get one, so that I end up with only five minutes before my first lesson. I duck into the refectory with Aaron, but the place is already emptying out. I wave at Cal going the other way, and spot Esi deep in conversation with Phoebe. They stop talking as I go up to them, Esi jumping up and saying, 'The bell's about to go,' then hurrying off.

So I take myself to Biology alone and try not to worry about it.

At lunchtime, Aaron's waiting in the corridor as I emerge from my lesson. We kiss and then he links arms with me as we walk towards the refectory. Some of the group are already there – Rach, Cal and Beth – but not Esi. I check my phone; she hasn't texted.

'Want to sit with us?' Aaron says – gesturing over to the knoboons. It's not hugely appealing; that is, until I see the blonde girl waving at Aaron and feel a little ripple of – not quite jealousy, but something that feels vulnerable.

I look back again, but still can't see Esi, only Cal looking my way. 'OK,' I say. I give Cal a quick wave, and follow Aaron over.

As soon as I get there, I reckon I've made the right choice just by the look on Blondie's face. She's definitely not happy to see me. Aaron introduces me around and everyone says hi. I sit next to Aaron, getting the measure of the group, and after a while I relax a bit. The lads, who seemed intimidating in their loudness from a distance are really just like Robbie Wellings from back at school and I know how to handle those. The one with piggy eyes – Jonny – leans forward and says, 'So guess who I saw in town the other day? Hayley Jones. She was well into me. Not that I'd go there, mate.' He makes a crude gesture and manages to raise a couple of laughs. Not on. Hayley Jones managed to get a reputation among some of the boys because she once, stupidly I agree, sent some topless pictures to a little arsehole just like Jonny, who then sent them round the whole school. There was a talk we had to go to about respect, cyber bullying, all of that. We all felt sorry for her – well, most of the girls did. Some joined in calling her a slag. Now I remember, it's one of the things that started off Esi's whole feminism thing.

'Are you talking about a wet dream or was this just a fictional conversation? Because last I heard, Hayley moved away for college,' I say to Jonny. 'And I'm not sure you'd be her type, to be fair.' The whole table erupts into laughter, the blonde girl, Selina, included. And just like that I'm one of the lads. Especially when I win three games of table football in a row.

I'm doing a little victory dance when I see Esi coming into the refectory, finally, with Phoebe. They're walking kind of close, which I wouldn't normally notice, except that Beth stands up in a hurry and walks off, Phoebe running after her. What's that all about? I want to go over, but lunch is nearly finished and I need to get to Psychology.

Later, Esi's already left on the early bus by the time I get out, so Aaron gives me another lift home.

When we're at the lights waiting to turn to go up towards the cliff road, Aaron looks at me softly and says, 'Did you want to come back to mine?'

I'm so close to saying yes. We stare at each other, my heart going hard in my chest. But something's holding me back. Maybe it's Jonny and the lads from earlier. It's not that I don't trust Aaron, I know he's not like that, but sleeping with him is … well it's a big step.

'I think … I'd like to …'

'But?'

'But maybe I'm not ready yet.'

Aaron nods, puts one hand to my hair and gives me a light kiss on the forehead. 'I just … I've never met anyone like you before and – this is something different. Rare, you know?'

He wraps his arms around me as best he can, given we're both wearing seatbelts, and it feels so right, like I'm safe with him, protected. Like my heart's singing. When he pulls over at the bottom of the track we kiss again, one of his hands sliding up under my top. 'You sure you won't come back with me?' he whispers in my ear.

'Soon,' I say, and he leans forward to kiss me hard.

Eventually, I manage to push a hand up between us and give him a little nudge. He pulls back and kind of groans. 'You're so gorgeous, I can't keep my hands off you,' he says.

I laugh, even though I feel the same. 'You're going to have to, mister – I need to get home.'

He groans again, then says, 'OK.'

Everything's still buzzing inside as I go up the track.

Chapter Nineteen

Gemma

'You can't park here,' Cal says.

Aaron grunts and swings his car in on some double yellows anyway. We're here, at the audition, which is being held in a posh-looking hotel, all shining glass in the sun.

'You two jump out and I'll find somewhere,' he says. 'I'll text.'

We get out and Aaron pulls off into the traffic as I wave and blow him a kiss. He toots his horn and I turn to Cal.

'Oh God, are you nervous? I'm nervous.'

'It'll be fine. You've written an amazing song, we've practised. I can totally do *twayang* …' He stretches out the word. 'It's all good.'

I square my shoulders, hoist up my guitar and in we go.

There's a super-glamorous girl on the reception desk, processing a queue of people with lightning efficiency.

'We're running ten minutes behind, but it shouldn't be too long to wait,' she says, and hands us some numbers to pin on our outfits. Before we know it, we're signed in and ushered into a holding room with a handful of other people.

I look around, wondering who might be going through. There are twenty slots for the regional final, but well over a hundred acts auditioning today, which I suppose is not the worst odds. And 'Sea Dreams' is such a good song, I can feel it. Good enough to beat the other people here? I scan the room again. The others are a mixed bag: some look like they were singing country before I was born – one guy with long grey hair and a beard strumming a guitar in the corner must be in his sixties at least. He has a seasoned air, like he's used to playing in pubs and clubs. Then two girls my age with matching cowboy boots and confident expressions doing some warm-up exercises. They sound really good – professional and slick. I bet they go somewhere like Portsmouth College. There's a lad standing on his own in a button-down shirt who looks a little bit like Aaron.

I put one hand in my bag, 'Oh crap.'

'What?' Cal says.

'Left my phone in Aaron's car.'

'Oh. Well, he'll ask at reception, won't he?'

I nod, annoyed I don't know his number off by heart, but then since when does anyone know any numbers by heart? I guess my grandparents did in the days before mobiles.

'Did you know people used to answer the phone with their number? So if your number was, I don't know, 111222 or whatever, that's what you'd say. That's bonkers, isn't it? My nana told me,' I say.

I know I'm gabbling, but I'm getting so nervous there's a chance I might pee myself in a minute.

'Fascinating,' Cal says, with only the tiniest hint of sarcasm, and offers me some chocolate.

'I'm going to puke,' I say, but I take some anyway. We lapse into anxious silence.

'Didn't Esi want to come today?' Cal says, more to make conversation than anything.

'Uh, she's working,' I say. I don't add that I've barely seen her all week, between rehearsals and seeing Aaron.

'Hey, do you know what's up with Beth and Phoebe?' I ask Cal. I tell him about Beth rushing off the other day.

To my surprise, Cal shifts uncomfortably. 'I think … if Esi's not said anything to you it's not really up to me …'

'Said anything about what? She never said anything's up,' I reply, deciding to ignore the memory of her trying to tell me something the other day, before Aaron came along in his car. There's a tiny swoop in the pit of my stomach, like you get when you know you've been caught out doing something wrong, and then irritation. 'Why does she have to be so secretive anyway?' I say. I look him full in the face. 'Go on, tell me what she's said to you.' I maybe sound a bit aggressive, but truth is, I'm hurt. Esi's usually so supportive, and instead she's decided she's got some issue with Aaron when she doesn't even know him. And now she's keeping some secret from me, that apparently Cal knows about and I don't. What kind of friends does that make us?

In response, Cal hands me a bottle of water. I take it, about to grill him some more, but at that moment a door opens and a girl comes through. She's wearing a red dress and holding a guitar, but unlike the confident girls in the corner, she looks like she's about to cry as she pulls off her number and drops it on the floor. I see her shake her head to herself. The older beardy guy asks her how it went.

132

'Not well,' she says, sounding on the edge of tears. He makes a sympathetic face.

'Yep, I'm going to be sick,' I say. 'I wish they'd tell you straight away whether you've got through. I hate waiting.' The information pack we were sent says that regional finalists will be notified at the end of the day. I suppose it's better than some *BGT*-style red cross halfway through your song. At least our slot is one of the last ones so we won't have to wait hours and hours to hear our fate.

'Deep breaths,' Cal says, and rubs my back.

Then a man holding a clipboard comes through the same door the girl did. He smiles around the room. 'Right then. Do we have Cal and Gemma?'

I clutch hold of Cal's hand as we make our way over. The man gives me a sympathetic look. 'Deep breaths,' he says. 'You'll be fine.'

'That's what *he* said,' I gasp out, but a second later I start to smile at how surreal this whole thing is. We won't be singing in front of The Greenwoods today – that's only for the national final – but there's going to be a producer, a record exec, and Niles Adam, the songwriter, which is pretty awesome.

And scary.

We follow the man into a surprisingly small room. There's two chairs and we both sit, me positioning my guitar on my knee. I glance at Cal. He looks slightly pale, but steady. My hands feel frozen. I don't think I could even pick out a note, let alone sing. Sweat starts to track slowly down my back.

'Hello. Who are you?' The man who's spoken has a kind face and with a jolt I realise it's Niles. Oh God.

'We're Cal and Gemma, from Ullington,' I say. It comes out a little high-pitched.

Fake it till you make it, Gemma.

I square my shoulders, sit up straight. Suddenly, I feel myself relax, my voice getting stronger. 'And this is the song I wrote, "Sea Dreams".' I smile. 'I hope you enjoy it.'

Next to me, I can sense Cal grinning too, urging me on.

'Fabulous. When you're ready then.'

I glance at Cal, who whispers, 'You've got this.' And my hand begins to move on the guitar, finding the familiar chords. My nerves crest then settle into a steady roll like waves crashing against rocks. Cal's eyes are telling me I can do it.

When it's time to come in, my voice hits the notes perfectly. We build through the new harmonies, locked into the moment together, and when we've finished there's that heartbeat stillness that tells you magic's been created.

When I turn back to the judges, they're leaning forward. And Niles is smiling.

There's only two acts left after us and then a nervous wait before we're finally all called into a conference room for the names of the finalists to be announced.

I grab Cal's hand as the woman from earlier stands in front of us with a piece of paper.

'The judges were blown away by the level of talent on display today, but sadly we can only take some of you through to the next round. I'm sure you all want to know so I'll get right on with it. The first regional finalists are The Devon Hearts.'

The two matching girls from earlier start screaming and hugging.

'I knew it,' I mutter to Cal. 'We should've come up with a proper name.' He squeezes my hand. I'm in agony as more names are read out, clutching Cal's hand tighter and tighter. Thank goodness I'm not doing this by myself.

And then, as if through a haze, I hear our names being read out.

I look at Cal, see he's grinning about as widely as I am. A man is filming everyone on his phone to put up on Instagram later – I can't wait to repost it to my channel. The last few names are announced.

'Congratulations, regional finalists!' the woman yells and the room erupts in cheers. I'm so busy jumping up and down and hugging Cal it takes me a moment to realise Aaron's even standing there, watching us.

Chapter Twenty

Aaron

Cal has enough time to see my face and step to one side fast, before Gem's running full speed down the room towards me, yelling, 'Aaron! Oh my God, we got through! I can't believe you weren't there – my stupid phone was in your car and then they took us all off to that room, but can you believe it?' She throws herself into my arms.

There's a lurching in my chest as I struggle with the sickening feeling of seeing her hugging Cal, then, conscious of Cal watching, I lift her off her feet and swing her around in a full circle, before placing her gently on the ground. 'I knew you would,' I say, and then I kiss her. It's a slightly harder kiss than I meant. Needy.

I pull her to me closer, wrestling the feelings back down and when I finally let her go, she's breathless and flushed, her lips a deep red. She has a half-laugh on her face, but her eyes are quizzical.

'Where were you anyway?' she says.

I shrug, tell the truth. 'They were only letting the people auditioning in, but I sweet-talked the girl on reception.'

Persuaded – eventually – more like. Not that Gem needs to know that.

Gem smiles, hugs me again.

Cal's giving a good go at seeming unconcerned. But I can tell. You got a girl as hot as Gem, you always know when someone else is looking.

I'm sure of her though.

Are you? whispers the little voice which laughs with Cherine's cruelty.

Yes, I am.

I am.

How sure? the little voice asks.

Chapter Twenty-One

Gemma

Aaron goes quiet once we've dropped Cal off. It's weird. One minute he's laughing and joking and the next, it's like he shuts down. It takes me a few minutes to notice, because I'm still on this massive high, but when I say, 'I couldn't believe it when they said we got through! And Niles said he thought it was a really special song. He actually said that – "really special". Niles Adam!' for admittedly about the twentieth time, Aaron says nothing, just drives.

'Aaron?'

Still nothing.

A minute goes by, which stretches out way longer than I knew a minute could.

'Are you OK?' I say. All of a sudden, I'm conscious I'm not wearing much, just the beautiful black dress Aaron bought me and my boots. I twist my cowboy hat in my lap. I look at the air con, which is set to low.

'I suppose I've been going on a bit,' I say, but it comes out uncertain instead of jokey. In response, Aaron goes a bit faster and then turns suddenly on to one of the back roads leading towards the beach. He pulls up at the parking spot we went to before, the day of the cave and switches off the engine.

Just as the silence is getting too much, he says without looking my way. 'Do you have feelings for him?'

'What? Who?'

Aaron looks at me and his face is so different to usual, closed and cold. 'You know who.'

'*Cal?*'

Aaron holds my eyes.

'Are you serious? No! Of course I don't.' My heart's suddenly going as hard as it was in the audition. Even though I haven't done anything wrong, there's this sense inside that I have, because Aaron looks so upset. 'Honestly, I really don't,' I say lamely. Then, maybe because it's been a long day and so much has happened, or because I can't bear to see Aaron staring at me that way, the sad, lost, disappoin-ted look in his eyes, my own start to fill up. 'As you wish, remember? I know we haven't known each other long, but … I really feel that. I do.'

Aaron gazes at me for an eternity longer, and then some-thing seems to break in his face and his eyes fill with tears too. 'I'm sorry,' he says.

There's something alarming and strange about seeing a boy cry – any boy, let alone one you love. I reach forward to put my arms around him and for a moment he seems to collapse into me, like a huge weight's lifting off him. 'Sorry,' he says again. 'I just couldn't bear it if … I've been here before.'

I pull back to look at him, put one hand up to the side of his face. 'When?' I say.

And that's when he tells me about Cherine. 'There was another girl back in London. Cherine. She was my first love, I guess. Or I thought she was.'

His first love. I can't lie; I get a flash of jealousy when he says the word 'love' but I try and contain it. I'd kind of thought I was his first. He pauses long enough that I say, 'What happened?'

He gives a bitter laugh. 'She cheated on me. Broke my heart. I guess that's why I got a bit ... oversensitive.'

'I'm sorry.'

'Don't be, I know you're nothing like her. What we've got ... it's not like with Cherine. I was stupid. She didn't really care about me. But you're different. I knew it as soon as I met you. I can trust you.'

'You can!' I'm so eager to agree with him, to see that hurt look gone from his face. I want to make things better for him. 'You can be sure of me,' I add quietly.

A different kind of intensity begins to fill the car as we look at each other.

Aaron breaks the silence first. 'Do you ... Would you come back with me?' And his face is telling me how hard it is for him to ask, how hurt he still is over what that girl did to him before. And if anything was going to make up my mind, it would be that. I want to show him he's right, show him who I am.

Who we are, together.

'Yes,' I whisper.

Back at his flat, I barely notice the chrome kitchen, apart from the way the light glances off the black tiles as Aaron unzips my dress. The soft touch of his lips as I stand exposed in only my bra and knickers. The look on his face as he tells me how beautiful I am before leading me to his room. This is it, we're really going to do it for the first time.

His bed is wide and firm and I can't stop looking at it as he kisses along my neck, but before I can decide if the shaking in my legs is due to fear or excitement, he's taken off my bra and the shock of his hands where no one but me has ever put their hands before makes me jump. Aaron doesn't seem to notice; he's pulling off his jeans and boxers in one movement and I'm staring at his penis and wondering about condoms, then he pulls me to him and somehow we're on the bed and he's taken off my knickers and he's on top of me, his breathing hot and ragged. When he puts one hand between my legs and his fingers push inside me, I gasp out. It's kind of painful, truth be told, and I'm not sure how to say slow down. He's whispering all the time, 'You're beautiful, you're so sexy, do you know how gorgeous you are?' and 'I want you,' and that, combined with his fingers which are rough but kind of hitting the right places, helps me get into the mood. Sort of. When he pulls back and fumbles in a drawer next to his bed, I take a deep breath and try to relax. There's a part of me that's wondering if this is right after all. But it's Aaron, I want to be with him. I'm ready, at least I think I am. I love him. Surely that makes me ready? Aaron seems to sense my uncertainty, because once he's got the condom on, he pauses above me.

'OK?' he says.

'Yes!' I gasp. He presses his mouth to mine, his kiss taking all my breath out of me. One hand is between my legs, kind of fiddling about down there and then he starts to push inside.

It feels harsh, like I'm being jabbed hard with a tampax, and I gasp out again, then kind of suck in my breath, holding on to his back as he thrusts all the way in and begins to move inside me. After a while, I start to get used to the sensation and think I should be making some noises, so I let out a couple of small moans. It's definitely starting to feel better, maybe getting to be more than better, so it's not like faking, but it seems to encourage Aaron and he grabs my legs and pushes them right back up towards my chest and pushes harder and it kind of hurts. Not just at the entrance bit, but somewhere deep in the pit of my stomach too.

I'm just about to tell him to slow up a bit when he shudders and collapses against me, his body slick with sweat. I can feel his heart thrumming against my chest, hear his long breaths. After a while he pulls out and peels off the condom, chucking it on his bedside table, then leans over to give me a gentle kiss.

'That was wonderful,' he says, kisses me again. 'You were wonderful.'

I kiss him back, making an *mmm* noise because I'm not sure what to say.

'Did you come?' he says.

For a second, I'm confused by the question, then I say, 'Yes.'

'Good. I wanted your first time to be special.'

I cuddle into him, ignore the soreness between my legs.

Afterwards, Aaron plants little gentle kisses around my mouth, my neck, my forehead. He wraps his arms around

142

me and I feel his skin on mine, warm and new. How connected we are. And he whispers it for real this time: 'I love you.'

Those three words are like a shot of energy, flowing through me. I look deep into his eyes and say it too, 'I love you, Aaron Weaver.'

He laughs then, and it feels like we're writing our own song, together. Then his face gets serious and he says, 'You know, when I first met you, I thought about this poem. It starts out, "I hold your heart." And that's how you make me feel – like there's something good in the world I can hold on to.' He kisses me again, draws me so close to him it's almost hard to breathe.

'I love you, Gem. And I promise I'll hold your heart forever.'

Part Two

Part Two

Chapter Twenty-Two

Gemma

I'm sure Esi or Cal or someone will notice there's something different about me, but no one does. Even though I feel like there's a neon 'I Just Lost my Virginity to the Boy I Love' sign over my head. A week goes by; a week where I spend nearly all my time with Aaron. We leave college as soon as our last lessons are over, to go to the beach and walk hand in hand, or more often back to his. I like it when we have a laugh, the feeling of being so close to someone you're almost the same person. I can't believe it's only been a few days since we started sleeping together; it feels like an eternity.

One day we're lying naked on Aaron's bed. 'What are you doing tomorrow?' he says, tracing a line up my arm. I have to think for a moment. This week's been a blur of dates with Aaron, sex with Aaron. I actually skipped afternoon lessons yesterday when he texted me to meet him out the front of college.

'Well, for a start I need to finish that Psychology essay – now I'm over my "migraine",' I say, making air quotes. We laugh. 'But seriously, I do need to do it. And I've got a shift at the cafe after Michael's match. So, unless we meet up super late … you might have to cope for a day without me. I know it'll be hard,' I say, only half teasing.

'How will I manage?' he says, all fake tragic, which makes me smile. He kisses me, then pulls back, his head on one side. 'Do you have to go to all of your brother's matches?'

'Most of them,' I say lightly. 'It's a pain some of the time, but Mum and Dad like him to have the support. We're a football family, after all!' I'm joking, but if I'm truthful, Aaron's hit a nerve. I'd rather be with him than sitting out in a field somewhere.

'But they didn't come to your audition last week,' Aaron says.

'No-o, Michael had an away game, otherwise …'

'You think they would have come?'

I shift on top of the bed, suddenly uncomfortably aware that no, they probably wouldn't. I grab the duvet and wrap it around my shoulders.

'And didn't you say your dad drives him to all his practices and matches, took a different job just so he'd be closer to training, but that Portsmouth College was out of the question for you, even paying for you to get the train up? Even though songwriting's *your* dream?' Aaron says.

'I—'

'Do they even recognise how talented you are? You've got a gift, you really have.'

'Thank you!' I say it in a jokey voice, but Aaron's still holding my eyes. He waits until I stop smiling, like he really wants me to understand, to feel what he's saying.

It strikes me then: no one's ever cared about me like this – not Mum or Dad, not even Esi.

'I just want you to realise how special you are, even if your parents are too blind to see it.'

'Thank you,' I say again, but this time my voice is full of tears. 'I guess … maybe they just don't … I don't know.' A wave of sadness overtakes me. I'm not sure I like thinking about this sort of stuff. Aaron pecks me on the nose, then stands up and pulls on his boxers.

'I'm going to get you a drink – stay right there,' he says. At the doorway he pauses. 'You know, if I were in your place, I wouldn't waste my time feeling sad about it. I'd be furious.'

While he's in the kitchen, I snuggle properly back down under the covers and think about what he's said. Gradually the sadness, that feeling of being small, that I'll never be as important to Mum and Dad as Michael, is shouldered away by something else: anger. It bubbles and boils, burning the smallness away, making me feel stronger.

I like it.

I still find myself at Michael's match the next day. The weather's starting to get pretty chilly now and, typically, it's raining. I sit under a massive umbrella, listening to the way the pattering of rain merges with shouts from the pitch, the ref's whistle. Mum's standing under her own umbrella, but Dad's not bothering to try and keep the rain off. He never does. Not even a hood. I think he thinks they're for girls or something. Whatever – he's the one with his hair plastered to his head. I flex my feet, which are getting damp, and tuck them further under my chair, shivering.

When Michael scores a goal, I'm so busy texting Aaron it doesn't even register until Dad's face appears under the brolly. 'You watching this? Come on!' he ducks back out and reluctantly I stand and jump up and down a couple of times, clapping the end of Michael's victory lap, before shooting back under the cocoon of the umbrella.

Aaron was right. I am angry. Maybe I have been all along, it just took someone who really gets me, who loves me for being me, to help me see it.

As the match ends, Dad's off for a word with the coach.

'Thought he wasn't supposed to be doing that any more?' I say to Mum. It comes out slightly on the grumpy side.

Mum squints at me through the rain. 'That goal was good though? He nearly got a second, too.'

Usually I'd join in, find something about Michael's performance to praise, a new hope to polish up. Or at least agree with Mum. But today I snap, 'Dad's not even here, Mum.'

I yank my brolly down and stalk off towards the car, before realising halfway there that I don't have the keys so now I'm going to have to finish my flounce by standing dripping while I wait for one of my parents to catch me up.

That is until I get closer and spot the unmistakeable shape of Aaron's car parked a bit down from Dad's.

'Aaron!' I'm grinning so hard as I run towards the car. Aaron steps out as I get there, but rather than swing me in for a hug or kiss, he just kind of waves at me, his eyes looking over my shoulder. I glance back, see Mum's coming up behind with her chair. Dad's still nowhere to be seen.

'Wait there,' I mouth at Aaron, then run back to Mum,

tell her I'm off to do some studying before my shift at the cafe and not to worry. I've dashed back to Aaron before she even gets a chance to ask any questions.

As soon as we've pulled out and around the corner, Aaron puts his hand on my thigh.

'I can't believe you came!' I say.

'Thought you needed rescuing,' Aaron says, and once again I can't help but think how in sync with me he is, how he knows things about me even I haven't seen before.

We go back to Aaron's and it isn't until we're in his bedroom and he's already started undoing my jeans that I realise I totally don't have any of my essay stuff with me.

'Oh my God!' I say out loud.

Aaron grins, waggles his eyebrows as if to say, 'You're keen.'

'Not that!' I punch him on the shoulder. 'My Psychology essay.'

'Do it tomorrow,' Aaron says in my ear.

'Looks like I don't have much of a choice now,' I say. But I'm kind of laughing as I do.

At the cafe, Esi is definitely not laughing and neither is Dora. OK, so I'm a bite late – me and Aaron lost track of time – but only by ten minutes.

'There you are,' Dora says, while Esi just stares at me.

OK, maybe it's more like twenty minutes, now I've seen the cafe clock. But I'm never usually late.

'Gemma, you know I expect you to be on time,' Dora says.

'Sorry.'

151

She purses her lips at me, then looks to Aaron. 'We're really sorry Mrs … uhh,' Aaron says, and flashes her that smile. It works. Dora says, 'You can call me Dora, but don't bring her late again, young man, understood?'

'Yes, ma-am,' Aaron says in a pretty good American accent.

Esi makes a noise that sounds like a snort and turns away. Her mood does not get better once Dora's gone, even though we're not exactly overridden with customers. It gets to the point where I can't be bothered to try making conversation, given I'm only getting one-word answers back, so I end up chatting to Aaron for most of the shift.

Just before locking-up time, Aaron disappears to the toilet. As soon as the door closes, I say, 'What's the problem?'

'You want an answer to that?' Esi says.

'I asked, didn't I?'

'Yeah, I don't think you do.'

I heave out a sigh. 'You've been acting weird for days now.'

'*I've* been acting weird? You know, I never thought you'd be the sort of person who dropped her friends the second she got a boyfriend.' Esi's voice is so sarcastic.

I seriously can't believe what I'm hearing. 'I've dropped you? You've been avoiding me. And anyway, it's not like that.'

'How have I been avoiding you? I've barely seen you.'

'Well, what about you? I know something's up with Phoebe and Beth. I saw Beth storming out of the refectory the other day. But you've not said anything. So what's going on with you?'

Esi puts her hand up to her cheek in a way she always does when she's embarrassed. 'That's not the point,' she says, her voice rising. 'Don't make this about me. It's about what's going on with you, and with *him*.'

I really don't like the way she says 'him' like that.

'Just because you don't get it,' I say. Then, even though I already know what she's going to say, I can't help adding, 'We're in love, OK? I love him.'

'You've known him five minutes.'

'That's not the point. You know when you know,' I say.

Esi gives me a hard look and then it's like all the anger drains out of her. 'You don't know anything about him, who he is, where he's come from. But hey. If you want to decide you're in love, then I guess that's up to you. Just don't expect me to wait around while you come to your senses. And don't bother pretending you care about my problems.'

'Wow. That's harsh.' I stare at her like she's morphed into this person I don't even know. But before I can work out how to defend myself, she gives a laugh. 'So you asked about me because you really want to know? Because I could've done with that weeks ago.'

'Yes. Of course I—'

But then Aaron comes out from the toilet and glances between our angry faces. 'Everything OK, girls?' he says.

'*Women*,' Esi snaps.

Aaron laughs. 'I forgot you were a feminist.'

'That's not an insult, you know,' Esi says. Then she bangs the keys on the table. 'I'll lock up.'

'Fine.' I'm still pissed off, also feeling slightly guilty. So taking off seems like the best option.

'Are you sure? It looks like you two gi— women …
need to talk? I can come back in a while?' Aaron says.

I look at Esi as if to say, 'See? Look how sensitive he is!'
but she's looking away.

'No thank you, I'll be just fine on my own,' she says
tightly, turning her back on the both of us.

Chapter Twenty-Three

Aaron

Sleeping with Gem for the first time was almost an out-of-body experience. Knowing I made her first time so special is like being in a different universe. Now it's finally happened I can't stop myself wanting her all the time. Even when I'm with her it's like I need her closer to me, I need to make her part of me. Sex is the one thing that stills that whispering voice, the one that says I'll never be good enough, that she'll wake up and see I'm still a loser underneath.

I was listening at the door in the cafe. If I didn't think Esi was out to get me before, I know she is now. I shouldn't be surprised; Gem told me she's a feminazi. I just don't know what Gem sees in her; she's not exactly a good friend. It's like Gem's family. They don't see her either, not like I do. They don't even know how special she is. But I'll show her and I'll keep showing her because we belong together.

It's thoughts like this that go through my mind at 2 a.m., on the nights I can't sleep. They lull me back off, at least some of the time. But other nights memories threaten to overload the good thoughts, drown the feeling of Gem's body or the smell of her skin, the way she laughs. Turn everything dark. I lie there, wishing she was next to me, that I had her all the time. It's then that I can't help texting her, hoping she's awake. Sometimes she replies but the nights she doesn't go black again. I don't know how to tell her though, not without her thinking I'm crazy. So I wait and wait and then by 6 a.m. she's usually texted me back, but if not I ping her or I go on her YouTube channel and I play the videos of her singing and that works.

Right up until she uploads one of her and Cal singing together.

Chapter Twenty-Four

Gemma

'Wait!' By the time I realise Aaron isn't going to be picking me up for college, it's almost too late for the bus and I have to run. The only reason Grumpy Sharon hasn't shut the door and left me in a cloud of fumes, I realise as I get to the bus, is because someone's blocking the doors from closing.

An Esi-shaped someone.

We haven't texted since Saturday at the cafe. Yesterday I spent a load of time around Cal's, practising for the regional audition. You have to play three songs, one of which can be the first one you used, to show your versatility. As well as 'Sea Dreams', we've got one upbeat song I wrote a while ago, but I'm thinking of writing a new one for the third. If I can find time from somewhere. We've been updating my YouTube and Insta like mad with pictures and videos of us rehearsing. We uploaded one the other day, filming the sunlight on the waves from my bedroom window while I talked about the inspiration behind my songs. I've picked up loads of followers and the main 'From Nashville ...' channel is nudging past 25k now. They're going to record us singing at the regional finals and put it on their channel too. It's all super exciting. And a bit daunting: only the twelve regional winners will go through to the final and get to win two days' coaching ahead of the national final.

I slide on to the bus, facing down Grumpy Sharon's glare, and follow Esi up the aisle. She sits on the outside seat so I take the one opposite and say, 'Thanks.'

'No problem.' She gets out a book. Camus.

We go up the road while I have a minor battle in my head about whether to say sorry first. I look over to where Esi's pretending to read her book and wait.

'What?' she says when she eventually looks up and catches my eye.

'I know you're not reading. You would've usually turned the page three times by now.'

Esi closes her book. We look at each other, then she shakes her head. 'You're not going to apologise, are you?'

'Are you?'

'I asked first.'

We face off for a minute and realise at the same time there's nothing to do but laugh. Neither me or Esi have much of a track record of backing down. After a moment, I say, 'Seriously though, what's going on with you?'

'You really want to know?'

Just then my phone beeps and it takes everything I have not to look at it, because it's so weird for Aaron not to show up and then not to text, and I've been getting kind of worried, but somehow I manage to keep focused on Esi.

'Yes, of course I do,' I say.

'OK then.' Esi takes a deep breath and looks out of the

window as if she's summoning the words. 'It's probably not going to be a surprise, I mean I expect you already guessed, but the thing is, I'm pretty sure I'm bi.'

'Uh-huh,' I say. I might've sneaked a quick look at my phone. Just a tiny one. Aaron has simply texted, **Meet me at the steps**.

No kisses.

What does that even mean? Is he breaking up with me? I'm glad I haven't had any breakfast because I feel sick all of a sudden.

'Did you even hear what I just said?' Esi's voice breaks into my thoughts.

'What? Oh … um yes, you're …' It's not until a second or two that what she's said actually goes in. 'What? Since when? I mean, are you sure?' My thoughts are going too fast, trying to think about Aaron and now about Esi. 'Is that why Beth was pissed off? Oh my God, are you and Phoebe getting it on?'

The words have barely left my mouth before I know I've said all the wrong things.

'Am I *sure*? Am I sleeping with someone else's *girlfriend*? What the hell is wrong with you?' Esi shouts the last part.

'Wait … I didn't mean …'

'Fuck off, Gemma,' Esi says, her voice about as cold as I've ever heard it.

I pull back, shocked. Me and Esi, we argue and bicker, it's what we do. It's us. But this … this is something else. I've never heard her use the F-word before.

'Esi …'

'I don't want to hear it.' She's opened her book up again.

I stare at her, not knowing what to say. Part of me is feeling pretty shitty, but another part is angry too. Before I can find the right words, Cal bounds on to the bus and plonks himself next to me.

'Did you see our video has over two hundred likes already?' Cal says. 'You want to see, Esi?' Cal says, but she shrugs his hand away. He looks at me, mouthing, 'What's up with her?' and I feel kind of bad doing it, but I just do an exaggerated 'Search me' expression. As soon as the bus stops, she ignores Cal's attempts to talk to her and stomps off in the direction of the refectory. I hang back deliberately; may as well give her a head start. Plus, there's Aaron's text to worry about …

For a moment I'd forgotten, but now there's that lurching in my stomach as we approach the car park, even though Cal's still chatting in my ear, laughing about something or other.

'You listening, Gemma?' Cal says. But I'm really not.

Aaron's standing by his car, arms crossed, watching us as we walk towards him. There's something in his look that makes me take a half-step sideways, away from Cal. A sudden prickle goes all down my back as I remember the conversation me and Aaron had the other week, right before we slept together for the first time.

Do you have feelings for him?

But I thought we'd sorted that out. There must be something else wrong.

We stop at the foot of Aaron's car.

'Hi, Aaron,' Cal says.

'Hi.'

Cal looks between us. 'Ahh ... so I'll maybe see you later?'

I smile at him. 'Sure!' I make it brighter than I'm feeling on purpose; I don't like Cal looking all awkward and unsure like that. He goes and I'm left facing Aaron.

For a long moment he doesn't say anything at all, simply stares at me, and it's like someone's drained out the Aaron I know and replaced him with a person I'm not sure I recognise at all.

'What's wrong?' I say eventually. I mean it to sound even, mature, but it ends up high and anxious, as though I have something to hide.

'You don't know?'

'No! I'm not a mind-reader, Aaron,' I say, and his eyes flash at this in a way that almost makes me want to take a step backwards. 'Is it ... Has something happened in London with your mum?'

Aaron gives a short laugh. The sort a teacher might give when you're trying to pull one over on them. 'Are you pretending to be stupid on purpose?'

The word 'stupid' lands so hard it takes the breath out of me. And now Aaron's waving his phone under my nose, scrolling along the video I recognise is the one I made with Cal yesterday and pausing it at a point where we're holding hands and kind of laughing into each other's faces.

Aaron takes a long breath, like he's trying to control himself. 'We already talked about this. Can't you see how it feels for me, to wake up this morning and see my girlfriend all over another guy?' His voice rises. 'I mean, you're practically screwing him in this one.' He takes another breath, pulls his voice down low again. 'How do you think that looks to other people?'

'But … I … that's not what I meant.' I feel like parts of me are crumbling under the weight of Aaron's gaze. Tears start up in my eyes. 'I'm sorry, I didn't think with the video. But there's nothing going on, I swear. You know it. You know me.' I grab my phone, log on to my YouTube channel and quickly delete the video, then hold my phone out for Aaron to see. 'Look, it's gone. Honestly, it was just a laugh, something for the competition. It really was.' My voice wobbles and I feel the first teardrop run down the side of my nose.

Then, because I don't know what else to do, I take a step forward and wrap my arms around him. It's like hugging a stone. 'Aaron, please … I'm sorry, I just didn't think … it's all part of telling the story of the song, that's all. I love you … As you wish, remember?'

Aaron pushes me back, not hard, but more holding me at arm's-length, his eyes searching mine. After what feels like forever, something in his face softens a notch. 'OK,' he says.

The relief that rushes through me then is so powerful it feels like I need something to hold me up, and as though he senses it, Aaron pulls me to him. He speaks to the top of my head. 'You can see why I was worried though, right? After what I told you about Cherine, I thought you'd be more sensitive.'

'I'm sorry,' I say.

'It's just … hard for me,' he says.

'Because of her?' I don't want to say that girl's name.

'Partly, but also …' He takes a big breath and looks at me.

162

'Listen, before all of that, back in London – I was …' He breaks off.

'What?'

'Let's just say Cherine wasn't the only one to betray me. You try being dicked over by your own mother.'

'What happened?'

He winces, like it's too painful to say and I don't want to push. Then he kind of pulls me to him and I feel the need running all through that hug. So I hug him back just as tightly, and I'm telling myself I won't be like those other people who have hurt him so badly. And as if he knows what I'm thinking, he says, 'I know you're different. I know you wouldn't hurt me on purpose.'

We go into the refectory. Esi's nowhere to be seen, but the rest of the gang is at the table.

'Hey!' Rachael waves us over.

'You want to?' I say to Aaron.

He looks at the table and then back at me. It's an expression I've started to recognise from the last couple of weeks. 'Come on, let's get out of here,' he says.

Cal: **You on your way over?**

Gemma: **Sorry – something's come up at home, can we rehearse at college tomorrow instead?**

Cal: **Sure, no problem.**

Gemma: **Thanks!**

Cal: **xx**

I don't send kisses back. I feel a bit bad cancelling on Cal, but after Aaron and I 'made up' at his, and then made up some more, we had a long chat. I guess I can see the Cal thing from Aaron's point of view. I was being insensitive. I never thought how it comes across before. And then there was the audition and all the hugging and stuff. So it's probably better if we rehearse all together in college when Aaron's around, so he knows there's nothing to worry about. I can't believe what that girl, Cherine, did to him. And all the stuff you read online says relationships are about compromise, putting the other person first.

It's worth it when you're in love.

Chapter Twenty-Five

Gemma

It's Friday morning. We've skipped out of college again and we're lying on a rug on our beach, another one wrapped around us because the weather is getting colder by the day. I snuggle in to Aaron while he strokes my hair and we listen to the waves. Behind us is the cave, the one we went to what feels like an ocean of time ago, when I first realised I was falling for him.

'I got a D for that Psychology essay,' I say to Aaron.

'The tutors are idiots,' he says. He picks up a rock and I feel his body tense as he throws it out towards the sea. 'Don't tell me you want to go back?'

'No, I'd rather spend the time with you.'

It's true, too. These times when it's just the two of us, when we hold hands and look at the shapes of the clouds racing past in the sky, when he tells me all the things he loves about me, are like some magical world where only the two of us matter. Although I can't help thinking about someone else too.

'Do you think I should text Esi?' I say.

He raises himself up on one elbow to look down at me. 'I think she needs to apologise to you. She's being massively oversensitive.'

'But—'

'You should stop worrying about people who don't value you for who you are. Esi, your parents,' he says. He takes hold of my hand. 'It must be hard, knowing they love Michael more than you.'

'What? That's not—'

'I know I don't have a sibling, but I do know what it's like to find out your own parents don't really give a shit, or not enough of a shit about you. And it's painful. But sometimes you have to be brave, you have to see what's in front of you. Face it, you know?' he says.

I stare at him, then up along the beach to the dark cave, and there's this sense that something is waiting for me in there.

'It's no good being in denial forever,' Aaron says.

Is that true? I wonder.

But now Aaron's said it, I can't stop a whole series of images playing in my head: Dad cheering Michael from the touchline. Dad and Michael talking endless football in front of the TV. Mum washing Michael's kit, making his food. When does anyone ask me what I want to eat? All those matches, week after week, and never once is it my turn.

'Don't get sad,' Aaron whispers in my ear. 'You've got me. I see how special you are.'

He pulls me close to him again, blocking my view of the cave, until I stop shivering and lie still, listening to the sound of his heart and the crash of the waves. Then he's moving

166

away, getting something out of his bag. 'Here. I have something for you.' He presents it with a half-bow and a little flourish, like he's trying to take the piss but not quite succeeding.

It's a sea-blue box with a white ribbon that can only have come from one place. I trace the lettering spelling TIFFANY & CO. with something approaching awe. I've never even been there, let alone thought I might wear something from Tiffany.

'Are you going to open it?' Aaron says, his usual crooked smile sliding away into a serious expression. When I do, there's this stunning rose-gold infinity necklace inside.

'It's beautiful,' I say, and it comes out kind of breathy because I'm pretty blown away.

'Here.' Aaron takes it out of the box and fastens it around my neck, then pulls me back into him so he's cradling me from behind. We gaze out to sea, Aaron with one hand over the necklace which hangs under my collarbone, a few inches above my heart.

'Look out there, at the waves,' Aaron whispers in my ear. 'They go on forever. That's how much I love you.'

Chapter Twenty-Six

Aaron

'All right, Weaver?'

'I'm always all right, Jonno,' I say.

'Here.' Jonny shoves up so I can sit down. I pull Gem on to my lap.

She's wearing the infinity necklace and I see Selina looking at it with an openly jealous gaze. Girls are hilarious sometimes. Gem spots it too; she fingers the necklace and I'm suddenly back on the beach with her. I tighten my arms around her waist and she leans her head back so it's resting under my chin. And there's Jonny, pretending not to look, me knowing he wants her too and how she'd never look at him.

Times like these, I'm so proud I could straddle the world.

'So when's your next audition?' Selina says to Gem. I feel her stiffen for a second, then she replies airily, 'Oh that? I don't know. Some time before Christmas?'

'I guess you'll have to do loads of rehearsing with Cal,' Selina adds, with heavy emphasis on the word 'rehearsing'. She glances at me, as if to gauge my reaction.

'Ooh, bet he'd love to—' Binners starts, before catching my eye.

'Don't be a dick,' Gem says, and I squeeze her tight, whisper in her ear, 'Bet Binners wishes he could find his,' and she laughs loudly.

Binners has got more bloody porn up on his phone and is waving it at Jonny, who barely bothers to look. Gem's rolling her eyes at Selina.

After I've walked Gem to her lesson, I slide, late, into a seat near the back of the Maths class. Jonny and Binners are waiting with a smirk. As soon as the tutor's set us some work and everyone gets going, Binners starts.

'Saw you got your girl a necklace. Sweet. That must've cost a mint.'

'Yeah, not to some of us,' I say. I'm not telling them I put it on a credit card. I've been doing pretty well with money from in-app purchases on Crow Stealer and I've got a new game getting good feedback in beta. It's not a Fortnite or a Candy Crush, but it's progress.

I don't like the look Binners gives me. Especially not when he says, 'She's got you here,' and mimes pushing his thumb down. Jonny laughs.

There's a small voice inside that knows they're trying to get a reaction out of me, that's telling me I don't need to impress them, but there's a larger part that can't seem to help it. I have to prove … something. Why do I even hang around with these guys? Why am I still that kid inside, watching everyone else get the invites to parties?

'Not sure it's that way round,' I say, striving for a light voice. Pretending I don't care.

'Whatever you like to tell yourself, mate.' Jonny laughs.

And I find myself suddenly saying, 'She looked pretty good wearing nothing but that necklace the other day.'

Jonny raises a pair of impressed eyebrows.

'Pictures or it never happened,' Binners says.

And that's when I do it. They were only meant for me, to have when she's not with me. My eyes only. Gem's not the sort of girl who'd want to do pictures, but I like having them, knowing I can see her whenever I want. She never knew I had my phone set up on the bedside cabinet. I'm going to delete them soon anyway so it's fine.

And now Binners is leering at me and Jonny has his eyes narrowed and I do it really fast, so it barely counts at all. I flash my phone in front of their eyes and smile. 'Some of us don't need porn, we've got the real thing,' I add.

'Looks like your missus needs a wax, mate,' Jonny says. Binners starts laughing and I feel myself clench up inside, my fist itching to plant itself in their faces. But then Jonny whistles and says, 'She's fit though, I'll give you that.'

Chapter Twenty-Seven

Gemma

'Just hop up here then, my lovely.' The woman's wearing a white jacket, which makes me more nervous. I kind of wish Esi was here, even though I know exactly what she'd say. I've already lied and said I'm eighteen, just in case, and luckily for me they didn't ask for ID.

'So, if you just take your bottom half off and cover yourself up with this.' She hands me a towel and goes out of the room.

This isn't a big deal. Definitely not. Loads and loads of girls get it done. Rachael, for one. Oh God, why didn't I get Rachael to come with me? I guess part of it was embarrassment, like I didn't want to let on to her I've never had a bikini wax before. Then again, I haven't actually seen much of Rachael the last week or two. And I'm still not talking to Esi. Or she's not talking to me, which is going to make our shift at the cafe tomorrow awkward.

The aesthetician's coming back in now.

'So,' she says as she starts putting on some gloves. 'Your first time?'

I nod. 'My boyfriend got me a voucher.'

'Uh-huh?' she says.

'Yeah, and I thought why not, you know?' I say.

Half an hour later, I know why not. Because it bloody hurts. And it's super embarrassing. And did I mention it hurts? I should definitely not have worn such tight jeans. Everything feels pretty weird down there. But I hand over the voucher and find myself making another appointment for a few weeks' time.

As I'm leaving, a text pops up on my phone from Cal asking about when we're going to rehearse again. We're still not there with the third song, and after my chat with Aaron I'm wondering if I should just write a different duet. The one we've been working on – 'Give' – is pretty much a love story. It's inspired by me and Aaron, but I don't know if he'll see it that way if I sing it with Cal. Finding the time to write something seems to be a problem too. I text Cal back and then go outside to wait for Aaron to pick me up, trying not to think about how much everything's stinging down below.

The next day's Saturday. I'm washing up the breakfast stuff, humming snatches of something that might work, but it's not coming as easily as it usually does. I'm still a bit, ahem, tender after the wax yesterday so I'm wearing loose harem pants. Michael's already gone for his shower and Dad's sitting in front of the TV in the other room while Mum wipes the table. She comes over with Michael's empty porridge bowl as I'm running water into the pan she used to make his breakfast. Bits of porridge are already glued on to the sides. She slides Michael's bowl into the sink, rinses her cloth out and goes back to wiping the table. I'm still humming as I pick the scourer back up, but then it's like I get an echo of Aaron's words: 'Sounds like your whole family revolves around your brother. When's it going to be your turn?'

I stop humming.

Then, very deliberately, I put the scourer down and step back from the sink. Mum comes up behind me. 'You've missed these.'

'I'm not doing them.'

Mum stares at me.

'Why should I? They're Michael's, not mine,' I add.

'Your brother has an away game today,' Mum says.

'So?'

She stares at me again, like she's totally at a loss for words, and I get this urge to laugh, or start screaming or something. It's like she can't even imagine why I might not want to be Michael's goddam pot washer the whole time.

'You know what? I've got stuff going on in my life too,' I say.

'Yes, I know, sweetheart, but—'

'But what? I don't matter as much as Michael? Is that it?' I'm shouting now.

'Hey, I'll wash it up.' It's Michael, standing in the doorway to the kitchen. 'No problem.'

He goes over to the sink. Before any of us can say another word, Dad comes in. He takes in my red face, Mum holding the tea towel aloft like it's her salvation, Michael sloshing water everywhere in the sink. 'What're you doing, son? We're going to be late. Leave that.'

'In a sec,' Michael says. Which is not the best thing to say to Dad.

'I said leave it!' Dad yells. 'You want to miss your coach?'

Michael drops the scourer, gives me a guilty sort of smile and follows Dad out of the room.

A moment later the front door bangs.

'I'm not doing it,' I say into the silence of the kitchen.

'Fine. If you want to be selfish, go ahead.' Mum plunges her hands into the water. So I do the only thing that's reasonable under the circumstances: I storm out, slamming the kitchen door behind me. Then I grab my stuff and head out of the house.

A few minutes later, Aaron meets me at the bottom of the track.

'I can't believe it. How didn't I see it before? All those bloody bowls I've washed up …' I'm ranting all the way to Aaron's place. It's not until he's parked up and paused, hands still gripping the steering wheel, that I stop and say, 'What's up?'

Aaron nods to the car I failed to see in the driveway. A sporty black soft-top that kind of hollers mid-life crisis. 'Oh. Is that your—'

'Dad's,' Aaron says and there's a grim note in his voice.

'Oh. Um. Well, we don't have to go in …' I begin, while at the same time wondering why Aaron doesn't want to introduce me to his dad.

You haven't introduced him to your parents either, I tell myself. But that's different. No way is Dad going to like me having a boyfriend, especially not one older than me. It's easier if he doesn't know, which means I can't tell Mum either.

They're so wrapped up in Michael they're not about to notice anyway.

I resist the urge to pull down the sun visor and check my reflection in the mirror. I put on make-up this morning, I know I look good.

'Come on,' Aaron says suddenly. He steps out of the car and comes around to open my door, holding out a hand to help me out. I love it when he does things like that; even if half the time it's just in a joking way, it still makes me feel cherished. Aaron gives me his smile, the one that always works. 'My lady. May I escort you from your carriage?'

It feels like a while since he's done that. I grin back and bat my eyelashes madly. 'Why, thank you, kind sir,' I say.

Aaron laughs too, but his smile fades when he looks back at his dad's car. He puts one hand tightly around my shoulders and steers me in through the front door.

Inside it's the same as always: spare decor, smattering of dirty dishes, one slowly dying spider plant in the corner. There's a generic picture of something abstract over the table of the kitchen diner and a lot of gadgets. I have enough time to glance at the bulging leather bag on the floor before a balding man comes in and grins widely when he sees us. Well, me, really.

'Ah, another one. You must be … ?'

'This is Gemma,' Aaron says, with a look at his dad like he wants to deck him.

Another one?

'Hi,' I say weakly.

'What happened to the blonde one? Selma or something?'

Aaron gives his dad a blank stare, then pulls me closer to him. 'You're such a fucking comedian,' he says, his voice flat.

His dad lets out a loud laugh, like he doesn't even care. I smile faintly, wondering what my dad would do if I swore at him like that. 'Don't mind me, just having a joke,' Aaron's dad says to me. 'He's too sensitive, always has been. Way too easy to wind up.'

I nod, because I'm not sure what else to do. Aaron shoots a very clear look at his dad before saying to me, 'Why don't you go to my room? Be there in a minute.'

It's not really a suggestion, but I'm happy to get out of there. I've barely got the bedroom door shut before I can hear Aaron and his dad start to argue downstairs. I put on some music and scroll through my phone. There's several texts from Mum, asking where I am, which I ignore. Today's match is far enough away that only Dad was going anyway, so why should she care what I'm doing? There's a text from Cal, which I quickly reply to, and one from Rachael just saying hi and asking if I'm out with Aaron. I text her back, pleased. Rachael gets it, at least. She doesn't give me weird crap for having a boyfriend. She likes Aaron.

Still nothing from Esi. We've never fallen out for this long before. For a minute I think about sending her a peace offering of some sort, but then I'm not the one who over-reacted. Like Aaron says, she needs to apologise to me first.

When he comes in, there's an odd look on his face. 'Well, Dad's officially moving out,' he says.

'What? Where to?' I tense up, wondering what this means for us. What is that look on his face saying? 'You're not going back to London, are you?' I say.

'London?' Aaron comes over and puts his arms around me. 'No way. Never.'

He strokes my hair as my heart races against his chest. My reaction's taken me by surprise; but Aaron's threaded through so much of my life these days. He always texts me good morning and goodnight, sometimes even sending me funny or cute messages at 2 a.m. And then there's the hours we've spent here, in this room, so close it's like we're one person. Like he completes me, if I was going to get Jerry Maguire about it.

I love that film.

'I'm staying right here. Literally,' he says. I pull back to look at him and he's smiling. 'Dad's moving in with C-minus Jack – he was just coming back to grab some more stuff – and he's said I can stay here until the lease is up, which is another six months.'

'What'll happen then?' I still can't keep the hint of anxiety out of my voice. It sounds like a different me talking.

'I've got money,' he says. 'I'll rent my own place if he doesn't want to pay.'

Relief melts through me and I hug him tight.

'You know, he's already gone out, so we've got the place to ourselves ...' Aaron says.

'Er ... the waxing lady said not to, you know, for a bit,' I say.

'That's OK, we can do other stuff,' Aaron says. He starts rubbing my shoulders and before I know it my top's off. Then he takes off the rest of my clothes and when he sees the results of yesterday he's so into it I don't want to tell him to stop. It's kind of sore, but I focus on the feeling of being close to him, how much he fancies me, and when that's not doing it I just think about all the homework I have totally not done, while I make the right noises. I know it's a bit fake but, well, Aaron's so sensitive, he might take me saying stop as a rejection. I don't want to hurt him or anything like that, so what does it matter if, every once in a while, I'm into it for his sake more than mine?

He finishes and lies on top of me for a bit, whispering, 'You're so beautiful. I love you,' and it makes me feel like I'm going to burst, to know how he feels about me. How cherished I am when he looks at me like that. He could have any girl he wants, but he's picked me.

'I love you too.'

And then he swears. 'Shit. I forgot …'

I look at him and then at the drawer where the condoms are. I've still not sorted out going on the pill. I've been meaning to, but it just … hasn't happened. I think my face is doing something suitably horrified. How can I not have noticed?

'I'm so sorry,' Aaron's saying, and he looks so upset I can't really get angry. 'We'll get you the morning after pill.'

A while later, I've not even got dressed, because Aaron's been talking all about how great it's going to be to have the place to himself properly, how I can sleep over any time. 'I'd love to wake up to you, not just here –' he puts one hand on his heart – 'but actually here, right next to me. I want you to be here with me, all the time.'

'Me too,' I say.

'You could, you know.' He sits up suddenly, looks at me with such a delighted face. 'You could move in.'

'I'm not sure what my parents would say about that,' I joke. Then my face falls. 'Probably wouldn't notice.'

'Oh, beautiful, come here,' Aaron says. 'You know, they're idiots for not seeing how special you are.' We hug some more, and then he says, 'You really could move in. Any time you want. No more football, no worries, just you and me and nothing else.'

'Well, I'd probably have to go to college some time,' I joke.

'Just college then. It'd be amazing.'

It would. I kiss him and he pulls me close.

Chapter Twenty-Eight

Aaron

There's a chorus in my head, singing her name over and over. Thoughts of the way she looked, how it felt to properly be with her, no condom messing up the mood. It makes my heart fill up and overflow until I don't think I can love anything more. Not ever.

But every time we finish, there's a part of me that feels lost, like I can only be happy in those moments in bed when she feels like mine, properly mine.

As I drive her to the cafe, Shiney wagging her tail in the boot, I'm thinking about that pill Gem just took and a part of me is sad, because would it be that bad if something happened? I think about her with my baby in her arms, linked to me for the rest of our lives.

'What are you thinking?' Gem says as she catches my smile.

'That I'd love to bring you breakfast in bed,' I say.

'Will it be a bacon butty with brown sauce?' She grins.

'If you play your cards right.'

She smiles, resting her head back. Then she winces and shifts in her seat.

'You OK?'

'Oh! Yeah, I'm more than OK, I'm great,' she says. But when I've come out of the next bend a quick glance at her shows she's frowning. She must be worried about being late; by the time we'd actually got dressed, we had to floor it to the next town up to get the pill.

I pull my attention back to the road. 'Don't worry, I'll speak to Dora,' I say.

'What? Oh, yeah … It's Esi who's going to be pissed,' she says.

'What's the deal with her?' I ask, even though I already know.

'Who knows.' Gem says it lightly, but I can tell she's upset.

'Well, if she's really your friend, she'll apologise and sort it out with you,' I say.

'I guess.'

'Just talk to her,' I say. 'She'll get over herself soon enough and if she doesn't, she's not worth it.'

'Why are you so great?' Gem says as we pull up.

I go around to open her door, and can't resist leaning in for another long kiss first. She has to push me off, laughing, in the end.

'I'm so late.'

And it's weird, but even the thought of letting her go for an hour or two so she can talk to Esi makes something inside me chasm open. Like she's a mirage.

I couldn't bear it if she vanished on me too.

181

Chapter Twenty-Nine

Gemma

Dora's not happy. 'Gemma. This is your last chance. If you're not going to be reliable, I'll find someone else,' she says as I run into the cafe, Aaron just behind me.

'Sorry,' Aaron says. 'It's my fault for losing track of time.'

Dora's face softens as she looks at him, but then she says, 'Well, young love or not, get her here on time, OK?'

'Got it,' Aaron says.

Esi stands there, winding a tea towel between her hands, tighter and tighter. She doesn't say a word.

Once Dora's gone, Aaron kisses me and then says quietly, 'I'll take Shiney up the beach. I'll come and check on you in half an hour.'

I watch him through the window, loving the way he leans down to pat Shiney as she wags her tail and gazes at him with complete adoration. She sticks like superglue to his side, until he tells her she can run up the beach for a bit. I guess she loves him almost as much as I do.

When I turn around, Esi is still holding that tea towel.

I'm about to say something, then I remember what Aaron said about how she should apologise. So I wait. Eventually, she says, 'What did he mean, he'll check on you? He has to keep tabs or something?'

'Actually,' I say coldly, 'he was worried about me. Or more precisely, you.'

'Why? Because I see what he's doing?'

'What's that supposed to mean?'

This conversation is getting away from me super fast. What happened to her apologising? I heft out a sigh. 'You're not going to say sorry, are you?'

'For what?' Esi's almost shouting now. I glance up the cafe to our only customer, an older man lingering over a pot of tea, but he seems deep in his newspaper. I go behind the counter anyway. Esi follows. She looks away, clearly trying to calm down, and says in a quieter voice, 'I have a right to be angry. If you weren't so wrapped up in yourself – and him – you'd see that.'

'Well, I'm sorry you're upset, but I don't see why it has to be that big a deal. Loads of people are bi.'

'Are you serious? You think my parents are going to throw a party if I tell them? Call all my aunties and uncles back in Ghana with the good news? Not to mention church … But you wouldn't understand anything about that. You've never bothered to ask.'

I'm staring at her now because I literally have no idea what to say, except there's a guilty voice telling me she's right: I haven't.

And then, because she seems so angry and because so much has been going on and most of it's great, but … well, it's all a lot … Aaron, the audition, the fact that I do miss Esi, but … I feel myself on the verge of crying.

Esi holds her jaw rigid for a moment, but then she lets out a long breath and says, 'Look. I don't want to argue. Let's just leave it all for now.'

Part of me doesn't want to, because nothing's resolved, but another part is actually really tired. I guess maybe waking up to texts a couple of times a night is bound to get knackering after a while. And I know I could put my phone on silent, but Aaron was so upset the other day when I didn't reply to a text because I'd fallen asleep, and I don't want to see that hurt look on his face, like he's lost or something. I've never known a boy could be so vulnerable before. I know he wouldn't be like that with anyone but me. It makes me feel wanted, loved.

'Tell me about him then,' Esi says on another sigh. 'You may as well. It's not like you've got anything else going on. Did you actually go to any lessons this week?'

'Er, yes,' I say.

Not really.

'And anyway, I'm doing loads of other stuff,' I say. I don't know why I'm feeling so defensive. 'There's the competition.' And I start telling her about the new song and my ideas, and for a while everything feels normal because she's listening and screwing up her nose and asking what it was like when we got the feedback at the first audition.

'Well, when Niles started praising my song, I thought I was about to fall over. I mean, wow! How many times do you get someone like that saying they could picture your song on a Nashville stage? I pretty much knew then we'd got through, even though I was so nervous. Cal was great, though, he just gave me this super-chilled look like he totally wasn't crapping it too – which he was, by the way – and it calmed me right down. He was brilliant. And Aaron too, of course, he was there to support us …' And somehow saying Aaron's name seems to divert my flow of thoughts, and before I know it I've started telling her how incredible he is, and showing her the necklace. 'Plus, he says he's got a surprise for me for my birthday,' I say.

Esi's lips have clamped together. I know I'm monopolising the conversation again, but I can't seem to stop myself talking. 'I take it you two have slept together?' she says.

I nod. 'I would've told you but …' I spread my arms. Esi puts one hand up to her mouth like she's stopping herself saying something, and I carry on quickly because I don't want us to start arguing again. 'Actually, there's a funny story about why I was late.' And I tell her how we had to go and get the morning after pill. 'He's really thoughtful,' I say happily.

Esi takes her hand away from her mouth. 'Shame he forgot about being *thoughtful* when he was getting his rocks off,' she says. There's real venom in her voice.

'It wasn't like that, he just gets carried away …'

'Let me guess. Because you're just so sexy, he can't help himself?' she says sarcastically.

'*We* got carried away then. Not just him. Look, just because you've never—'

'You're right,' she cuts in. 'I would never have sex with someone like Aaron. Because I have too much self-respect.'

My mouth drops open, but Esi's not done. 'Gemma, have

you listened to yourself? Your bar is so low it's through the floor. You say you're in love, that you want to move in with him, that he's your soul mate. Do you know how deluded that is? You've known him for a nanosecond, but you're happy to ditch your friends for him. Cal told me how Aaron will only let you rehearse in college when he's there too. And now you're saying you're having sex and he isn't even wearing a condom? That's not love. It's … I don't know, like sexual obsession or something. It's not healthy.'

'Why are you being such a bitch?'

'Me? What about—'

'Hi-hi, girls. How's it going?'

Aaron's back. He looks from Esi's face to mine and says, 'You all right, Gem?'

'No.' My voice is full of tears. 'I'm leaving.'

I go around the counter. Aaron immediately puts his arm around me.

'I'm not going to lie for you if Dora asks—' Esi begins.

'No one's asking you to,' Aaron says coldly. 'Come on, Gem.'

'Her name's Gemma,' Esi shouts at our retreating backs.

Something about it makes me stop. 'I'll be there in a second,' I say to Aaron. He looks between us, but eventually shrugs and goes outside to untie Shiney.

'Esi …'

She makes a sharp movement with her hand. 'I can't watch this any more, Gemma.'

I take a quick breath and then I turn to leave.

Esi mutters something, just as I'm going through the door. I can't be totally sure, but I think she's saying her old catchphrase.

Don't do anything I wouldn't do.

But this time she's crying.

I walk out without answering.

A while later, I'm all cried out. Aaron drives us up to our usual beach and we walk along the seafront, his arm wrapped around my shoulders, until I feel better. Then we go back up the cliff path, Aaron piggybacking me some of the way.

Once we're at the car, I realise there's still half an hour to go before my shift finishes and Dora comes back. I could still make it. Despite what Esi says, she wouldn't tell Dora, I'm sure of it. I'm also feeling pretty guilty for calling Esi a bitch, even if she was sort of acting like one. 'I should go back,' I say.

'You really don't need that job.'

'Yeah, I guess I could get something else.'

'No. I mean you shouldn't have to work. I've got plenty of money if you need anything. If you want something, let me know and it's yours.'

'I can't just take your money, Aaron,' I say.

He turns me in my seat to face him, looks into my eyes. 'Yes, you can. I want you to have things. In fact, here –' He gets out his phone. 'What do you want?'

'Nothing. Just you.'

He kisses my nose, then pulls back and says, 'Come on, there must be something. You could do with an upgrade on that.' He gestures at my phone, which is in my lap.

'Honestly, don't worry.'

'Well, it's your birthday soon so you'd better let me treat you then,' Aaron says.

'Won't argue with that,' I say, and we laugh.

'So no more cafe?' Aaron says.

'No more cafe,' I agree. And it's like a weight has lifted off me.

But there's more to come when I get home. For once, Mum's waiting for me when I get in.

'Where have you been? You didn't answer your phone. And when I called the cafe, Esi said you weren't there.'

I take her in, how she's looking all fake concerned for me, and suddenly all the anger I've been holding from earlier fizzes up. 'I was out,' I say.

'Who with? Esi said you were with your boyfriend? What boyfriend?'

I take it back. Esi is totally being a bitch. She's stitched me up on purpose. I manage to force out a laugh. 'Does she mean Cal? Oh my God, Mum – as if! We were just rehearsing for the audition. But he's not my boyfriend.'

Mum's face relaxes. 'Oh, Callum? OK then. But you really should have texted me back.'

'Sorry, Mum,' I say. To my surprise she gives me a hug. It feels oddly squashy.

'I had a boyfriend at your age, you know.' She smiles.

'Urgh, I don't need the gory details about you and Dad.'

'I'm not talking about your father.'

This is interesting. I'm about to ask her to tell me more, when Dad comes in.

'You're late,' he says.

I bite back a reply along the lines of I didn't think he'd notice – I'm actually a bit surprised he did – but Mum jumps in: 'Oh, she was doing some extra studying.'

'Good, good,' Dad says vaguely, reaching into the fridge to pull out a can of lager, while I stare at Mum like she's just told me she's taking up rally driving. She winks at me and nods for me to go upstairs so I make my escape.

I guess just once in a while, Mum can be all right.

Chapter Thirty

Gemma

Cal: **Hey! Want to come to mine to rehearse?**

Gemma: **I can't tonight, sorry. I'm going to the cinema with Aaron.**

Cal: **Tomorrow?**

Gemma: **Can we do it in college?**

Cal: **Sure, if you're planning to come this week, ha ha.**

Cal: **Sorry, only joking. But you've not really been in this week. Are you ill?**

Cal: **???**

Gemma: **Sorry, got distracted. I'll be in tomorrow** ☺

Cal: **Are you 'with me' today?** ☺

Gemma: **If you don't mind …**

Cal: **Sure, but you know mums do that talking thing every now and again right?**

'Who are you messaging?' Aaron says as he decants a takeaway on to some plates. Somehow it's Thursday, and I've barely been in college. Again. I've also had a 'sleepover' at Rachael's and a lot of 'studying/rehearsal sessions' at Cal's. It's not that I think Mum wouldn't be OK with me seeing Aaron, but I'm not sure how Dad would react, so it seems easier to make excuses. The night I spent at Aaron's was amazing though. He took me out along the coast to this restaurant where they served these huge gourmet burgers and chips. After they took away the dessert plates, he brought out this box which had an infinity bracelet to match my necklace. And then a brand-new iPhone, some gorgeous new cowboy boots, a ton of make-up and vouchers for the salon.

I just wish it had been on my actual birthday, which was yesterday and mainly consisted of a super-boring meal out with my family, in our usual football celebration restaurant, where Dad talked about transfers, UEFA and training, and Mum pushed her food around her plate as usual. At least they got me a load of Amazon vouchers which is what I asked for. Well, I'd have preferred driving lessons, but no chance Dad would stick his fist in his pocket for those. Amazon vouchers came second – that way I can save them up for something special for Aaron for Christmas, now I'm not earning any money.

I told Mum and Dad I'm cutting back on my hours at the cafe to spend more time studying, which is a bit ironic given I've seen more of the inside of Aaron's bedroom the last two weeks than I have the inside of the refectory, let alone an actual lesson. But the first term barely counts anyway. It's all on exams now, so there's no coursework and I can totally catch up on anything important over the holidays.

I look down at my new bracelet on my wrist. The rose gold colour catches the light and glows as I trace the two loops. It's beautiful.

'So who were you messaging?' Aaron says again, as he comes over with two plates of chicken korma and pilau rice.

'Oh, um. Just Rachael. I told Mum I was going to be at her house tonight.'

He puts both the plates down, not saying anything for a moment. I get a sudden sense he knows I'm lying. I just don't want him to get upset, that's all.

'Um, Cal WhatsApped too … I thought maybe we should do a rehearsal in college tomorrow?'

'Sure,' Aaron says. He starts to eat and, relieved, I do the same. 'If you really want to,' he adds after a moment.

'Well, it's just the audition's getting closer now and we haven't really rehearsed for ages so …'

'You know, I thought before, Cal's a bit of a hanger-on, isn't he? Your voice is way better than his. And you're the songwriter. Do you even need him any more?'

'Well … we entered as a duo,' I say lightly. 'And we got through as a duo, they wouldn't let us change now.'

Cal brings something else too … not just the vocals, more like moral support. But I don't want to tell Aaron that.

'It's a shame you didn't audition on your own. I mean it's your talent, not his,' he muses.

'It won't take long, honestly.'

'No, of course. We'll definitely go.'

I smile, but there's a knot in my stomach that's making it hard to force the curry down. I push the plate away after I've eaten half.

'That's all you're having?' Aaron says when he's finished. I get up and take our plates to the kitchen and start to clear up.

'It was really nice, I'm just not super hungry,' I say. A moment later, Aaron comes over and pinches me on the bum.

'Guess it's not a bad idea to keep this in check,' he says.

'What do you mean?' There's a flash of irritation in my voice. This week's been incredible, but I'm pretty tired. I ended up FaceTiming Aaron until 2 a.m. this morning, then I still had to get up for college even if he took me off after the first two lessons, all because that arsehole Jonny said something stupid that pissed him off.

'Nothing! Jeez, I just meant you girls are always trying to watch your figures or whatever. You don't need to shoot me down,' Aaron says.

I wasn't shooting him down. Yet I find myself saying, 'Sorry, I'm just a bit …' I'm about to say 'tired', but then Aaron might get upset I don't want to talk to him. So I say, 'Hormonal. Think I'm due on.'

Aaron wrinkles his nose. 'I thought the pill was supposed to help with girl moods or whatever?'

I finally sorted going on the pill, to Aaron's relief. He really hates condoms.

'Er, yeah, but I think it takes a bit of time,' I say. I have no idea really, but Aaron nods.

'Poor baby, come here,' he says and kisses me. Then we cuddle up together on the settee to watch *Nashville*. It's so cool Aaron's a fan too; we've been re-watching right from season one. We're midway through season three now. I already know what's going to happen, but I still love curling up with my head on his chest, his arms around me.

But later, when he's dropped me home and I'm up in my room, I get my laptop out and start to search '*Can someone love you too much?*'

Tons of hits come up, but before I can read the first one, there's a knock on my door. I shut my laptop. 'Yeah?'

Michael comes in.

'Oh! Hi. I thought you were Mum.'

Michael pretends to look himself up and down and says, 'Nope, just me.'

There's a pause.

'What's up?' I say.

Michael's kind of moving around my room. He looks a bit shifty.

'Everything OK?'

'Yeah, pretty much. I just wondered, um … how's college?'

'What?' I stare at him.

He comes and perches on the edge of my desk chair. 'I just wondered what it's like. You know, A levels and stuff?'

'It's OK, I guess. Why?'

It's not like Michael's going to go to a normal college. By the time he's my age, he'll be in the Under-21s if all goes how it's supposed to.

'I just wondered …'

Just then, Dad's voice floats up the stairs. 'Michael? Match is on.'

For a second, Michael's face falls, but then the next minute he's his usual self, bouncing out of the room like he

194

hasn't got any worries at all, throwing out a 'See you later!' over his shoulder.

I lie back on my bed, the laptop forgotten, thinking about my brother and his insane talent, and the next thing I know it's dark outside and the house is still and there's a noise at my window.

Chapter Thirty-One

Aaron

When she doesn't answer her messages, or her phone when I call her, that's when I look. Not before. But I know how to get into her WhatsApp; it's easy if you've got someone's number.

The first thing I see are the messages from Cal. Way more of them than she said. The winky faces. Kisses. Little in-jokes from a time before I knew her. I read through each one, feeling the nausea rising. There's a rational part of me that's aware her messages indicate nothing more than friendship, though his are screaming he wants more. But a larger part of me feels like a vortex, as though my lungs are collapsing in on themselves and I'm struggling for breath, fighting to pull up and out.

Fighting to remember who I am.

Before I know it, I'm dressed and driving, taking the corners on the wrong side of the road, not bothering to brake at red lights, the night a blur of looming hedgerows and cat's eyes flaring at me from the middle of the road. I kill the engine at the bottom of her track and sit there, holding on to the steering wheel.

Go home, a voice is whispering in my head.

I try her number again but there's still no answer.

And the need to just see her, to touch her hair, is over-whelming. Too big for me to fight.

I step out of the car and jog up the track.

Chapter Thirty-Two

Gemma

'Wha——?' I grunt out, still half asleep and wondering if perhaps I'm actually dreaming. But it comes again, a rattling sound like something hitting my window.

I sit up, the duvet pulled close to me as though I'm little and I've had a nightmare. I can feel my heart pounding. The noise comes again, and this time I don't cringe. A flash of annoyance goes through me instead. Whatever bird is pecking at my window is about to get the worst fright of its life, because I am over being woken up in the middle of the night.

I throw the duvet off me so hard it slides to the floor, switch my lamp on and jump out of bed, then yank the curtains open in time to see something hit the window and bounce away. I peer out and then stop, my mouth dropping open.

It's Aaron, standing under my window looking up, his face illuminated softly by the moonlight. I unlatch the window and lean out. 'Aaron?' I whisper.

He waves. I can't work out the look on his face in the half-light. It's full of shadows.

'Hi,' he says quietly.

'What are you doing? My dad …'

'I'm sorry, I had to see you.' He tilts his head slightly and as he does, I think I see something shining on his face. Is he … crying? Then I notice he's holding something in his hand.

'Are those flowers?'

Aaron looks down as if surprised to see them there himself, then back up at me. 'Come down.'

'What? I can't. I'll wake the whole house up.'

'Not if you're quiet.'

Oh God. This is insane. Then he moves and a moment later I realise with horror he's trying to climb up the drainpipe. 'Aaron!' I hiss. 'Stop it. You'll fall.'

'Come down then,' he says, still climbing, his feet scrabbling for a purchase on the wall. He gives a sudden smile up at me, his teeth flashing wolf-like in the dark.

'Oh Jeez … OK, wait there.'

I duck back into my room and grab my dressing gown, then my phone to check what time it is, which is how I realise I've forgotten to put it on charge and the battery has died at some point overnight.

Slowly, I creep downstairs, wincing at every little noise as I ease the back door open. I'm met with the faint rush and roar of the sea, and the night air, and then a moment later Aaron's mouth and arms. He's been waiting right by the door and he kisses me like he never wants to stop.

There's a hefty part of me that's annoyed, confused. But Aaron's kisses seem to override everything until my head starts to swim and I can't think of anything else. Eventually he pulls back, and I try to catch my breath. 'You know, you shouldn't have come here. If my dad finds us he'll basically ground me forever.'

Aaron dips his head. 'I'm sorry. I just … I needed you.'

'Why?'

'I – I can't …' He looks up, like there's answers somewhere in the stars above us, and I remember the things he hinted at before, with his mum. How she basically rejected him. Perhaps it's too painful for him to talk about. Then Aaron goes on, 'And then, when you weren't answering your phone it reminded me of …' He breaks off and I remember how much Cherine hurt him. Still, I purse my lips because for real I am going to be in so much trouble if we get caught out here. But just then – maybe it's some sort of cosmic timing – the little piece of cloud that had drifted across the moon clears and I see his face giving that small smile I know so well, ghostly and loving and wholly mine. I can't help the rush of love that comes over me then.

'You muppet,' I say, but I'm smiling even as I shake my head.

'I should go. I'm sorry I woke you,' Aaron says.

'It's OK.'

'No, it's not. I shouldn't have worried you like that. I'm such an idiot sometimes. I don't even know … all I know is when I'm around you, all the bad things just go away. I love you so much.' He gathers me up in his arms and I can feel how he's shaking, and suddenly this conversation out here in the moonlight feels like the most real thing that's ever happened to me.

'I love you too.'

'Am I forgiven?' Aaron whispers into my hair.

'Always.'

The letter rounds off a painful morning the next day. Painful because Aaron stayed for another half an hour and by the time I'd got back to sleep it was practically dawn. Mum had to bang on my door three times before I managed to get myself out of bed. I was seriously thinking about faking another illness, but I've missed so much college already and there's only so many times you can have period pains, stomach upsets and migraines.

So I haul myself into the shower. About twenty minutes later I'm massively glad I did because as I'm going out of the front door, the postwoman comes up and hands me a pile of letters. I'm about to leave them on the side and go, but something makes me stop and flick through, and there it is: a letter with the college logo, addressed to Dad. I shove it in my bag, put the rest of the letters on the side and yell goodbye to Mum, then bang the door closed.

Aaron's not at the bottom of the track. I leave it as long as possible, then run for the bus and take a seat right at the very back, looking the other way as I pass Esi. Which is fine, because she's ignoring me too. Once Grumpy Sharon's got going again, I slide the letter out of my bag.

Sometimes you pretend to yourself that things aren't going to happen, which I suppose accounts for the shock when I see that I've been put on to Stage 2 of the disciplinary procedure, and that they want Mum and Dad to come into college for a meeting to discuss my absence. There's also an email on my college account saying I have a meeting with the College Manager, Mr Bowyer. Today. It was sent last week, but of course I've somehow been too busy to check my emails properly.

I sit back in my seat, the letter crumpled between my fingers while my tired brain tries to work out how to get out of this one. The only reason Mum and Dad don't already know about the lessons I've skipped is because Dad would never bother with the ParentPal system and Mum is too technologically incompetent. And, I think with a flash of guilt, because it would never occur to her I might skip out.

I text Aaron, but for once he doesn't text straight back. I put my phone away and sit there, feeling weird, like there's this space I've got so used to being filled and suddenly it's empty. Then we get to Cal's stop and I'm slightly worried in case Cal comes to sit with me, because I know Aaron's got a thing about him, but he doesn't; he sits with Esi, which somehow makes me feel worse. I don't know if he's actually seen me, but it still stings.

When we arrive at college I do what I do best: I shove my shoulders back, put on a smile, and breeze down the bus as Cal and Esi are getting off. 'Hey!' I say, only looking at Cal. Esi hurries away and Cal stares after her for a minute before turning to me.

'You're not going to apologise to her?' he says.

I'm so taken aback by this, I don't say anything for a minute. Then I turn the smile up and say, 'I don't know what she told you, but I'm not the one who needs to apologise.'

202

'Is that so?' Cal holds my eye and I get a seriously uncomfortable feeling, like he knows things I don't. 'You don't think she has a point, about Aaron? He's taking up pretty much all of your time, isn't he?' he adds.

I feel like a comedy cartoon character, mouth hanging open while my brain goes totally white. Cal doesn't say stuff like that to me, especially not about Aaron.

A moment later, Cal's giving me an awkward half-pat, half-guy-punch on my shoulder and saying, 'Think about it, 'K? And let me know if you want to rehearse,' before walking off.

I watch him go, wondering how everything, everyone, has changed so fast.

'Hey, Gemma! You standing there all morning?' It's Rachael. I've never been more relieved to see her. Rachael is just … well, Rachael. Uncomplicated. 'Oh my God, is that Tiffany's too?' she says, looking at my bracelet.

'Oh … yeah, Aaron got it for me for my birthday,' I say.

'You guys are like some Hollywood couple. It's totally, grossly unfair,' she says.

'I know,' I say and try not to sound smug, but I'm so … relieved, I guess, that Rachael's not in a pisser with me, because everyone else seems to be. Then I let out a huge yawn without meaning to.

'Lover boy keeping you up at night?' Rachael says.

'Something like that,' I say, and then I can't resist telling her about last night. Not exactly because I want to make her jealous, but because I want to maybe … check.

She listens with wide eyes, then sighs. 'He threw stones up to your window because he missed you? That's so romantic. I can't believe how into you he is.'

'Oi,' I say, going for a smile, but I'm so tired it fades out before it gets properly started.

'You know what I mean. There must be something up with him, though?'

'Like what?'

'I don't know. He's like the model boyfriend. He's not making up for something, is he?' She wiggles a little finger.

'Nope,' I say. Then I glance around to check we're alone and say, 'He does text quite a lot though. Says he misses me.'

'Urgh!' she screeches. 'You're killing me. He doesn't have a brother, does he?' We go into the refectory, me trying to work out how to put my feelings into words.

'It's, like, a *lot* of texts. Most mornings … well, every morning and—'

'Wish I had someone texting me good morning,' Rachael interrupts as we get to a table containing Phoebe, Cal and Beth. Aaron's friends – mine too now, I guess – are gathered in the usual corner.

Everyone looks up and says hi.

'Long time no see,' Beth says, not in a horrible way.

'Hi, guys …' I say, but trail off, distracted because I've just seen Aaron coming through the door.

'Hey, if you're not into it, pass him to me,' Rachael says, with what's pretty much a leer on her face.

I grin properly this time. I can't lie, it feels good knowing she wants what I have. Then she's yelling, 'Hey, Romeo, your girl's here,' and I'm nudging her to shut up because suddenly I realise Aaron might not have wanted me to tell her about last night. I say a fast goodbye to Rachael and go to intercept Aaron before she can say anything else to him.

Aaron gives me a kiss, then says, 'Sorry about this morning, I had to have a little lie-in.' His hair is still wet from his shower and he smells really great.

'How come you look so perky?' I say, a little grumpily.

Aaron shrugs. 'I never sleep more than four hours. That's all you really need. All this bollocks about eight hours is a total myth,' he says.

Doesn't feel that mythical to me, but I make myself smile back because I don't want him thinking I'm moaning. Why do I feel like I need about ten?

We're just going over to the football table when Mr Bowyer, the College Manager, looms in front of me.

Crap.

'Ms Bellfine,' he says. Urgh. I got the 'Ms'. This is not a good sign.

'Hello!' I reply, too bright.

'You're due in my office in two minutes, I think?'

Aaron's looking between us. I haven't had time to tell him about the letter yet. 'You want me to come with you?' Aaron says.

'I think she can manage on her own,' Mr Bowyer says. I pull a face at Aaron from behind Mr Bowyer's departing back and trail after him, feeling seven rather than seventeen, painfully aware of people watching and whispering. I look the other way as I pass the old gang, but not fast enough to miss the fact that Esi's there too now and she's looking over with a serious expression.

It's not good news in Mr Bowyer's office.

'We expect your attendance to be ninety per cent, minimum,' Mr Bowyer starts. Then he gives me the whole spiel about commitment and working hard. 'You had a good report from your school and your GCSEs are solid, so you have an excellent foundation, if you put in the effort.'

I nod along, trying to look contrite but I can't keep my mind from wandering.

'… anything at home I should be aware of?'

I tune back in. 'Sorry? Um, no. It's all fine,' I say.

'Well, then. Sort out your priorities. If your attendance doesn't pick up immediately, then we'll need to assess whether this is the right place for you. And you also need to catch up on every single lesson you've missed, and any work set outside the classroom too. I'll be speaking with all your tutors in two weeks but until then consider yourself on probation.'

I gape at him. I mean, I know it's been bad, missing a few classes, but he's talking about kicking me out! I can't find the words to defend myself, so instead I let him usher me from the office and then I run upstairs to Psychology.

My phone goes three times in the lesson, but I manage to sit and actually take notes rather than looking at it.

Aaron's waiting for me outside, but as soon as I've kissed him quickly, I say, 'I have to get to Biology.'

'Ahh, you can be a bit late.'

'No, I really can't,' I say. I tell him about what Mr Bowyer said.

Aaron gives a low whistle. 'That's harsh.'

I nod, feeling suddenly so miserable and tired, I don't know what to do. Aaron puts his arm around me. 'It's OK,

I'll help you study. Come on,' and he pulls me along the corridor and into Biology.

The next two weeks pass in a blur of studying. I have to go to all my tutors and apologise and get the work I missed, which is totally cringeworthy. But slowly I work my way through it all. I'd never manage without Aaron: he says he blames himself for taking up all my time, so now he sits over me and makes sure I study, even when I'm so tired I can barely see the paper. We start spending every free period together: in a corner of the library, at a coffee shop a short drive away. Then we go to his house and do another couple of hours after school, as well as during my pretend shifts at the cafe over the weekend. Mum and Dad just accept I'm at Rachael's or Cal's.

It's like Aaron says: if I'm going to be in the shadows for them, I might as well take advantage of it.

Aaron's keeping me so busy that I somehow kind of forget the regional final is coming up. Or I push it to the back of my mind, at least. So it's a shock to realise there's days to go and me and Cal still haven't rehearsed a third song properly.

I'm at Aaron's house on the last Friday of my two weeks' catch-up time. It's already dark outside and he's going to have to drive me home soon. I close my Psychology text-book with a long sigh and look at Aaron across the little table. 'That's it, I'm all caught up.'

'Well done, baby,' he says, and comes over to give me a long kiss.

After a few moments, I pull away.

'What is it?'

I look at him, 'The audition's in less than a week.'

Aaron frowns for a second, then says, 'You still going to do it with Cal?'

'Yes – I told you, I can't change it now,' I say, struggling to keep my voice light. It's been a long couple of weeks.

'No.' He looks far away. 'I suppose not.'

Chapter Thirty-Three

Gemma

The next day, I knock on Rachael's door early.

I had to send about twenty grovelling texts to Cal, but we eventually set up a time to meet. We're using Rachael's house so we don't disturb Cal's mum.

Rachael opens the door. 'Jesus, you look like you need to go back to bed for about ten years.'

'Thanks.'

She gives me an uncharacteristically concerned look for a second, then her face clears. 'You've been up doing filthy stuff with you-know-who, haven't you?'

I see Cal standing behind her. 'Hey,' I say. 'I'm sorry I haven't been around much. It's just …'

'Shall we rehearse then?' Cal sounds stiff.

I follow them inside. 'Aaron's picking me up in an hour,' I say.

It stays weird for the first ten minutes, but Cal soon softens, especially once we've done some silly warm-up exercises, including the duck voices.

By the end, we're laughing. 'Right. Now we've got

our twang on, shall we go?' I say.

We run through 'Sea Dreams', which sounds great, as always, then the more upbeat number, which works well after a few adjustments. It's the new song, 'Give', I'm the most worried about.

I play it to Cal, showing him the music, the bits where he comes in.

Cal nods when I finish. 'Wow. I like it. I mean, it's got an edge compared to your usual stuff. Beautiful, but, like … darker, you know?'

I look at him in surprise. I hadn't thought of it that way.

'Where did you get the idea from?' Cal says thoughtfully. I hesitate. It's about me and Aaron, but that feels somehow private.

'Oh, you know …' I say.

Cal's still looking at me as though he wants to say something else, but then he smiles. 'Shall we give it a try?'

We run through it and Cal seems to get straight away the intensity I was looking for. After another few times through, we've got it down. I sit back, relief rushing through me.

'That went OK, actually,' I say.

'Well, I think it sounds amazing,' Rachael says, and she's not taking the piss. 'You're like a dark Taylor Swift singing that.'

That wasn't entirely what I was going for, but I know she means it as a compliment. 'Thanks,' I say.

I check my phone, see several messages from Aaron and hold in a sigh. 'I need to go. We're good for next Saturday though?'

'I think so,' Cal says. He looks at Rachael. 'I've got to go too. Mum.'

She nods, and I see a look pass between them that seems kind of private. I gather up my guitar and music, and walk Cal to the bus stop, keeping one eye out for Aaron's car.

'I'm glad we rehearsed,' I say to Cal, and he nudges my shoulder.

'Just next time don't leave it so late, Gemma.'

It's a slight shock to hear him say my full name. I've got so used to 'Gem'.

I smile to cover it up. 'OK, Callington Cal-Cal.' He laughs and I do too, realising suddenly how much I've missed him. Then I see Aaron's car coming up the road towards us. I stop laughing and step away from Cal. Aaron pulls up and opens his window.

'Hey, Aaron,' Cal says.

'Hi.' Aaron gives him a smile, but I notice his eyes seem kind of tight around the edges.

'Uh … I'll see you later,' I say to Cal.

He touches my arm. 'That new song is something special. You're going through to the national final, I can feel it.'

'Thanks.' I smile. Then I load my guitar into the backseat of Aaron's car and get into the front.

As soon as I lean over to kiss him, I know he's upset. 'Hey? You OK?' I say.

'Yeah, fine,' Aaron says in a voice that is definitely not fine. He accelerates away, me still trying to get my seatbelt on. We drive in silence back to his place and I feel my heart starting to pound. I know what's coming.

By the time we've shut the front door to the flat and sat down, I'm braced for Aaron to yell, to say I was flirting with Cal.

But he doesn't. He puts his hands over his face and starts to cry. Big sobs, shoulders shaking, the works.

I'm so shocked I do nothing for a moment, and then I go over and touch his rigid shoulder. 'Aaron?'

Slowly Aaron takes his hands away to look at me. There's so much in his gaze, but above all, this awful look of betrayal.

'Is this about Cal?'

He gives a short laugh.

'You know I don't think that way about him, don't you? Of course you do. I love you.' I try one of my confident smiles but it wobbles. I hate seeing Aaron like this.

'And do you think that's what Cal thinks? Because it didn't look like it, the way he was touching you.'

I open my mouth. There's a part of me that wants to scream, *He's just a friend, that's all*.

'I just … I can't trust you. Do you know how awful it is to feel like you can't trust the person who has your heart?' Aaron says.

I want to hold him and reassure him, anything to get that look off his face. And then, with a flash of guilt, I remember the other week, that feeling when Cal didn't sit on the bus with me. How pleased I was to see him today. Aaron knows me better than anyone. What if he's seen something I haven't? But I love him – Aaron. Not Cal.

'I love you, Aaron.' I say it out loud. And we both hear that question in my voice.

His eyes are saying, *Prove it*.

There's another long pause, and then I hear myself say, 'I won't go to the audition. It doesn't matter to me anyway.'

212

Gradually the desperate look fades out of Aaron's eyes, and then he reaches out to me. 'You'd do that?'

I force everything I have, every bit of conviction I can, into my voice. 'Of course.'

I feel like I'm barely breathing.

'Come here.' I get up and he pulls me roughly into his lap. Then he's kissing me, hard. He pulls back, leaving me breathless. 'I knew you were different, I did. It's just been so hard for me …'

'I know. But it's you. It's us. "As you wish", OK?'

He nods. His Adam's apple bobs in his throat.

I rub one finger on his wet cheek and we both smile a little. Then I whisper it again.

'As you wish.'

Chapter Thirty-Four

Aaron

She keeps her word. I check, but she ignores all of Cal's increasingly frantic messages through the week. And slowly I begin to relax, to feel that trust building between us again.

Jonny's his usual dickish self in college. Him and Binners are still taking the piss about Gem's 'rehearsals' with Cal, but I laugh it all off. I can't even be bothered to tell them she's given up the songwriting comp for me. That's how much she loves me. The thought of it's like liquid gold, a precious gift I keep close to my heart. My heart that holds hers. Hers that could do so much to shatter mine. But she doesn't waver. I know she'll do the competition next year, on her own. She's so much better as a solo singer anyway.

On the Friday before the audition, I get her to tell her parents she's at Rachael's and she stays at mine. We get a takeaway and then stay up most of the night talking and making love, and it's almost as perfect as it was in the beginning, when the world was me and her, and no one and nothing else to get between us.

I drive her down to her house early in the morning. Her brother's got a home game and she says she has to go, that her brother and her parents want her there. It's pathetic really, but it makes me love her more, how she still tries to get their approval, even though she knows the painful truth now: they'll always prefer Michael, they'll never put her first. How I understand that. Except my own mother didn't even have the excuse of blood before she threw me under the bus because of Cherine. She chose to believe Cherine's lies over her own son. Because that's what they did best, after all – Cherine, my mother: betrayal.

But not Gem. She's the one. Someone better. I know I can make her see that she doesn't need any of them. We don't need anyone else.

I watch the morning light catching her hair, the way she moves, how she stops and blows me a kiss before she rounds the corner, my chest expanding with happiness.

Chapter Thirty-Five

Gemma

My smile fades after I blow Aaron a kiss, to be replaced by a heavy feeling as I go through the front door. I run straight upstairs to grab a jumper. When I get back down, Mum's standing in the kitchen, gazing out into nothing.

'Hi, Mum.'

Mum blinks, like she was somewhere far away, and takes me in. 'You're coming to the match?'

'Oh, yeah, thought I would.'

'What about your audition? Isn't that today?'

Now it's my turn to look surprised. 'Umm, yes, but I'm not going. I've decided it's not for me after all.'

Mum frowns. 'I thought you wanted to go?'

Michael appears, followed by Dad, and I let Dad hustle us all off into the car. It's easy to let Dad take over the conversation, but when we start setting up at the side of the pitch, Mum comes to stand next to me.

'You haven't seen much of Esi recently,' she says.

Jeez. Why does Mum have to pick the worst possible day to decide she actually wants to know about my life?

'Been busy with college,' I say.

'And the cafe,' Mum says. There's something probing about her voice I don't recognise.

I drift over to Dad and set him going with a comment about the opposition while Mum hovers on the other side of him.

About ten minutes into the match, I'm just starting to relax when someone comes up behind me and pokes me right between the shoulder blades.

'Hey!' I turn around and stop.

Cal's standing there, looking royally pissed off. 'Hey yourself,' he says.

I glance at Mum, who's looking over at us, then walk off to the side where I collapse into a chair. Cal follows and stands in front of me, his arms crossed. 'What the hell's going on? I've been calling and texting. Why haven't you picked up?' He stares down at me. 'You're not coming, are you?'

I open my mouth, but I have nothing to say. Whatever I do, it seems I'm letting someone down.

'I thought we were friends,' Cal says.

I take a deep breath. 'I am your friend. It's just … complicated.' How can I make Cal understand what it's like, with Aaron?

'I'm not thick, Gemma. Everyone's worried about you. Ever since you started seeing Aaron, you're like a totally different person. He doesn't want you to go, does he?'

I'm trying to find a way to explain, without raising my voice in case Mum overhears. She's standing a way away, but then she's got supersonic ears. 'It's not that … It's just complicated.'

'Yeah, you said that already. But actually, it's very simple. You say to my face you don't want to go, right now, and I'll drop it. You tell me this isn't the opportunity you've been waiting for, maybe one that will never come again. Who knows if they'll run this competition next year. Did you know The Greenwoods' manager is one of the judges today?'

A massive jolt goes through me. The Greenwoods' manager! I would give almost anything to sing my songs in front of her. How come I didn't know? Then another, uneasy pulse goes through me as I realise that I would have, a few months ago.

'Tell me you don't want to go. Tell me you want to give this chance up.'

He waits.

I look him in the eye, but I can't make myself say the words. I made a promise to Aaron. But … it's been my dream for such a long time, to become a singer-songwriter. I stand there, feeling like something's tearing me down the middle.

'You can't say it. Because it's not true. Come with me. Don't throw it away over some guy. That's not you, not the Gemma I know.'

'I can't,' I say, and my voice feels foreign. 'I don't know how to …'

Tell Aaron.

I say instead, 'I have nothing to wear, and I don't have my guitar. I'm sorry, Cal. But I've made up my mind.'

Cal shuts his eyes for a second. Then he opens them and gives me a long look. 'OK, I'll tell you what. My brother is

218

here with his car and my guitar. Rachael, too – which I'll tell you about another time – but she's got a couple of dresses and make-up and stuff, and we're leaving in ten minutes, with or without you. I think you want to come, in fact I know it. And you do too.'

He walks off.

I slump back in my chair.

What do I do?

At that moment, Michael scores a goal. Dad does his usual roar, and Mum's cheering too, and suddenly I feel like I've spent my whole life sitting in this goddam chair, watching. Waiting.

That's when I know I have to go.

But how can I, when I made a promise to Aaron?

Then a little voice starts to whisper. *Does he need to know?* If I text him and say it's gone to extra time, invent a post-match meal, maybe some food poisoning, I could go to the audition, come back, and he wouldn't be any the wiser. I could bring it up later on, when everything's died down a bit, sort of ease him into the idea. There's ages before the national final. And if we don't get through, or The Greenwoods' manager hates my songs, then none of it will matter anyway. It just means I get a chance. A tiny one, but a chance. To get my songs out there. And I definitely will tell Aaron as soon as the time's right.

So, it's not like *lying* lying. Is it?

I stop feeling guilty a few junctions down the motorway and this is for a couple of reasons: (1) everyone is so over-the-top excited it's hard not to be too; (2) me and Cal are having to go over everything in the car to make sure we can bring it all together, given we only rehearsed 'Give' for the first time the other day; and (3) it's really hard to get changed in a moving car when two boys are trying not to look, and your sort-of new best friend is killing herself laughing while 'accidentally' letting the blanket she was holding up to the window slip just as you're pulling a dress over your head.

Oh, and (4) said new sort-of best friend has apparently been getting it on with none other than … Cal.

This news is imparted by Rachael about half an hour into the journey, along with way more info than I ever needed to know about Cal's willy size. Cal is beetroot-coloured and horribly pleased all at the same time. It's a little bit gorgeous, actually.

I can't lie, it also makes things five times easier for when I tell Aaron about all this. Because I'm totally going to tell him, just as soon as today is out of the way. Once he realises Cal's got a girlfriend now, he'll see there's nothing to worry about.

'I wish you guys had told me before,' I say to Rachael, but she just grins and stares at Cal like a lovelorn puppy.

Nothing about today is going like I expected.

We finally arrive. My make-up is on: bonus points to Rachael for somehow managing to help me with my eyeliner in a moving car. That girl is a genius. And thanks to Cal's brother, Sean, we're on time, too.

I send a fast text to Mum to let her know where I am. We say bye to Rachael and Sean, sign in, and are taken down a long corridor and into a room which is serving as the holding area. The same guy from last time's here, but this time we're instructed to follow 'the boss', a black woman called Deena who looks impossibly sophisticated. It's this more than anything that tells me the stakes have gone up. Not only will the judges be there, but other scouts and industry people too. She sees me fiddling with my dress and says in a posh accent, 'You look fabulous.'

Inside the holding room, there's a group of about ten people milling about. I spot the two girls from the first audition in another set of matching outfits. They still seem supremely confident. In fact, everyone here looks really professional and stylish.

'Right.' Deena looks at a list. 'You two are fourth.' She walks off.

The first act leave the room and a few short minutes later they're back, smiling. Guess it must've gone well. I tap my hands on my knees, remembering how they called us into a room to tell us the results of the first audition. This time, we'll find out on stage, in front of an audience. The next act come back in, looking shell-shocked and white.

'Oh no,' I whisper to Cal.

'That won't be us,' he says, and I seriously hope not because my stomach is churning so badly I think I might be in danger of puking.

'It really won't. I mean, we're—'

'I want to see her! Move.'

The shout floats through the closed doors to the reception area.

I freeze.

Cal looks at me. 'Is that … ?'

221

'Oh my God,' I whisper. I know that voice. 'It's Aaron.'

'How the hell did he know you were here?' Cal says.

I'm already moving. I can hear more shouting outside. What if he does something – gets into a fight? Cal grabs hold of my arm. 'Talk to him after.'

But I shake him off.

I'm trembling, aware of how quiet the holding room has gone. But I can't stop.

'Gemma, please don't …' Cal says.

I pull open the door.

Aaron's being held by a security guard. He's shouting and struggling, but when he sees me, he goes still.

I walk up to him in slow motion, while my brain flashes through what to say like a magician with a deck of cards. But no aces turn up. I've lied and somehow he knows and there's nothing to say.

I try anyway. 'Aaron, I'm sorry. It was a last-minute decision and I was going to tell you just as soon—'

'You're on in five.' Deena's appeared next to me. She looks at Aaron, then back at me questioningly. I realise I haven't taken a breath for a good long time. I do now, in a short gasp. Aaron seems past the point of anger because instead of yelling any more, he just looks at me, and that look's enough to let me know I've shattered his heart.

'I'm sorry,' I whisper.

'I don't even know who you are,' he says, and for the most terrible moment I think he's going to cry again right in front of everyone.

'Gemma.'

It's Cal. The next moment, Aaron's wrenched himself

free of the security guard and lunged towards us. I don't even know where his fist is heading – Cal or me – I don't think Aaron knows at this stage, but Cal drags me backwards out of harm's way and keeps on pulling, tugging at my arm while the security guards bundle out a screaming Aaron.

Cal pulls me through the door to the holding room and it shuts behind us. I turn, to see the other contestants staring at us. I'm sobbing, hard, but then Deena comes in and says, 'Right, uhh, you two are supposed to be on next. Do you think you'll be OK? I'm not supposed to change the schedule around …' She flicks through her paperwork, bites her lip.

'Just give her a second,' Cal says.

A minute, maybe two, go past. I'm still crying. Cal sits me in the corner, gets tissues and a bottle of water. Then he kneels in front of me and begins to talk. 'Listen, Gemma, I know this didn't go to plan …'

I let out a laugh despite myself, but it turns into a sob.

'I think we should do it. This is who you are, not whatever it is he's trying to make you into.'

'He'll think I've betrayed him.'

'Well, you haven't, for one, but anyway I'm pretty sure it's too late for that,' Cal says. 'So you've got nothing to lose, have you? But maybe something to gain.'

'People are going to think—'

'No one's going to think anything bad. Well, not about you. But who cares? Screw what anyone thinks. Get up and show them who you are.'

Suddenly I know he's right. I have to sing my songs.

I take a massive breath and reach inside, to a place under the layers of fright and sleep deprivation and worry, searching for Confident Gemma, the me I've always been sure of. She's still there. Maybe a little heartbroken, but there nonetheless. And so I wipe my face, and push my shoulders back, and I look at Cal. 'All right, let's do it,' I say.

Cal breaks into a relieved smile and gives me a quick, gentle hug.

Deena comes over. 'I'm sorry but I think it's now or never,' she says. 'Can you manage?'

Cal grabs my hand and doesn't let go, all the way down a corridor, and then we're waiting in the wings of an actual stage, much bigger than the last little room we went to. When I peek out, I can see the judges, and then a fair few rows of other people. Some look like family and friends – I can see Rachael and Sean – others must be the industry people, scouts.

I start to shake, clutching Cal's guitar. Cal puts one arm around my shoulders.

Then it's time to walk on. There's lights set up, microphones. Two chairs. The faces in front of us are suddenly a blur. I see a woman to the left of the judging table I recognise. The Greenwoods' manager. OhGodohGodohGod.

'Hi. Welcome back! I remember "Sea Dreams" – very fresh. We're looking forward to seeing what else you have for us today.' It's Niles. His smile is still warm.

There's silence, then Cal says, 'Yes. Gemma's written two new songs but we're going to start with "Sea Dreams".' He gives me an encouraging nod. I curl my fingers over my fretboard.

I look out into the crowd. Everything's too bright. All I can think about are the lights, and the people watching, and what if I mess this all up? What if it's all been for nothing? Hurting Aaron.

Aaron. Just his name makes my heart twist so hard I'm breathless.

'It's OK, just focus on the music,' Cal whispers.

I feel my fingers start to move automatically, strumming the chords, pulling the music from somewhere.

Cal holds my eyes. I can feel him, willing me on.

But I'm remembering. Long nights looking out of my window and seeing the sun glinting on the sea. The stories in the music, weaving around me. All the hours teaching myself to write music, to play. To sing. Listening to my heroes singing of love lost and found. The way it transforms people. How I thought I'd found my very own story and it was even better than a country song. I think about Aaron, about what we've had. How badly I've let him down.

My cue comes. I open my mouth, fill my lungs with air.

And nothing comes out.

Chapter Thirty-Six

Aaron

I take off as soon as the security guard loosens his grip; I'm not about to get arrested. Been there once. Never again. They chase after me half-heartedly for a few paces, then give up, the fat bastards that they are.

My head is like a radio tuned to the highest frequency, ears ringing with it. I run faster, get to my car and take the road back at ninety. Then I push it to a ton. I'm in the outside lane, the central reservation a blur of steel, and it occurs to me how remarkably easy it would be to tweak the steering wheel to the right.

Then she'd be sorry.

But I don't. I drive all the way to our beach. To the cave she once showed me. I stand in its mouth, listening to the sea pulse against the shoreline, then walk in, to the very back where it's dark and still. Where there's space for the howling in my head to take over.

Chapter Thirty-Seven

Gemma

Cal: 'It wasn't your fault.'

Rachael: 'He was being a complete arsehole.'

Sean: 'Dude's got issues. You see the way he went at the security guard? Thought he was going to take his head off.'

Cal again: 'It's not as bad as you think. Maybe we could … well, there's always next year. If they run it. I mean, they probably will, right?'

They carry on half the way home, before everyone lapses into silence. I just sit there, unable to speak. Everything feels numb. I've lost them both: Aaron, the competition. And it's all my fault.

Every so often I try Aaron again, but none of my calls or texts are getting through.

When we draw up near my front door, I look at Cal and say, 'I'm sorry.'

'Hey, don't worry about me. I was just along for the ride. You're the one who writes the songs. And I promise there'll be another chance. You're too good for there not to be,' Cal says.

'Yeah,' adds Rachael. 'It'll all sort itself out.'

But I don't think I'll ever sing a country song again.

I nod and tell them goodbye.

I'm so exhausted, I just want to crawl into bed, yet part of me is scanning everywhere, as though Aaron will appear through the front gate, or at least text me, tell me where he is. That he's OK.

I nearly turn around to go straight back out. Maybe he's at his flat. But the front door swings open, and both Mum and Dad are standing on the doorstep, looking grim in the face.

What now? I don't think I can handle faking my way through some football-related disaster. But then Dad says, 'Who's Aaron?'

'What?' I say, and sidle past them, into the hallway. Dad bangs the front door and positions himself at the foot of the stairs, arms crossed.

'You heard,' he says.

'Where have you been?' Mum asks, her voice softer, timid. Dad shoots her a look.

'At the audition. I did text.' It hurts even to say the word 'audition'.

'You still haven't told us who Aaron is,' Dad says.

'He's …' I pause because the most ridiculous thing is, I don't even know. 'Who said … ?'

'I bumped into Esi,' Mum says. 'She's worried about you. Cal is, too.'

'Well, it's none of her business, or yours,' I snap. It comes out of nowhere, or perhaps it doesn't. Maybe it's all the stress of the last few hours finally making its way out, but

I'm really angry, in a way something cornered is: ready to fight my way out.

I don't have time for this. I need to find Aaron.

A new, horrible thought comes to me as I remember something he said once, one night after we'd slept together. 'After Cherine left me for that guy, I thought I'd do something stupid to myself ...'

What if he has?

Everything in me goes cold.

'How long have you been seeing him?' Dad's demanding. He starts pacing back and forth, winding up to one of his explosions, and sure enough, when I stare at him and refuse to answer, it comes. 'Your mother logged on to that parent thing and found out you've barely been in college!'

'I made up the work,' I shout. But shouting back makes Dad ten times worse.

'And your job? You jacked that in too?'

'So what? You said yourself it paid peanuts. And anyway, I wouldn't have had to do it if you'd given me the same allowance as Michael.'

'Leave your brother out of it,' Dad shouts. 'This is about your behaviour, young lady. It's disgusting—'

'Disgusting?' I hiss. 'I'll tell you what's disgusting. You and your goddam football. And the way *you* —' I jab a finger at Mum, who's actually got her hand clamped to her heart in some parody of a bad actor having a heart attack – 'go along with it. Neither of you give a shit about me. Maybe if you weren't so wrapped up in Michael all the time I'd have talked to you.' I'm screaming so loudly.

'That's completely ridiculous …' Dad begins, but I shout across him so loud it burns the back of my throat.

'No it's not! You don't love me. You've only ever loved Michael!' Tears run down my face. I see Dad getting ready to shout me down and I can't bear it. I push past him and run up the stairs, crying so hard I can barely see.

Dad shouts something up the stairs – it might be 'Get back here!' – but at the same time a voice comes from just above me, saying, 'What's going on?' and I let out this huge scream that ends in a 'Fuck you!' and bring my hand down hard on the banister, just as Michael draws level with me. I don't even know who I'm shouting at now. Michael does a sort of sideways jump to avoid my fist, which bursts into pain as it connects with the wood, and then through my haze of tears, I see him miss his landing. Only by maybe two millimetres, but it's enough. The side of his foot keeps going, off the stair, twisting underneath his ankle and we both hear this horrific crunching sound, and then Michael's tumbling down the stairs, yelling out and scrabbling to hold on to something. Mum screams as Dad lunges forward to catch Michael just before his head hits the wall, and then my brother's writhing in pain at the foot of the stairs while I watch, a block of horror.

Michael's foot – oh God, his foot – is at an angle it was never meant to be, and he's crying with the pain of it while Mum shrieks, and Dad yells at her, 'Call an ambulance, you stupid cow.'

I still can't move. Then, slowly, as I hear Mum ask for the ambulance, I inch my way down the stairs. I crouch next to Michael, who's quieter now, but almost entirely white, and I whisper, 'Michael? I'm sorry, I didn't—'

'Get away from him. You've done enough.' It's Dad. He yanks me away so hard I stumble and hit the wall, cracking my elbow and sending another stream of pain down my arm. No one speaks for a second, and then Michael says weakly, 'It's OK, Gemma …'

'No it's bloody not!' Dad roars out, and I can't bear it any more – the way he's looking at me with pure hatred in his eyes, before he crouches down and cradles Michael's head in his lap, like he's never once done to me, and all the time Mum is just watching, and she's silent, silent, silent.

There's nothing here for me.

I push past Mum and run out of the front door, and if anyone calls after me, I don't hear them.

Chapter Thirty-Eight

Aaron

How long passes in the cave? I don't know. The stars are out when I emerge. I haven't cried, haven't thought, haven't felt. Just sat and listened to the ringing in my ears until it merged with the waves into the bitterest of songs.

For once, I drive slowly back to the flat. My phone has so many missed calls, voicemails, WhatsApps from Gemma. I listen to all of them, and delete them one by one. Her pleas to give her another chance, to let her explain, are all drowned out by the image of her with him. Her lying to me. The tracker on her phone showing her driving away, out of town, on to the motorway.

I knew as soon as I saw it.

How much like the others she must be, after all.

And yet a part of me can't bring myself to admit it. To see how wrong I was. I could take my revenge. Maybe I should. I still have those photos in the Cloud. A few quick messages to Jonny and Binners would be all that's needed.

And still.

I don't.

Not yet.

Something inside is telling me to wait, as though there's still a chance, a way to fix this. Because if I let her break me like Cherine did, like Mum did, I might stay broken for good.

These thoughts all go through my mind as though there's another Aaron whispering them to me, and it's not until I get to the flat that I know why.

I feel her before I see her, huddled with her arms around herself outside the entrance, her face streaked with old tears and mascara, deathly white in the fluorescent light coming from the lobby.

She looks so small. So fragile. And part of me loves her still, and part of me hates her for it.

Chapter Thirty-Nine

Gemma

'Thank God you're OK.' That's the first thing I say. Aaron looks as bad as I feel, which is saying something. After I ran away, down the track, I called him, again and again, and each time he didn't pick up, I started getting more scared he'd done something terrible to himself. It feels like days have passed out here. There's no one else I want to talk to. Esi's out of the question. Underneath my exhaustion there's a bubble of anger at her growing because she's the one who started all this, telling Mum about Aaron. If she hadn't, we wouldn't have argued and then Michael …

I squeeze my eyes shut as that cracking noise sounds in my head again.

'I had to see you,' I say.

Aaron looks down at me and I can't read his expression at all.

'Please? Just talk to me. That's all I'm asking,' I say.

He leans across and unlocks the door, then steps past me without a word, but he doesn't shut it. I unlace my stiff fingers from around my knees and pull myself up. Everything aches; my elbow, my fist, my legs. My heart.

I pull the door closed quietly behind me and walk slowly into the flat.

Aaron's sitting at the kitchen table, his fingers resting on top of it. Opposite him is a chair, pulled out a little. I sit in it, across from him, and wait. Moonshine whines quietly from the corner, her tail moving in a greeting to me, but she quiets at a look from Aaron.

'Tell me. I want to hear it from you. But if you lie, even once, then that's it,' Aaron says, his voice eerily calm.

And so I do. I tell him about Cal coming to the match, how he talked me into going to the audition. Aaron doesn't react when I explain Cal and Rachael are a thing now. I tell him about the audition, and going home, and the fight with Dad, and then Michael falling … I have to gulp back tears as I do. Aaron makes a movement with his hand, as if to comfort me then, but stops himself.

Finally, I say how I walked to his flat. 'I know you might need time, but … I can wait.'

'Where?' Aaron says now, and it's the first time I've seen some colour come back into his face.

'I don't …?'

'Where will you wait? You can't go back to your parents, can you?'

'No … I – I thought … if you'll have me, I want to stay here. With you.'

Aaron sits back and considers me. I chew on my bottom lip, trying to meet his eyes, but they're so dark and unreachable.

'Maybe. But first I need to tell you a few things,' Aaron says. And then it's his turn to talk. It feels like hours go by, with me sometimes crying, sometimes apologising, as Aaron explains what is was like for him, to find out I'd lied. What a betrayal it was. But eventually his voice slows and then stops. I'm so exhausted I can barely see.

And then … and then he reaches one hand across the table, and his fingers, touching mine, feel like pure salvation. 'I think …' he says after a long silence, looking down at our hands, 'I want to try.'

I let my breath out so hard I think I might be sick.

'I want to try to forgive you,' Aaron adds. 'But it's going to take some time.'

I nod.

'You'll never speak to him again?'

'Of course not! No, never, I promise.'

Aaron lets out a sigh, too, then looks me in the eyes, and this time I see the old Aaron, my Aaron. 'Come here,' he says.

The relief is so huge, I practically fly around the table and collapse into his arms and then I'm crying and crying, and Aaron's stroking my hair and kissing me and holding me and whispering it'll be OK, how we'll find a way through together, as long as I prove he can trust me again.

'Of course I will, I will,' I say between sobs, and he kisses my tears.

Then, I pull him into the bedroom.

Chapter Forty

Gemma

I wake a couple of hours later. Aaron's still asleep. I'm sore from earlier – not just from at home, but from sitting on the step and also because Aaron was … It wasn't gentle make-up sex. But then I remember after, when we cuddled and he told me he loved me. The closeness of him. I go over to stand by the window, look out into the dark. You can't see the sea from here, but that's OK. I'm with Aaron and he forgives me and that's all that matters.

I slide into bed and push my body as close to Aaron's as I can, feeling the warmth of him. Tomorrow I'll make a start on getting him to trust me again, and one day all this will be like a horrible dream.

'I love you,' I whisper into his sleeping ear.

Aaron mutters something and shifts in his sleep, one arm falling so that it's resting heavily across me.

'Gem. Wake up. Someone's here.' I wake slowly. It feels like I've barely had two hours' sleep, but it's light outside. I look for my phone to check out the time, but it's not where I left

237

it on the bedside cabinet. 'You need to get dressed,' Aaron says from the doorway.

I half fall out of bed and struggle into my clothes while Aaron watches. 'Who's here?' I say.

'The police.' Aaron's voice is grim.

'Why?' For a panicked second I think it must be because of Michael. But that was an accident. 'What do they want?'

'Your parents reported you'd run off. I think they're doing some check. Don't worry, you just need to tell them it's all fine,' he says.

'OK …' I still feel a bit dazed as I walk into the living room. Two police officers are sitting there, a man and a woman. The woman smiles when she sees me.

'Are you Gemma?'

'Ye-es.'

'Take a seat. Can we have a few minutes alone?' she says to Aaron.

I exchange a look with him, and somehow I know this is going to be the first test. I have to persuade the police officers to leave.

So I summon up Confident Gemma, and she's a little ragged around the edges but seems to work on the policeman, at least. I explain how I'm staying with Aaron for a bit, how I've fallen out with my parents, but I'm safe and happy here.

The policeman's ready to go after five minutes; his face says he has better things to do with his time. 'Well, as you're seventeen, we wouldn't usually … We can't make you go back home. But maybe speak to your folks, eh? Don't let a little spat fester.'

Spat. I remember Cal, joking about *Queer Eye*, what feels like a century ago.

'Oh yeah, sure, I will,' I say.

The policeman's already standing up. But his colleague leans forward, glances at the door to the kitchen which is slightly ajar, and says, 'Are you happy in your relationship?'

'Oh yes, very,' I give her my biggest smile.

'Nothing that concerns you?'

'No, not at all. We're really happy,' I say.

She looks at the door again, and then nods. 'Well, OK. But if you need to, there are organisations I could signpost you to. Just for a little independent advice,' she adds.

'I don't think I'd need that,' I say firmly. I can see she's about to ask me something else, so I raise my voice a bit and say, 'Aaron? I think the officers are going now.'

A moment later he comes in and we see them off, smiling. When the door's shut, Aaron kisses me. 'I can't believe your parents sent the cops round. It's not like they were bothered before, is it? You'd think they'd want to see you happy,' he begins.

I'm still staring at the blank face of the closed door.

'I mean, did they even try to call you first? Talk about an overreaction.'

I need to check Michael's OK. 'Hey, you seen my phone?' I say as we go back to the living room.

Aaron goes into the kitchen, then comes back holding it.

I blink twice. 'I thought I took it to bed last night?'

'Nope, you left it here.'

Did I? I was so tired ... still am. I let out a gigantic yawn. Aaron comes over with a blanket and tucks it around me.

'I'm getting you a hot chocolate,' he says as he hands me my phone. I take it with a grateful smile and snuggle in under the soft grey wool of the blanket.

While he's making the hot chocolate, I quickly scan my phone. There's no texts from Esi, or Cal, thank goodness, and only one from Mum:

It's a clean break so we're hoping.

I look again, thinking I've missed something, but that's it. No kisses, no asking where I am, or if I'm coming home. When I show the text to Aaron he sighs.

'They didn't even want to talk to you face to face. Imagine if the police took you home.'

'Yeah, so they could ground me forever and not speak to me,' I say. I'm trying to sound upbeat, like I don't care, but before I can stop them, a couple of tears run down my cheeks.

'Oh, baby, come here.' Aaron gathers me, blanket, hot chocolate and all, into his lap. 'You don't need them anyway. We've got each other now.'

Chapter Forty-One

Aaron

It's a fresh start. I watch her sleeping under the blanket, her hands curled up against her chest. The way her breathing sounds. That urge to touch her, to shake her awake, to make sure, rises in me. I go into the kitchen, drink a glass of water.

It should be this way, just us, only us. Everything will be like it was before. Better, even. She sighs in her sleep, shifts so the blanket slips off one shoulder, and I see her phone nestled in her hand. I take the phone and put it on the coffee table, then tuck the blanket around her, kiss her forehead.

Back to the kitchen. Laptop's open on the side. I do a bit of coding. Think about money. I've started doing some investing. When you get enough, it can grow without you looking: interest rates and share prices. And it can disappear on you too, if you're not watching hard enough.

I keep working.

She sleeps on, oblivious to my third cup of coffee, the jitter running through me.

So peaceful.

I think about the cops, about the texts and WhatsApps on her phone. She doesn't need her family and so-called friends hassling her, putting confusing crap into her head.

My eyes go back again and again to that square of metal on the coffee table. It lights up once more.

She sleeps on, peacefully.

The message is from Esi. If I didn't think she was a bitch before, I do now. I hit delete without pausing.

Then I watch my arm raise high, like it has its own momentum, until the phone is over my head.

My fingers release.

The phone takes its time falling, spiralling over and over like a coin deciding whether it's heads or tails. So it's really the phone's decision, in a way, to shatter its own screen, not mine. It could've landed face up. Gem wakes with a start as I crouch down to pick it up.

'Shit, Gem, I'm sorry. It must've slipped out as you were sleeping. Why didn't you have a screen protector on it?'

She's half awake, looking at her spider-web phone, gazing blearily up at me. I take the phone from her. 'Don't cut yourself on it. We'll get you another one. Actually, I've got an old one you can have. We'll sort it.'

'OK.' Her voice is sleep-filled, confused. I slide on to the sofa next to her.

'I'll get you everything you need, don't worry. This is the beginning of something new, just you and me.'

I pull the blanket tight around us.

Chapter Forty-Two

Gemma

If I'd known how easy it was to move out, I would've done it way sooner. We spend the best day in Plymouth, shopping for new … well, everything. By the time we're finished, we look like one of those paparazzi shots you get of celebrities with arms full of bags from exclusive shops. I've got new bras, pants – loads of those – and jeans, shoes, make-up. It's like being on *Queer Eye* or something, with Aaron standing in for the Fab Five.

I'm shattered by the time we get back, but Aaron helps me unpack my stuff into a space he makes in the wardrobe in his room – our room. The thought of it gives me a thrill.

Later, I go into the kitchen where he's working on the laptop. I want to do something to pay him back, apart from the sex of course, which Aaron jokes is all the payment he needs. I start looking through the cupboards.

'Whatcha doing?' Aaron says. I love the way that smile is back on his face, how he's looking at me like he did before. It's like being in a warm bath, safe and relaxed.

'You have zero food in here,' I say, laughing.

'We'll order takeaway.'

'But I want to cook for you … I'll go and get something in Tesco …' I break off because I've realised I don't have any money. I left everything at home – at Mum and Dad's and Michael's house – except my phone, which I've managed to break, and it feels a bit weird asking Aaron for cash to cook him a thank-you dinner. Plus, for a moment there's an expression on his face, this hardening, like he's afraid. Then he taps on his laptop and brings up an online menu.

'Chinese?' he says.

Later, when I've got rid of the leftovers and washed up, we sit on the sofa looking for something to watch. It feels weird not being able to check my phone. I wonder for a bit whether I could Sellotape the screen, but Aaron's worried I could cut myself on it, and anyway, I've got an old PAYG of his, which is fine for now, I guess. It's not like I've got anyone I want to call anyway.

We put Netflix on, and Aaron finds some sci-fi thing. It's not really what I'd watch, but Aaron seems totally into it, so we watch four episodes. Just as the countdown begins to the next one, I say, 'I think I might go to bed. College tomorrow.'

Aaron doesn't look away from the screen.

'Aaron? I'm going to bed,' I say.

'We can't leave it there!' Aaron says. He's like a little boy, all excited. I can't see the appeal myself; it's obvious the man who's pretending to be a human is actually one of the aliens, but I let Aaron pull me in close to him for a snuggle.

Three more episodes later, it's 2 a.m. and I really need to get to bed. I can barely stop yawning long enough to brush my teeth with my new toothbrush. I give the Gemma in the mirror a quick smile as I'm brushing.

When Aaron reaches for me in bed, I move away. 'I'm knackered,' I say.

'OK,' Aaron says and rolls over. But just as I'm almost asleep, he rolls back and starts again.

'Oi,' I whisper.

'Can't help it, you're too sexy,' he says.

I sit up. 'Seriously. We've got to get up in, like, four hours or something.' I am properly pissed off now.

I feel Aaron freeze beside me, then he says, 'Sorry. I didn't mean to hassle you or something,' and there's so much hurt in his voice. 'I just wanted to be close. After everything that's happened …' He trails off.

Guilt and something else crawl through me. Annoyance maybe? But this is not how I want things to go when we've only just found each other again. So I kiss him and coax him back into it and, well, we don't get much sleep that night.

Which is possibly why I'm in a real grump as Aaron drives me into college the next day, though I'm trying not to be. We're running late and it's just occurred to me I don't have any of my textbooks or work because they're all at home. There's no time to stop by the refectory and see everyone, because I'm still basically on probation, so Aaron runs me up to my first class, which is awkward because it's Psychology and usually I'd sit next to Cal. I make sure to choose a desk at the front and not even look Cal's way, before waving to Aaron through the glass portion of the door.

'Are we in the room or outside?' my tutor says to me.

'Sorry,' I say.

When the lesson finishes, I bolt for the door, where Aaron's waiting again.

At lunch, we're on our way out of college to go to the beach, when I see the old gang across the car park. Cal's gesturing to Esi, who looks over. She raises one hand, as if to wave or beckon to me, but I turn away. A moment later, I hear Rachael calling my name. I exchange a look with Aaron. He's never liked Rachael, because of the whole club night thing and also probably now because of Cal, so I hesitate, then throw back a quick 'Hiya!' and keep walking.

But Rachael jogs over. 'Hiya yourself,' she says. Then she looks at Aaron. 'You mind if I talk to Gemma for a second?'

I don't like the way she says it. 'Whatever you want to say to me, you can say in front of Aaron.'

Rachael gives a tiny snort, which makes me want to slap her. But Aaron says, 'Hey, it's OK. I'll wait in the car. See you later, Rachael.' He gives her a smile and me a quick kiss, and moves away.

'So, what do you want?' I say. I don't mean for it to come out quite so rudely, but I'm exhausted. Rachael doesn't seem bothered though.

'You've run away from home?' she says.

'Bloody hell, I'm not twelve. I've moved in with Aaron, yes,' I say.

'Bit fast, wasn't it?'

'Like you and Cal?' I shoot back.

Rachael laughs. 'Cal's nothing like Aaron. You know it, too. Look. I've got no skin in this, but as your friend I'm

246

telling you this one time that you're making a huge mistake. He's controlling.'

'Really? *You've* changed your mind.' I cross my arms and stare at her. 'You fancied him about three days ago.'

'Well, that was before his little performance at the audition the other day,' she says. I'm opening my mouth, ready to argue back, but she goes on before I get the chance. 'Your parents are worried about you, they've been calling everyone. And you didn't even bother to text them back?'

But I'm looking over her shoulder and I can see Esi and Cal and Phoebe and Beth in a little knot looking over at us.

'They put you up to this?' I say.

'We're worried about you,' Rachael replies. Then I see Cal begin to walk towards us. No way can I talk to him, not with Aaron nearby.

'Well, you don't need to be. I'm happy. If you want to be jealous of that, then that's your problem. And if you're not going to support me, then leave me alone,' I say.

'It's your funeral,' Rachael says. She turns away. I hear Cal call after me, but I'm already walking fast towards Aaron's car.

'You OK?' Aaron says as I get in.

'Yeah. No. I don't know,' I say.

When he's driven us away I lean back against the seat and close my eyes.

'They're jealous, you know. People don't get it, what it's like to be really, properly serious about someone,' Aaron says.

I open my eyes and watch the high hedges fly past. Soon we'll be on our beach, just us and the waves, and I know this feeling will stop.

The rest of the week goes better. Aaron gets me all new textbooks and makes sure he's taking me to each class so I don't need to worry about seeing the others. The more I think about how they've ganged up on me, appointed Rachael, of all people, their spokesperson, the angrier I get. But I love the feeling of me and Aaron against the world. We eat takeaways most nights, then cuddle up in front of the TV. Sometimes we go down to the beach to take Shiney for a walk, which she loves. Her fur is so soft.

On Friday night, just as we're celebrating the weekend's here, there's a bang on Aaron's door. I'm not dressed, because of the celebrating – so Aaron pulls on his jeans and goes to answer it. A moment later, I'm horrified to hear my parents' voices floating into the living room.

'We want to see our daughter.'

That's *Dad's* voice. I grab the nearest blanket and blow out the candles I lit earlier. The remains of dinner – a bucket of KFC – are still on the floor.

'She doesn't want to see you,' Aaron's saying. I crack the living-room door a tiny amount and peer through. Aaron has, thank God, got the door on the chain.

'Please, I'd just like to check she's OK, that's all.' This time it's Mum talking, and for a second I nearly run straight out, because suddenly I want her to hug me in a way she hasn't since I was about five.

But then Dad's shouting, 'Open this bloody door before I kick it down!' I hear a thump as he bangs on it, then sound of my parents having some sort of argument in the hall, before Dad's voice says, 'Shut up!' and Mum falls silent. I draw back.

Aaron says, 'If you come here again, we'll consider it harassment and call the police. She has your number. If she wants to get in touch, she will.' He pushes the door closed. There's two or three more bangs on it and then everything goes silent.

He finds me in a ball, the blanket around my shoulders. 'Hey, don't cry. Are you OK? Hey, you like baths, don't you? I'll run you one.'

And he does. He dumps about half a bottle of shower gel in it, because we don't have any bubble bath. I climb in and settle back. It's super hot, but after a while it kind of does the trick. I start to relax and close my eyes. The next minute, though, Aaron's decided to chuck off all his clothes and jumps in with me. I shriek, laughing, as water sloshes all over the floor.

'Oh my God, you wally!'

He grins, and then scoops up piles of bubbles to make me a bubble crown. 'My queen,' he says, in his fake posh accent.

I smile, feeling the old rhythm between us. 'Kind sir,' I say.

Then he leans down to give me a soapy kiss, his mouth pushing hard on mine so that the back of my head sinks into the bubbles.

The water makes shushing noises in my ears.

Chapter Forty-Three

Gemma

We develop our routine: we go to college, we go to the beach. We eventually get bored of takeaways, so we work out an online shop, just easy stuff like fish fingers and instant mash. We watch a lot of Netflix. Aaron clears a space for me to do my college work at a little desk while he does his app development.

The only thing I miss is my guitar. 'I wish I could play something, it always helps me concentrate,' I say without thinking one Friday as I'm trying to work through a really stupid essay for Biology. There's certain topics we don't talk about, like we've kind of agreed not to, without words. And music is one of them.

'I mean, I don't really *miss* miss it. Just a bit,' I add quickly. Aaron nods and goes back to his work.

But the next day, after I've cooked him a fry-up, Aaron comes up behind me while I'm washing the pans and says, 'Leave that,' in my ear.

'Won't take a moment,' I say. I have discovered Mum was right about one thing: you leave a pan with a load of stuck-on egg and bacon, and it's ten times harder to wash up than if you did it straight away.

'You need to get out, get some fresh air. Why don't you take Shiney down to the beach?' Aaron says. I look at him in surprise. Apart from when I'm in class, or in the bathroom – and not even always then, to be honest – I haven't been away from Aaron for weeks.

'You're not coming?' I say. There's a strange feeling inside, like panic almost.

'You go,' Aaron says firmly. 'It'll do you both good.' Then he gives me a pinch around the waist, like he's feeling the fat there.

'Hey!' I'm laughing, but also slightly self-conscious because maybe I have put on a bit of weight.

'You're so squidgeable though,' Aaron says, and I kiss him, then wriggle out of his arms to get the lead.

The walk down to the beach is quiet. It's drizzling and I don't have a coat, only one of Aaron's fleeces that doesn't keep the wind out. We totally forgot to get me a coat when we did our shopping spree. I go down through the grey streets towards the beachfront, choosing the end away from the cafe. Here the bay curves out against a white sky, big boulders piled up near the seafront wall. I trace it around, jogging on the damper sand where the tide is on its way out, Shiney running ahead of me and barking at seagulls. After a while, my shins start to hurt and I have a stitch so I slow to a walk. I wander further along and round a crop of rocks towards the end of the bay. At low tide, you wouldn't be able to get through this way, but I can always cut up the cliff path at the other end if I needed to. I breathe in sea air, feel my face get sticky with salt. It's nice to be out on my own, I realise, then a moment later I feel guilty. Aaron's done so much for me the last couple of weeks.

Far away in the distance, I can see a couple of little dots huddled on the cliff edge: mine and Esi's houses. For a minute, I wonder what would happen if I went up and knocked on my door. Probably a whole load of shouting, for a start. I think about Michael's broken ankle, but that just summons up a world of awful feelings and I can't face it. Can't face the what-ifs that will come if I think about it all for too long.

I call Shiney back and turn for home.

I've been gone well over an hour and my legs are aching when I ring the bell to get back into the building. Aaron needs to sort out another key. Then I wonder how my parents got in. Maybe one of the neighbours let them up or they tailgated someone or something. But that belongs in the category of stuff I don't want to think about.

'Gem?' I'm so relieved to hear Aaron's voice, in a way I can't really explain.

'Yes.' The door buzzes.

Upstairs, Aaron's waiting at the flat door. He takes Shiney's lead from me, unclips it and ushers the dog inside. Then he closes the door and comes behind me, putting his hands over my eyes.

'What are you doing?'

'Just walk forward, I'll tell you when to stop.'

With Aaron's guidance, I walk up the hall, his hands still

clamped down so I can only see snatches of the floor from underneath his fingers. Then he says, 'Stop.'

I do.

'Open your eyes.'

Aaron lifts his hands, but for a moment I can't speak. 'Oh my … Aaron,' I whisper.

The entire room is covered in flickering candles and flowers, and in the middle, on its own stand is an acoustic guitar. Not just any guitar. This is a Gibson. I've dreamed about playing one of these. It's a rich mahogany colour and the scratchboard is painted with the trademark humming-birds, butterflies and flowers. It's beautiful.

Aaron's grinning. 'You like it?'

I throw myself into his arms. 'It's perfect. I love it. I love *you*.' I kiss him, feeling tears and dried salt on my face. 'This is just … It's amazing. I can't believe you did this.'

'You're worth it,' Aaron says. 'You going to play me something?'

I sit and strum a chord. The sound is sweet and clear, filling the room like a bell. And then the oddest thing happens. It's like all the music, all my original music, the songs I wrote, have disappeared from my head. In the end I settle for strumming some old country songs I'll probably still be able to play in my sleep when I'm ninety.

A thought occurs to me as I rub my fingers, waiting for them to warm up properly. I've just been playing a Janie Wynell song, badly, but it's made me remember. 'Hey, do you think her new album's out yet?'

'Who?'

I laugh. 'Janie Wynell, that's who I was playing. You told me about her new album, remember?'

'Who?' he says again. Then he laughs. 'I think you're confused.' I open my mouth, but Aaron says, 'Play something else.'

There's an urgent voice, somewhere deep inside me, telling me I need to pay attention, that something's wrong, but Aaron's looking expectant so I begin a new song, stumbling over it a little, maybe because my fingers are still cold from the beach, but Aaron claps at the end. 'You're so talented,' he says.

Slowly my fingers warm up as I remember other pieces. But I don't do any of my own songs. And I don't sing.

The weather lets us know Christmas is approaching. It dips colder and colder as we go into December. I'm still wearing Aaron's old fleece to college. It's not really a problem. I mean, I basically go straight from his car up to my lessons now, and anyway … I feel bad always asking him for stuff. Like when my foundation ran out and he made a comment about the price of the replacement so I put a cheapo one on the online food order instead.

And then there's Christmas presents. I want to get him one, but how? I don't have any money of my own. I never added my Amazon gift cards to my account and they're still in my room back home.

One evening over pizza I say, 'I'm thinking about getting another job.'

Aaron puts down the slice he was about to take a bite out of. 'Why?'

I avoid his eyes, because if there's one thing I've started to learn with Aaron, it's that it's easy to get confused talking to him. I can't always keep my thoughts straight. 'Well, I think I need my own money – you know, just for things,' I say.

'But like what? We've got everything we need here, haven't we?' he says.

I meet his eyes then, and the next moment I find myself agreeing. But later that night, alone in the shower, I think about it some more. I want to be able to get Aaron stuff, too. And, well, the foundation that I want, without having to worry about it. Then I wonder if I'm being petty. I mean, most girls would love this, wouldn't they? He bought me a guitar. It feels ungrateful to complain.

Then I give myself a shake. Why am I even worrying? I just need to explain this to Aaron and he'll understand. I wrap myself in a towel and pad over to where he's tapping away on his laptop, frowning.

'Hey,' I say.

'Hey.' He sounds distracted. Probably something up with his new investment stuff. I know I should leave it, but Confident Gemma – or Stubborn Gemma maybe – suddenly surfaces. It's a surprise to find myself saying, 'I need my own money. For starters I want to be able to buy—'

He slams the laptop closed so hard I think it might crack. 'Buy what? You girls are all the same. Always wanting more!' he shouts.

Buy you a present.

That's what I'd been going to say. Instead I find myself staring at him, paralysed, Confident Gemma shrivelling

255

away to nothing. 'No, I …' I begin, but I can't seem to find the words when he's looking at me like that.

He jumps up and comes past, whacking into my shoulder as he does. I gasp, because it hurts, but he doesn't stop, just grabs Shiney's lead and bangs out of the flat, the dog trotting meekly by his side. I consider running after him, but it's dark and I'm only wearing a towel. So I put on some clothes and I clean up a bit, and I pace and rub my shoulder and wait.

After half an hour, when he's still not back, I start to comfort eat, scooping out bites of ice cream from the tub in front of the freezer with a teaspoon.

When the door goes I put the nearly empty ice-cream tub back in a hurry, the spoon still inside. Aaron comes into the room just as I'm straightening back up. I'm sure I must have a guilty look on my face, even though it's only ice cream.

But as I say, 'I'm sorry,' he does too. There's a tense moment where we look at each other, and then he starts to laugh and so do I, though mine has this relieved edge to it that feels wrong, like someone else is laughing.

Later, in bed, Aaron explains how I interrupted just as he really needed to concentrate on his work. 'It's complicated stuff. I need to keep a lot of things in my head if I don't want to lose a shedload of money,' he says. I feel a flash of guilt. The guitar must have cost loads, even if it was second-hand.

'Maybe … could I help?' I say. 'I'd feel less like I'm … I'd be making a contribution,' I say.

Aaron laughs, then kisses me on the nose. 'It's pretty

complicated, Gem. But you do contribute. You cook and clean, and stuff. Well, sometimes,' he adds in a jokey voice. 'I mean, I'm pretty sure the kitchen floor's a health hazard but hey, only Shiney eats off it so …'

'Oi,' I say, and poke him.

And of course it goes the way it always does, except that when we're done, I don't fall asleep like I usually do. Instead I stay awake for ages.

In the morning, I get down on my hands and knees and clean the kitchen floor.

He's kind of right; it *was* pretty manky.

Chapter Forty-Four

Aaron

'Can I have a word?' It's Mr Bowyer, the College Manager.

Shit. Gem gives me a questioning look. When I nod at her it's OK, she goes into her Music class. I notice she sits at the very front, right by Mr Higgins. He's older, but not that old, and I don't like the way she looks at him, there's something doglike about it, but I haven't got time to watch because Mr Bowyer is hustling me down the corridor towards his office. There's not much point following him, but I'd rather do it in there than out in the open, where someone like Jonny might see.

In his office, he gets straight to it. 'You've already been notified of the decision to expel you for non-attendance. You are no longer a student here. So may I ask what you're doing on college premises?'

I shrug, because I don't owe this guy jack.

'If you continue to come on to the premises I will call the police to have you removed. Am I clear?' he says.

There's no point answering, so I just go to walk out, but

not before he says, 'What's your relationship to Gemma Belfine? You're living together, I understand?'

'Hardly your business, as I'm not a student any more,' I grind out through a clenched jaw.

'Yes, but Gemma is,' he says, and his voice is musing.

I don't wait to carry on the conversation, just get out of there. Mr Bowyer makes a movement as if to stop me, but I push past him. My brain is racing. Has she said something to someone? That Music tutor of hers she was making eyes at? Isn't she happy? I think back to her asking for more money, to the way she seems to eat all the time now. The extra weight was sexy at first, but it's really sitting on her face. I don't get it. What more does she want? Am I not good enough for her? Is she complaining about me to people at college?

The thoughts spin round in a blur, mocking me.

Nothing you do will ever be good enough. She's stopped making any effort.

I think about the dinner she tried to cook and burned the other night. The dog food uncleaned on the floor. Her demands for more this and more that.

Binners saying I'm under the thumb.

Is she taking the piss?

Then another part of my brain tells me to stop being an idiot, that she loves me. She's always saying it. But she's never written a song for me, has she? Not like the ones she did with Cal. I thought she would when I got her the guitar. And it cost so much. More than I could afford, really. As soon as I sell another app it'll be fine, but the point is, she doesn't have a clue. Does she still secretly care about him? Or someone else? My thoughts keep coming back round to that look she gave her music teacher. Could something be going on?

I wait outside college in the car as lessons kick out. She doesn't appear. Ten minutes go by. Why isn't she here? Is she flirting with him – Mr Higgins? Laughing? Leaning down as he hands her an assignment, so her hair brushes against his arm …

There's a tap at the window.

It's her.

She grins, gives a little wave. I press the button to unlock the doors and wait until she slides in. She smells like the perfume I got her, and like something else I can't work out. Is it aftershave? I lean in to kiss her, but really I'm taking in a long breath through my nostrils. And this time I'm sure of it. Man's deodorant. Faint, but there.

For one horrible moment my hand itches, like I want to punch her, but she's already talking, saying in a rush, 'I was so confused when you weren't outside the room, then someone said they'd seen you in your car so I came down here and—'

'Who said?'

'What?' Is that a guilty look on her face?

'Who were you talking to? The mystery person who saw me in my car?' I say.

Her expression falters. 'I don't remember. I just … Are you OK? What did Bowyer want?'

In reply, I turn on the engine. I can't do this here. I need to think, need to plan what to say to her. But partway home I can't help it. It bursts out. 'Who were you with, Gemma? I can smell you,' I shout.

260

Out of the corner of my eye I see her jump, and it makes me angrier, like it's a confirmation. I accelerate and change direction, head towards our beach. The flat's too small for this conversation. I want her face to face, out in the light. I want to look into her eyes and get the truth.

At the car park, I get out and stride down the cliff path, Gemma following behind, calling my name.

The sea's a frothing grey, wind pushing gulls about overhead, the scrubby weeds lining the cliff path bending one way, then another. I hit the sand and keep going, on up towards the cave. Gemma's running behind, the wind taking her words. All I can hear is the echo of my name and the sea crashing. I was right; this place is a bitch now it's winter.

I stop in front of the cave. Turn to face her.

She stumbles up, her hair plastered across one pasty cheek. Her make-up's run into two lines tracking her cheeks. She looks like crap.

'Aaron,' she gasps out, and then doubles over, holding her side. I wait while she straightens. 'Please, I don't know what's going on,' she says.

And at that my fury subsides into something cold, clinical, like all my feelings are frozen. 'It's very simple.' I say it loudly, so she can hear over the sound of the sea. 'Who were you talking to and who were you flirting with?'

'What? No one. I wasn't.'

'Then where were you after your class?'

'This is insane! I was looking for you,' she's shouting now, crying again.

'Don't get hysterical. I know, OK? I smelt it on you. Some man's aftershave.'

'What?' She's really sobbing now, looking completely confused. Is she lying or telling the truth? Then she says, 'Oh my God, Aaron, I used your deodorant this morning, mine ran out. Is that what you mean?'

I hold her eyes, searching.

'I swear it's the truth. Why don't you trust me?' she says.

'Well, what about Higgins?' I say.

'What about him? You can't be serious, he's forty or something,' she shouts.

'What does that matter?' I grab one of her wrists, and she flinches. 'Tell me you don't fancy him.'

'Of course not, of course I don't! Aaron, please look at me. I love you, no one else.' She's still yelling, tears pouring down her face.

And suddenly the thing I thought I saw – that shadow of Cherine, her hand on that guy's arm, her smiling into his face – lifts away and I see her again, my Gem, crying on a beach as I twist her wrist in my hand.

I drop to the floor so fast it's like my legs have been kicked out. And I'm crying and dry-heaving and telling her I'm sorry, and she's got her arms around me and she's telling me how she won't go back to college, how we'll be together all the time.

How much she loves me.

It takes a long while, but slowly the storm inside calms and I'm me again, on the beach, our beach, while the girl who holds my heart rocks me in her arms.

Chapter Forty-Five

Gem

'It's *Chrissssstmas!*' Slade blares out on Aaron's laptop as we hang up all the paper chains I made. Everything's all ready, except for one thing: Aaron's present.

The last two weeks have been weird without college. Aaron told me about how he decided to quit after that awful day on the beach, and it made sense for me to stop too. I mean, he's been making more than enough money to support us, and like he said, it'll give me more time to focus on my songs. I don't really need A levels anyway to be a singer-songwriter. Besides, I've been so busy planning Christmas and getting the flat ready. We're having Aaron's dad and Jaquie round in the morning and it's the first time they've come, so I'm super nervous. I was a bit surprised when Aaron said he'd invited them, but then he put his arm around my waist and pulled me in tight, saying, 'I can't wait to show you off.' I like the idea of us hosting too, it's the sort of thing serious couples do. Aaron wanted me to sort out the food so I've got what I hope are all the right things in. Even though I don't really know what a 'Christmas brunch' is.

This will also be the first Christmas Day I've been away from my parents and Michael, but there's too much to do to spend much time thinking about it. Especially in this weather, Shiney gets muddy paw-prints everywhere; Aaron's always forgetting to towel her off in the lobby, and I don't want to be a nag about it, so I go over the floors of the flat with a cloth on my hands and knees most days. I sometimes take her out in the evening, or go with Aaron, it all depends.

And now here we are, on Christmas Eve. I never brought up the job thing again and so I've had to get creative about Aaron's main present. I'm feeling a bit nervous about it. I don't know why I've found it so hard. I run through it all in my head one last time in bed, and I think about all the other Christmas Eves I couldn't sleep, waiting for Santa to come.

I'm up first on Christmas morning. I shower and do my hair and make-up. Then I get the gingerbread biscuits out. I bought them rather than made them, but I got some of those coloured-icing pen things to decorate them with, and if I shove the packets in the bin no one needs to know I didn't actually bake the biscuits. I should've done it yesterday.

I glance at the closed door. I want this all to be perfect. I've bought proper coffee, the same brand as the one we have in the cafe, some Pringles and a pack of dips, and a plate shaped like a Christmas tree for the biscuits. I tried to check with Aaron if it was the sort of thing he had in mind, but he's been a bit distracted with this investment thing he's doing. He keeps saying it's all fine and that he trusts me.

Trust. It seems that word comes up all the time with us. I wish that Cherine girl hadn't been such a bitch to him. Then he wouldn't get so upset about things. But I'm not going to think about that today. I squeeze a wobbly line of icing on to a gingerbread man, then hear Aaron call out from the bedroom.

I speed up. The icing looks a bit rubbish, but I can't leave half of them done and half not. Then Aaron calls out again. I put the icing down and go into the bedroom. Aaron's sitting back in bed, arms behind his head, watching the TV.

'Happy Christmas!' he says.

'Happy Christmas,' I kiss him and then snuggle up to his shoulder, one eye on the clock, which is already reading nine.

After a moment, Aaron says, 'Look under the bed.'

I reach down and pull out a parcel wrapped in layers of tissue paper, tied with a bow. I sit on the bed to unwrap it. Inside is a set of underwear, beautifully delicate and lacy.

'Oh, wow … it's gorgeous,' I say, but some doubt creeps into my voice.

'Don't you like it?'

'Yes I do, it's lovely, thank you,' I say and kiss him.

'Try it on.'

'In a minute – I need to clear up before your dad gets here,' I say.

'Wow, you know how to turn a guy on,' he jokes. Well, it's more or less a joke, but there's this thing I've noticed sometimes recently, where he's joking, but not in the way he used to. I can't put it into words and I know he'd be hurt if I say anything, so I gather up the flimsy lace and go into the bathroom.

It's too small. The bra cups barely cover anything and they bite uncomfortably into me. And the knickers are worse … For a moment tears come into my eyes. I know I've been eating a bit more, but … I check the label. They're a size eight. I've never been that size. It's such a boy mistake to make that I nearly laugh.

Aaron calls from the other room, 'What are you doing in there?'

'Umm … it doesn't quite fit,' I say.

'Let me see, I bet it's gorgeous,' he says.

'Not really …'

Then the door rattles. 'Come on, I'm sure it's fine,' he says.

Reluctantly I open the door. Aaron stands there, looking me up and down. For a second I think I see disappointment, and I feel heat rushing up to my face. Then he says, 'It fits fine. Very sexy,' and moves towards me. I don't feel sexy. I slip to one side.

'I have to get the stuff ready for your dad and Jaquie,' I say, by way of apology, and go back to the bedroom to get dressed.

'You're taking it off?' This time he's definitely disappointed.

'Um, no … just …' I grab my dress and put it on over the top. The effect is pretty, erm, busty, but I haven't got time to worry because Aaron's dad said he'd be here at ten and I have to finish the biscuits. While Aaron's getting showered and dressed, I lob the rest of the icing on and put the crappier ones at the bottom of the Christmas tree plate, then set out the dips and Pringles in bowls, next to a couple of candles. It all looks pretty cool on the table.

'What do you think?' I say, as Aaron enters the living room.

He looks at the table. 'Is this everything?'

'Yeah, why?'

The buzzer goes. Shit. I'm a total mess from running about.

'Oh my God, I look like a state,' I say to Aaron as the buzzer rings again. He glances at me, and then says, 'Well, no time now,' which isn't totally the reassurance I wanted. I run into the bathroom and put on some lipstick.

Aaron's dad and Jaquie are already in the living room when I come in.

'Gemma.' Aaron's dad comes and gives me a kiss on the cheek, standing a bit too close for my liking and getting an eyeful of my boobs while he's at it. I step to one side and smile. Jaquie gives me a broad smile back and a little wave.

'The paper chains are very sweet,' she says.

I see Aaron clench his jaw. Then he says, 'Drinks?' and looks at me.

'I've got some coffee? It's the proper stuff,' I say, a hint of pride in my voice.

'Sounds lovely,' Jaquie says. Maybe she's not so bad. Then she laughs. 'It'll go with the little biscuits, I suppose.' Aaron's dad looks amused.

I take it back, her being nice. I go into the kitchen and Aaron follows.

'Aren't you cooking anything?' he says.

'Like what?'

'Well that's what Christmas brunch is, isn't it? My mum used to do these eggs with a sauce, and salmon and stuff.'

'Sorry, I didn't know,' I mutter, fiddling with the bag of coffee next to the brand-new pot. The next minute, it splits, and beans go flying out all over the floor. I try not to swear.

'Gem, why have you bought beans?' Aaron says as I push it all into a pile with one hand.

'It's what we used in the cafe – Dora always used to say it was the best …' I trail off because I've suddenly remembered that you need to grind the beans first and of course we don't have a grinder here. There was one built into the machine at the cafe … How could I have forgotten something that simple?

'Can I help?' Aaron's dad and Jaquie are standing in the doorway.

'She's bought coffee beans for a cafetière,' Aaron says, and all three of them laugh.

I can feel my face flushing. I open my mouth to defend myself, to explain it's not that I didn't know, but Aaron's dad is already saying, 'We'll just have instant.'

I make the coffee and we go back into the living room. Aaron's dad takes a Pringle and Jaquie nibbles on the edge of one of the biscuits before examining the icing and popping it back down.

Aaron frowns.

'Does anyone want some dip?' I say, in slight desperation.

'Oh, are the Pringles for the dips?' Jaquie says, her eyebrows high in surprise. I swallow hard. I don't think when Aaron said he wanted to 'show me off' this was exactly what he had in mind.

Somehow we make it through an hour. Aaron's dad spends most of the time on his phone, showing us pictures of a second-hand Audi TT. 'It's a twelve-reg,' he says. 'Pretty tidy for 10k.'

'Well, I guess nothing says mid-life crisis better than a TT,' Aaron says. I glance at his dad, but he just smiles. It's like nothing Aaron does bothers him one bit. I make what I hope are the right admiring noises even though I know nothing about cars.

Eventually Aaron's Dad and Jaquie go. When the door closes, I stare at the dining-room table, the Christmas plate with its sad-looking gingerbread men and the half-drunk cups of coffee. The dips and Pringles almost untouched.

Aaron comes to stand next to me.

'I'm sorry,' I say. To my horror, tears are welling up. I wanted this all to be perfect. To show how I could do Christmas. To make Aaron proud. I thought I'd bought the right things. But now I feel small and the underwear is hurting me and I feel like …

I want Mum.

The realisation makes the first tears spill over.

Aaron puts his hands around me. 'You silly thing,' he says. 'Who gives one about my dad? This was all perfect because you tried your hardest.'

But it doesn't make me feel better because I know he's disappointed in me.

Slowly, I clear up. We watch a couple of films, eat our Christmas dinner – a Tesco Christmas ready meal for two, because neither of us have a clue how to cook a turkey from scratch – have sex. But the sense of failure is still there, like nothing I do is right. I mess it all up.

Later, I remember Aaron's Christmas present. The song I've been working on the last couple of weeks, the one about him completing me, about how beautiful our lives will be because we're together.

'Aaron?' I say.

He's half asleep on the sofa. 'Yeah?' He mumbles.

I stand up, ready to get out my guitar, but then I stop.

It's like the words are sealed up inside me and they don't want to come out.

'Never mind,' I say. 'It's nothing important.'

Chapter Forty-Six

Aaron

Why is she so mopey? Ever since Christmas she's got quieter and quieter. It's like living with a mouse. Sometimes I don't even want to have sex with her any more. She never wears the underwear I got her, all she does is clean, and try to cook and clean some more. And the place still looks like shit most of the time.

One day, I'm out shopping, looking at a new smart TV. I've been getting a good upturn from the new app – BungeeMayhem – in the last couple of weeks, and they just upped my credit card limit, but I need to develop more apps, find out more about investing and shares. I go out to cafes some of the days, just so I can concentrate. Gem never wants to come anyway. If she's not going to bother wearing the stuff I get her, then I'll spend some of my hard-earned cash on myself. Maybe a new car …

'Aaron!' I turn, and there's Selina from college. God, I forgot how fit she was. We end up going for a coffee, and she's as smart and funny as I remember. She fills me in on all the gossip from college. Binners has a girlfriend, if you can believe it.

When the coffee's finished, she gives me a kiss on the cheek and a long hug. She smells amazing, and I can feel the lines of her body, she gets in so close. We swap numbers and I can't help watching her legs as she walks off.

At home, Gem's standing over the sink, scrubbing some potatoes. Her hair's pulled back into a greasy ponytail and she has a few spots. She never bothers putting make-up on for me any more. A flash of Selina's lips go through my mind as Gem kisses me, especially when she pulls back with a frown.

'What?' I say, and it's hardly my fault if it comes out a little harsh. She jumps, as if I've scared her, but it doesn't make me worried, or sorry. I want to laugh. She looks like a flabby little rabbit.

'Nothing,' she says.

Chapter Forty-Seven

Gem

January is cold, February worse. I know it because we only have the heating on in the mornings and evenings. Aaron's reasoning is I can wear a jumper anyway if I'm lazing about the flat while he goes out to work. He works all the time now, in cafes. And the other day, I could have sworn he smelt like perfume. He keeps his phone on him all the time too and whoever's texting him, he won't say.

Another day, when I'm putting some of his clothes in the washing machine, I find a hair on his jumper. It's long and blonde and definitely not mine. I can't find the words to ask him about it. Instead, I stand in front of the washing machine, holding the hair up to the light, trying to convince myself it's brown. When Aaron comes in to grab a drink, I stuff it in my pocket. I don't know why I can't throw it away.

I stop sleeping. I wasn't really before, when Aaron used to call and text at all hours. But this is different. Now I'd give anything for him to wake me up in the middle of the night for sex, or to talk, or whatever.

In my heart, I know there's something wrong.

I start to talk to Shiney, when Aaron's out. Just for someone to chat to. She rests her soft nose up against my face and on the days I cry, she tries to lick my tears. 'Where is he?' I whisper. 'Is he with someone else?' The thought of Aaron with another girl fills my head. The same images run through my mind, like sea sucking at sand under my feet, until I don't know anything any more.

He comes in one evening, face flushed and eyes sparkling from the cold.

Or from someone else?

I'm on the sofa. I haven't moved all day.

'Where's dinner?' he says, barely even looking at me.

Where have you been?

'I thought … we could go out?' I say eventually.

He laughs, and there's no mistaking it now, the tone of it. The way he's looking down at me as if to say, 'With you looking like that?'

It's true. I haven't even washed today. I get up and try to cuddle him, but he pushes me off and goes for a shower, but not before I catch the perfume smell again.

The days when he won't speak to me are the worst. Sometimes I don't even know why. I'll ask and ask, and he'll carry on with what he's doing like I'm not there, no matter if I shout, or plead, or cry. It could be over anything: a meal, the state of the house. The state of me. All I want is for him to smile how he used to. Or look at me like I exist.

I'm crying when he comes back out of the shower. He sighs, heavily. Opens his laptop.

'Do you even love me?' I say, wondering who he's

emailing. Even a month ago, if I'd asked the same thing, he would've been all over me, showing me how much he loves me. Now, he doesn't answer. 'I'm taking Shiney for a walk,' I say.

He barely looks up from the screen.

On the beach, I run and run, everything hurting as I do, the wind freezing my face. I'm wearing Aaron's fleece, but it doesn't smell like him any more. It smells like me: stale sweat and tears.

I watch Shiney chasing the waves in the semi-darkness. She's so happy. Why can't I be happy like that? I think of the things Aaron says, how I'm ungrateful, how I always want more. Is it true? What's wrong with me? I think about Mum and Dad, Esi and Cal. How none of them care about me. How maybe I'm not worth caring about. Then I imagine him with his arms around someone else, telling them how beautiful they are, how much he loves them. I can't stand it.

Back in the house, I towel Shiney off and mop her paw-prints from the floor. Aaron's still on his laptop, like he hasn't even noticed I was out for ages in the dark.

I try to reach out to him. To bring him back from wherever he's gone. 'Hey.' I make my voice soft. 'We never finished watching *Nashville*. You fancy putting one on?'

'*Nashville*? You know I can't stand it.' He goes back to typing while my shocked brain tries to process his words.

'But … we watched it. Before. I thought you liked it?'

'I think you're confused,' he says coldly.

I try to remember back, to us cosy together on the sofa, watching episode after episode because we couldn't wait to find out what happened next. Didn't we?

The hair's still in my pocket from the other week. And suddenly I have to know.

'Are you sleeping with someone else?' The question just comes out.

Aaron finally looks up. 'What?'

'You heard me. Are you?' My voice sounds all wrong, too harsh, too accusing. Aaron slowly closes the laptop lid.

'Well, it sounds like you've already made your mind up. That's a bit rich, coming from you,' he says.

I feel myself falter as Aaron warms up. 'What about all the guys you were flirting with? Cal? Higgins? That bloke up the hall? I saw you laughing with him the other day when you were supposedly taking the dog out for a walk. You sure you don't have anything you want to tell me? You expect me to believe you stay in every day while I'm working? Never sneak out? Knock on his door?'

'That's crazy.' My voice is faint because my head's spinning. Aaron comes up so he's right next to me.

'*I'm* crazy? Have you heard yourself? How insane you sound? Have you looked at yourself? What are *you* hiding, Gemma? What is it you really want to say?' The way he uses my full name like that hurts even more than what he's saying. I can feel tears coming. I try to hold them back, but it's no good.

'I don't even know that guy. He just stopped to ask me a question.'

'Like what?'

'I don't even remember! It wasn't anything.'

'Seemed pretty cosy for an "I don't even remember",' Aaron says, mimicking my voice.

And on it goes. Me trying desperately to defend myself, Aaron talking on, the night stretching out as he paces and I cry. In the end, I'm so exhausted I start to agree with him, to say I'm sorry, anything to make it stop.

When he finally goes to sleep, on the sofa, because he's too hurt to sleep in the same bed as me, I take a long shower. There has to be a way to make this all better. I think about the things I've given up, for him. Wonder if there's anyone I can talk to, apart from Shiney, and remember there isn't. The only person I have is Aaron. There has to be a way to make this better, make him love me again. There has to be.

Chapter Forty-Eight

Aaron

I type into the search engine:

Q: *What to do when your girlfriend's let herself go.*

A: *Have you tried talking to her? Perhaps she's depressed. Get her to see a doctor.*

I don't read any further. What's she got to be depressed about anyway? That's just an excuse. She's got everything she needs, everything I've given her. All she has to do is ask and she gets stuff. I think about the shopping trips, the guitar she doesn't even bother to play. She doesn't have to work or go to college or anything. Then she accuses me of cheating, when she's the one who flirts like crazy with anything with a dick. She can't be bothered to make the effort for me, that's her problem. And so what if me and Selina have had a couple of kisses? Everyone knows that doesn't count, not for a guy. Especially not when his girlfriend's sitting there, lazing about the house without even bothering to do her make-up. She doesn't bother to learn how to cook me nice food, she barely bothers to shower, and sex? What a joke.

Men and women are different. Men are visual. She's trying to put me off by not making any effort any more. Like she wants me to go off with someone else. That's the real cheating because it's heart cheating, not a kiss or two, or a quick feel-up.

I miss her. I miss her smiles and the way she looked at me like I was her world, not like I'm some huge disappointment. If I want someone to look at me like that, I've got my mum. I can't believe she's throwing away everything we have, after all I've done for her. I've even given up Selina for her. Me and Selina haven't even slept together, though Selina has made it more than clear that's on the cards. And I said no because I'm faithful. Unlike some.

I look again at the word 'depressed'. Could that be it? Or is it just being a girl that does it?

Slowly the rage falls away. It's the middle of the night, and I want my bed. I go into my room and there she is, asleep like nothing's wrong at all. I can't work out if I want to kiss her or throttle her. She stirs as I lean over. Her hair smells good from her shower. Before she's even fully awake I'm there on top of her and she lets me in, moves the way I like, and if I'm thinking about Selina some of the time, that's my own business, no one else's.

Chapter Forty-Nine

Gem

I wake up the next morning with Aaron's arms around me. The relief is so acute it feels like my whole body is melting into the covers. I wriggle in closer to him, breathe in his smell.

The next day is even better. I know he's sorry because he brings me a huge bunch of flowers, and even breakfast in bed. Then we spend hours together, just like before, ordering new clothes and make-up with his credit card.

Maybe this is the start of a whole new phase. I make sure I'm up early every day, do everything I can to look as nice as possible. When he's working, I find exercise videos on YouTube on his new smart TV and spend hours doing them, or watching cookery programmes so I can cook him different things.

It seems to work, except maybe there's a part of me still watching, on high alert, even if I don't ask him any questions about where he's been. Or who with. I can't stop smelling his clothes before I wash them though, looking for hairs or traces of make-up, especially when he's been out late. And I still can't sleep. I keep trying to sort all the Aarons I know out from each other. The hurt, vulnerable Aaron, and the angry, shouting one. The loving Aaron and the Aaron he is sometimes in bed, like it's not even me there with him. I don't know how to talk to him about it. I remember the time he quoted Bowie, the thing about being the person people believed him to be.

Who do I believe Aaron is? I try to keep that question for night, when only I'm awake.

My face breaks out in even more acne, although at least I've got the right concealer to cover it all up. I layer it on each morning, top it up before he comes home. Slowly I start to feel like the bad times have passed, that whatever was going on with Aaron, he's back to his old self again.

And then, one day, the guy up the hall stops me as I'm coming in with Shiney.

'Hey,' he says. 'Haven't seen you about for a while.'

'Hi.' It's the briefest thing, and my eyes don't even meet his, but he carries on anyway.

'So … how long have you been living here? Is this your dog? You're with that tall dude, aren't you?'

'Um, yeah. Sorry, I need to …'

'Sure. I've got some post for your guy, though, picked it up by accident the other day.'

'Oh. Um, can you just slide it under the door?' I say. I look up the hallway.

Aaron's home. Shiney knows it too, because she gives a little whine, wanting to get back for her food.

'I'll get it now.' The guy gestures for me to follow him.

281

He's only two doors down. I stay where I am. Then he pokes his head out of his door.

'Here we go.'

I glance at our door, mine and Aaron's. I can't ask this guy to bring me the letters, that'd be too rude. But I can't go in there and get them, because what if Aaron comes out and sees?

That's when I realise I don't know how to make a decision on my own any more.

'Oh, hey …' The guy's come back down the hallway. 'You crying?'

I shake my head, even though I am.

The guy puts the letter in my hand, but at the same time places the other hand lightly on my arm, and I can't lie, it's nice to feel a soft touch, to hear the concern in his voice. He looks into my eyes. 'You OK?' he says.

'I—'

The door opens.

Aaron.

I jump back from the guy, the letters dropping to the floor. Then I'm scrabbling to pick them up, hearing my voice high and nervous. 'He was just giving me these for you.'

'Sure, thanks. Dude,' Aaron says. He smiles.

'Any time.' The guy goes back into his flat.

Shiney dives for our door.

I let her go, look up into Aaron's face, but I can't read it. I go inside, even though something in me is shivering and shivering. I feed Shiney, get the cloth for her paw-prints. All the time, Aaron stands over me, watching. As I

282

straighten, he takes the cloth from me, and that's when I start to feel afraid.

These past few weeks, I've been desperate sometimes, but I've never felt scared the way I do now. I know what's coming. I know it even as I sit down while Aaron begins to pace. I stare at his feet going back and forth, waiting for it to start. I don't even know if I have the words any more to try to explain.

'He was just giving me some letters,' I whisper.

And Aaron roars. So loud I let out a little scream. His face up close to mine, spewing out insults. 'You fucking bitch. You've been dressing yourself up for him, not me, haven't you?'

'I'm sorry.' I keep whispering it, my back pressed against the sofa as he rages on. Shiney whines, and he aims a kick towards her, not to hit her, but to send her running. It's as though his foot is kicking me.

'I knew it. I fucking knew it. You've been laughing at me all this time, haven't you?' Aaron shouts.

'No,' I whisper again, but he can't even hear it, can't see me.

I can't reach him.

It's so much worse than before. The shouting lasts for an eternity. He jabs my chest with his finger, hard enough to hurt. When I get up and try to go, he stands in the doorway. 'Don't you walk away from me,' he hisses.

And I sit back down. I watch as he takes out every item of make-up I possess and smashes them to the ground in front of me, all the time raging about how I did my make-up for that guy, the guy whose name I don't even know.

The one with the kind eyes.

I'm so numb I can't even cry, can barely feel my heart racing. I stare and stare at my guitar on its stand, remembering the song I've never sung him, hoping I can hold on to that, and so it takes me a while to realise he's screaming, 'Going to answer me?'

'What?' I say through frozen lips. I'm shaking.

He follows my gaze, takes in the guitar, and gives this awful hard laugh. 'I was worried about you. Thought you might be depressed. But you're a nasty, manipulative little bitch, aren't you? You never cared about me, just what you could get.' His face is so full of hatred and disgust he barely looks like himself. It freezes me so badly I think my heart might stop. 'You want to know the truth? You're ugly, boring, and you know what else?' He pushes his face close to mine. 'You sound like a fucking screech owl when you sing your shitty songs.'

I gasp out loud and put my hands up to my ears, as though I can block out what he's said, the cruelty of it sounding in my head like the aftermath of a bomb detonating, but that seems to make him angrier. He turns and aims a kick at the guitar and, unlike Shiney, this one connects. The guitar topples from its stand.

'Stop!' It comes out as a wail.

But it's like he's not even there any more. He lets out another low roar, like a bear about to attack, and he grabs the guitar, lifts it above his head, and then crashes it into the ground. There's the sound of wood splintering. He's stamping on the guitar, kicking it, smashing it into a thousand pieces. And then Shiney starts to bark and howl, and it's like the howling in my head, and somehow that unfreezes me.

I snatch my phone up and run. Past Aaron, past Shiney, straight to the front door. In the hallway I barrel past the guy who sparked it all off, who's standing there looking sleepy. 'You OK?' he says. But then Aaron crashes out of the flat too, and runs right past him, towards me, and I think I see true violence in his eyes.

'Hey!' The guy yells behind us.

But I'm still running, as fast as I can, in a blind panic now, Aaron behind me, his heavy boots making solid slaps on the ground. I duck down an alleyway and then another, hear him shouting my name. I run harder, down towards the beach, not understanding why there, just knowing I have to run and that my feet are in agony with no shoes. I hit the sand and step up my pace, realise Shiney's next to me. I'm sobbing, a stitch in my side, but I keep on.

Eventually, though, I can't run any more. I'm walking as fast as I can, wondering what next, thinking I should double back, try to knock on a door. I get out my phone, but it's going in and out of reception. I'm walking like I'm on autopilot, and suddenly I know why I've come here, to a place I always thought was magic.

I don't think I can carry on any more. I'm so tired of it all.

I walk right up to the shoreline. The tide's way out, the edge of the cliffs looming far away in the distance to one side. The water is so cold on my toes. I stare out to where the stars meet the water in the distance. It would only take a few minutes to swim out, to let myself fade away, because that's how I feel right now.

285

Like I don't even deserve to be here any more.

One of the stars is winking at me. To call me to it or to tell me something else? And perhaps it's that star that does it, or the fact I'm freezing cold, but it's like I'm hearing an old song we used to sing in assembly when I was a little kid. It's a song about love. Not of a person but of God, and even if I don't believe in one, I do believe in music. Despite everything, I still believe in that.

And I know I could never swim out into those waves.

That's when Shiney growls, and the next moment, Aaron rugby tackles me and we spin into the surf with a splash.

Chapter Fifty

Gem

I'm coughing and spluttering, with the cold and shock as much as the water filling my mouth. Aaron's arms are tight around me. The next moment, he's hauled me up. I stand there, soaking wet and shivering in front of him.

'Gem. Oh God. You're wet. Here –' He takes off his fleece. Holds it out to me.

I take it slowly, hold it close, trying to read his expression in the moonlight. My arms are shaking.

Aaron's talking, saying how sorry he is, that he lost control. That he thought I was about to do something crazy, and while he's not totally wrong there, it's like the water has woken me up from the longest dream. Or nightmare, I guess.

'Come on, you're cold. Let's get you inside,' he's saying. He picks up my phone which has fallen into the sand, the screen still glowing. I reach out automatically for it, see him go to put it in his pocket, hesitate, and then hand it to me. I curl my shaking fingers around it like a lifeline as Aaron starts to lead me away, and even though my brain's awake

287

now, my body still follows him. We start up the beach together.

And then I look back and I see it: that pinpoint of light in the house next to mine, close by where my room is.

Was.

And I stop.

Aaron tugs on my hand. 'Come on, we need to get you in and dry. We'll talk … Maybe we can go away. A mini-break? You've always wanted one of those. Or to London. We could move. This town's a shithole anyway. We could have a new start.'

Part of me is so tempted. I would have given anything for him to say that to me a few days ago.

And another part, the part that loves music, that still knows who I am, is looking at that tiny light in the distance. But I'm so cold, I can't think.

Aaron's pulling at me, propelling me up the beach. We're almost at the path now.

I stop again. Under the street lights my bare feet look like two pale ghosts.

'I'll carry you,' Aaron says gently. 'I'll always carry you, I promise. I carry your heart, remember? And you carry mine.'

And my frozen brain's stuck on the word 'carry', because Aaron always used to say 'hold' and it seems important somehow, but I can't work out how. Then, suddenly, I get this memory, like the music but even stronger, of being a kid standing at the tip of the diving board, Esi yelling, 'Jump, it's now or never!' and me grinning, then leaping in with a huge Doctor Who-style 'Geronimo!'

I don't say anything. I just yank my arm free and take off back along the beach, sand kicking up in wide dark arcs behind me. And perhaps Aaron's too surprised to react, or there's some small piece of him that knows too, but he doesn't follow me. When I've put some distance between us, I can't help but turn and look. He's just a shadow on the horizon. He doesn't move. Shiney's next to me, and I put one hand on her coat, like it will give me strength.

Then Aaron lets out a piercing whistle.

Shiney quivers under my hand and I can feel her indecision, wanting to stay with me, but Aaron's trained her so well.

'Don't go,' I whisper.

But he whistles again and she gives a kind of shudder under my hand, then trots slowly up the beach, leaving me standing holding on to nothing.

Chapter Fifty-One

Gem

'Gemma?'

It's Esi who's opened the door. I'm soaking wet, my feet cut from the long walk up the cliffs, shivering so hard I can't speak.

'Shit,' she says, and it's so unlike Esi to swear. Then she yells, 'Mum!'

A moment later, I pretty much fall into Baaba's arms.

The next few moments are a blur. I hear Baaba exclaiming, 'She's soaking wet. Get a blanket.' I hear her calling for Esi's dad. And Esi looking at me with such worry in her eyes that I can't stop crying.

'Should we call someone? What's happened?' Baaba's saying.

'N-n-no.' My teeth are chattering. 'Please. I don't want to go home. I just need …' I'm crying too much to finish.

They push a mug of hot tea into my hands, then Esi says, 'You've got to get undressed. Put this on.'

'She's exhausted,' Baaba says. Then she sucks in a breath. 'Her feet.'

And Esi is helping me strip off my clothes, taking the tea and putting a nightie and a dressing gown on me. Wrapping the blanket over that. Sitting me back on the sofa. And now I'm crying, because she's being so kind to me and I know I don't deserve it.

Slowly I start to warm up as the tea and the blanket take effect. The shivering calms down so I can use one hand to drink the rest of the tea without spilling it. Esi and Baaba wait while I drink.

Esi breaks the silence first. 'What the hell—' She glances at her mum. 'I mean, what happened?'

I shake my head. I can't seem to get the words out now. I'm drowsy, more exhausted than I can ever remember feeling. My eyes keep closing. Baaba shakes her head.

'We should tell Lucy she's here.'

I force my eyes open. 'No. Please don't tell Mum. Not yet,' I say. I'm too confused, too ashamed of everything that's happened, to talk to her.

Baaba looks at me a long while, then she says, 'I need to check with my husband.' She goes into the next room to talk to Esi's dad. I can hear their voices, low, talking in Twi. Eventually Baaba comes back in holding a bowl of water and a first-aid kit. 'OK. I'll make up the spare bed in Esi's room,' she says, 'But first, your feet.'

I'm too tired to do anything but nod in gratitude. I sit still while Esi helps Baaba clean and bandage my feet, then I crawl up the stairs.

'Should I ask her … ?' Esi begins as I start to drift to sleep.

'We'll get some answers in the morning,' Baaba replies.

I wonder about answers, about who Aaron is, who I am, but I can't even begin to think how I'll understand. And so I close my eyes, and sleep.

When I wake up, I'm alone. I lie for a while until I can't put off going to the toilet any longer. I creep out to the bathroom, pee, and go back to Esi's room. She's left me some towels and clothes on the desk. Next to them is my phone, switched off. I wonder if I did that or Esi. I wash and dress, feeling vaguely more human, and then I steel myself to go downstairs.

But I can't make myself walk past the bedroom door. It's not just my bruised and cut feet, or the fact my whole body feels like it's been whacked with rolling pins. It's the embarrassment. I wonder whether it might be possible to die of shame. I think about all the arguments I've had with people, the way I treated Esi, Cal, Mum and Dad, Michael …

'Let me guess. You're wondering whether you can just crawl back into bed and stay there forever?' Esi's in the doorway, arms folded. And somehow the fact that she's pissed off with me makes things better. Like there's some way back.

'I'm so ashamed,' I say.

Esi sits down on her bed. 'Tell me.'

So I do. I don't leave anything out, I tell it all, as much as I can remember. How I can never work out which Aaron is the real one. How I've thought I might be going crazy. How frightened I've been.

Esi listens, asking for more information here and there. At one point I'm wondering if she's going to take notes – it

292

would be such an Esi thing to do. And then I remember what a me thing it is to do, to think like that. Have I ever really valued Esi's friendship at all? I think back to all those hours mucking about at the Beach Cafe. To making paper aeroplanes and flying them out of her window for hours one summer. How we cried when we got put in different classes in Year 4. Then I realise I've stopped talking, and so has she.

'So … um, that's it, I think. I've been a total idiot, haven't I?'

Esi leans forward and takes hold of my hand. 'No.' She seems like she's picking her words with care. 'I think … you've been through a lot.'

I look at my phone. The urge to call Aaron is so strong, here in Esi's bedroom. I remember before, how worried I was he might do something to himself. 'I just don't understand,' I say, and start to cry. 'What did I do wrong?'

Very gently, Esi says, 'I think you're asking the wrong question. Or at least using the wrong pronoun.' She shakes my hand, makes me look at her. 'He's abusive, Gemma. He's been abusing you.'

I turn my head away. 'It's not like that. We're not like … like those people you see on TV.' I mean those women you see who get beaten up, the ones who go back for more. Me and Aaron aren't the same as that. 'He's never been violent. He's never hit me or anything,' I add.

'Well, let me see.' Esi starts ticking things off on her fingers. 'He's pushed past you, he's trapped you in a room, he's shouted in your face, destroyed your property, stopped you seeing your family and friends. Oh yes, and chased you for miles. But you're saying he's not violent? You think none of those things matter? That they aren't bad enough to leave? Because they are.' She's lost the soft voice and somehow it's reassuring, listening to her rant, like old times. But I still can't say she's right. I mean, yes, it sounds so bad when you add it up like that. But what about all the other times, when Aaron made me feel safe? When I felt so loved?

I try to put it into words. 'Don't the good times count too? Aren't those the real him as well? He just has a problem controlling his temper. I mean, maybe he could get some counselling or something?'

Esi shakes her head. 'The good times can never excuse the bad. You think you're only worth someone who treats you well some of the time? That's not love. It's not about words, it's actions too.'

'If I hadn't – if that guy hadn't talked to me just then … We were getting back on track …' I say, but part of me knows we weren't, not really.

'OK.' Esi looks like she's trying to keep herself under control. And I don't know what I feel. I look around her room. One shelf has an entire section of feminist books. How does she know more about this than me? She's never lived it. I mean, books and theory are one thing, but she's never been in love, has she? As if she's reading my mind, Esi says, 'I did some research these last few weeks. I think you should have a look.' She brings up a screen on her laptop, but I whip my head away.

'I don't want to read it.'

Esi says nothing.

294

'It's not ... it's not so simple as you're making out, Esi ... Maybe I need to talk to him. We could find a way to work it out ...' I start.

Esi bites her lip, not through worry but because she's physically trying to stop herself saying something. Eventually she just says, 'Why don't you think about it for a while?'

I nod.

Then she says, 'I turned your phone off.'

And I know why. 'Thank you,' I say.

We go downstairs, to where Baaba is making toast. I take a slice, but my stomach is twisted up so hard it's difficult to get it down. I'm missing Aaron already. The real Aaron. It's like a physical hole that's opened up inside. I can't help remembering the breakfast in bed he got me the other day. How he kissed my forehead so tenderly.

Baaba comes over to sit down. 'Gemma. I need to tell Lucy you're here. She's been so worried these last few weeks.'

'Has she?' I say, and hear the way harshness mixes with hope in my voice.

'Yes. She's your mother, she loves you. You need to consider that,' Baaba says, and although her expression isn't angry, it is very firm. I don't know how to explain to Baaba about everything that happened, how it felt like Mum and Dad only care about Michael. I'm not sure she'd understand even if I tried.

'Can I ... ?' I look at Esi. 'You have a phone charger?'

Esi exchanges looks with her mum.

'I think that would be unwise,' Baaba says.

But I need to know. I can't help it. Esi sighs and gives me her charger and I go back upstairs. I plug my phone in and turn it on.

There's over thirty voicemails.

Even more messages.

I sit on the bed holding the phone. Esi taps at the edge of the door and comes in, looks over my shoulder. 'You don't need to listen to those,' she says.

But I do.

Esi sits with me while I listen. They're all the same. Aaron crying, pleading with me. *'I'm sorry, Gem,'* he says in one. *'Please come home. Or just call me. I'm worried about you, what you could do.'* Then the worst one of all: Aaron crying and crying, and saying, *'I don't think I can go on without you.'*

I let out a massive sob and then I can't stop. Eventually Esi takes the phone off me and listens herself. Then she does the strangest thing: she starts to laugh. I'm so surprised I stop crying for a moment and look at her.

'Listen to this one. He couldn't manage to keep it up in the end.' She hits the Speaker button, and then Play. It starts like the others, a long message going on about how he misses me, how he's frightened he'll do something bad to himself, he needs me.

'Why are you—' I wail.

'Shh. Listen,' Esi says.

A moment later, Aaron's voice changes into a shout. *'How could you do this to me? I hope you die, you bitch!'* he yells. The message ends. I sit there, completely frozen, his words, the viciousness of them ringing in my ears. A moment later the next message starts. *'I'm sorry, I didn't mean that, I*

296

*love you. I just got so frustrated, why won't you at least talk?
Don't throw everything away, we're better than that, more than
that ...'*

Esi hits the button to end the call. 'And if that doesn't tell
you what you need to know, I don't know what will.'

I swallow hard. Deep inside, I know she's right. But it's
more painful than I could have imagined. I miss him. Even
hearing that, I miss him.

Baaba knocks on the door. 'Gemma? Your mother is
downstairs.'

Chapter Fifty-Two

Gem

I limp down slowly. Not only because my feet hurt, but because I'm afraid.

Mum's in the living room, her back to the door when I come in, looking at a photo on the mantelpiece. I go up and look at it over her shoulder. It's of our two families. Mine and Esi's arms are around each other, and Michael's dressed in his football kit. He must have been about seven then, so around the time he was scouted.

'Your dad never knew how to relate to girls. Football was something he could understand, you know. We – I – didn't realise how much it had taken over all our lives. I'm sorry,' she says. And then she turns to me, and I want to cry because she looks like she's aged about ten years. 'I'm sorry, Gemma,' she says again. 'I let you down.'

Then she holds out her arms and I fall into them and it feels like I'm a little kid again and I realise how much I've missed her.

'I'm sorry too, Mum,' I cry.

Eventually, we sit down on the sofa. There's an

awkwardness between us still, because so much has happened. Some stuff I don't think I'll ever be able to tell her. But I know she loves me.

I have to ask though. 'Mum ... what about Dad?'

She looks pained for a moment. 'Your father and I have been having some issues ... You know he doesn't like to talk about feelings. But he's sorry for the way he was when Michael had his accident.'

I stiffen, then ask another question. 'Is he ... Will he play football again?'

'His ankle will be fine in time. But I'll let him talk to you about the rest,' Mum says.

I swallow. 'I don't know how to tell him I'm sorry.'

'Gemma, it was an accident. And perhaps things happen for a reason ... Like I said, your brother will talk to you. He's missed you. We all have.'

'But you never called!' It bursts out. 'You left me one weird message and that was it.'

I thought Mum had gone past the point of shock, but now her face goes pale. 'What do you mean? I called and called you. I sent texts. I even loaded up that ... WhatitsFace thing. The green one.'

I smile despite everything. 'WhatsApp?'

'Yeah, that one. I did it on my own too.' Mum looks proud for a minute.

I smile gently. 'Maybe there's hope after all.'

Mum touches my hand. Then her face darkens. 'You never got the messages?'

I think back. It's all blurry. 'Well ... my phone broke, and

I got a new one, and before that, I remember Aaron showing me one message, that first night but …'

Mum gets out her phone. 'I still have them here. Look.' She scrolls back all those weeks and I can see them now. The weird staccato way she's always had with texts. And the whole series starts like this:

Gemma?
Where are you? Mum
We're at hospital, Mum
xxx
Michael's ankle is broken but we're hoping
Sorry
It's a clean break
Where are you we're worried
Love you
Mum xxx

And about twenty more just like that. 'Oh my God. Aaron must have changed them,' I say. I remember … I can't work out what I remember, what he said. It's like some sort of fog. But cutting through it is about a whole ocean full of anger. 'I can't believe he'd do that …' I start.

Then I stop. Because yes, I can.

And even so, I still miss him.

Or the person I thought he was.

I realise I'm shaking, and Mum gives me a cuddle for a while as I cry. 'Everything's such a mess. I don't know how to face it all,' I say. Mum hands me a tissue.

'A bit at a time,' she says and nods to the living-room door.

Michael's standing there on crutches.

Chapter Fifty-Three

Gem

'Michael.'

I don't know what else to say.

He comes over, using the crutches like a pro. His foot's in one of those massive boot things. I can't stop staring at it.

'They didn't even give me a plaster cast, or I'd ask you to sign,' he says.

'I'll find Baaba,' Mum says, and goes off towards the kitchen.

Michael sits down and puts his crutches to one side, then looks at me.

It's the hardest thing to meet his eyes. 'Michael ... I'm so sorry—'

'You should be,' he says.

I gulp.

'Not for this. For running away. Mum and Dad were so worried ... Dad even cried.'

'Dad cried?'

Michael nods. 'We all did.'

I bite down on my lip, shake my head. 'I'm sorry,' I say again.

'I don't get it. Everyone thought Aaron was an idiot,' Michael says.

'They did?'

'Well, I did.' He smiles, shifts awkwardly on the sofa. I look down at that boot.

'Your football. Will you …?'

'Maybe, with physio, in time, yeah.'

'OK, that's good—'

'If I decide to,' Michael adds.

I stare at him, and he smiles back.

'I'd already been thinking for a while about talking to Dad. Football was taking over … It was my whole life, you know?'

I nod.

'Yeah, I guess you did know. It was all our lives … too much. I mean, I love it, but maybe I want to do other things too.'

I can't stop staring at him. Is he saying this to make me feel better? But then I realise he's not. Michael's always told the truth.

'… so it sort of helped to have the conversation with Dad. He'd already had to deal with the idea I wouldn't be able to play, at least not at Premiership level. Although … I could've thought of a less painful way to do it,' he says, but with a smile that lets me know he's not angry.

'How did Dad take it?'

Michael twists his hand back and forth in a 'So-so' way. Which is better than I could've imagined, really. 'To be honest, he was freaking out so much about you, too, it kind of took the heat off me,' he says. Then his face gets serious. 'I don't love that it happened. I still want to play football. But if it turns out I can't, I'll deal with it.' For a moment, I see a familiar look in his eyes, like a hurt that's been sanded over, but a part of you knows the wood's crumbling underneath. It reminds me of Aaron. Then it's gone, and it's just my little brother in front of me again.

We talk a little more and then everyone comes in for a cup of tea. Everyone except Dad, that is. I know I'll need to face him sooner or later, just not right now.

When we've nearly drunk our tea, Baaba comes to sit next to me. I see Mum looking nervous as she nods at her.

'Gemma, we've been talking and we wonder ... We need to go to the police.'

I immediately shake my head. 'No. I couldn't do that to him ...'

'He was abusing you!' Esi bursts out. 'He deserves to face the consequences.'

'Esi!' Baaba says sharply, but I'm already running upstairs in a storm of tears.

Chapter Fifty-Four

Gem

I keep on crying. The amount of tears Aaron's pulled from me … and still I can't imagine talking to the police, them going to knock on his door … My heart hurts thinking about it.

My phone starts to ring: Aaron. Voicemail clicks on. Then a message comes through, and another. I put a pillow over my head.

A while later, there's a tap on my arm. Esi, with more tea. It's like someone died.

'They're arguing about you downstairs. They won't let me in but I've been listening at the door,' she says in that direct way of hers.

'Why are they arguing?'

'Your mum wants to go to the police and take your phone away – is that him now?' She grabs my phone, hits the button to answer it, shouts, 'Piss off!' then puts it down before I've even had a chance to do anything but stretch my hand out.

'Esi, what the hell?' I say.

'I agree with your mum, by the way,' she says. But she tosses the phone back to me. A minute later, a text goes again. Then a notification from Instagram. I haven't even been on there for weeks.

'My mum thinks we need to let you come to your own decision. That if you're pushed too hard, you'll run back to him,' she says, rolling her eyes to let me know what she thinks about that option.

I pull my knees up to my chest, loop my arms over them. 'Glad everyone's got an opinion about my life,' I say. I don't mean to sound harsh, but everything's so confusing. I just want to go to sleep.

'Well, I think you should go to the police,' she says. 'For all you know, he's done it before. He might do it again.'

And suddenly I remember Cherine.

'What?' Esi says,

'I'm not sure. I just need … some time, I think,' I say. Esi nods and goes back downstairs.

I sit for a while on the bed, cuddling one of Esi's teddies, thinking about Moonshine slinking back to Aaron on the beach, how much I wish she was here. About Michael and Mum. All those messages she sent me. And I think it's that which makes me look at the website Esi has left open on her laptop. I read the whole page fast, as if it would hurt less that way. Signs and symptoms of coercive control, emotional abuse.

Me and Aaron, we tick each box.

It takes another two days at Esi's house before I know what I want to do.

I'm crying again when Esi comes in one morning. She doesn't say anything, just sits next to me until I'm cried out. Then I look at her through tear-blurred eyes. 'I need your help with something.'

It doesn't take too long for us to track down Cherine's Facebook. Her name is fairly unusual and I remember the area of London. Esi helps me send her a message and then we wait. Mum and Michael pop over for a while, but I'm not ready to go back home, not yet. Lunchtime passes, then dinner. I don't eat much, not even Baaba's jollof rice, which is always amazing, the smell of spices and tomato filling the house.

We're watching something on Netflix early evening when Cherine messages Esi. My own phone is off for now, but every so often I look at it. I miss Aaron so much it's taking everything I have not to call him, not to believe all his messages telling me things will be different if I just give him another chance, that I owe him another chance.

'Hey. It's her,' Esi says. She grimaces as she reads the message. 'She doesn't want to talk, she's just said to call Aaron's mum. There's a number.'

We look at each other, then I shake my head. 'I can't.'

'I will then. I'll put it on speaker,' Esi says.

The phone rings as my heart speeds up. I don't know what I'm afraid of, just that I'm afraid.

'There's no one there,' I say after about twelve rings.

Then, 'Hello?'

I clap one hand over my mouth.

Esi springs into action. 'Hello, Mrs Weaver, we wanted to talk to you about your son, Aaron?'

There's a long pause, then the woman says, 'Who is this? Has something happened?'

Esi explains briefly who she is. And then who I am. That we got the number from Cherine. And Aaron's mum lets out a long breath that crackles down the line. 'I was afraid this would happen.'

I'm holding on to my mouth so hard as I hear Aaron's mum talking. Words like 'Harassing her ... she went to the police ... caution ...' filter through. Then she says, 'We argued about it a lot. I tried to explain how he couldn't treat her like that. All those phone calls ... the other things.' Her voice catches. 'But he saw that as a betrayal, especially when I wouldn't ... He wanted me to back him up. Then he left to stay with his father. I haven't heard from him in months.'

Esi thanks her and hangs up, then looks at me for a long time.

'I think that's your answer,' she says.

I can't sleep that night. I play everything over and over in my mind. I hear Aaron's voice whispering, 'I love you,' feel his arms around me. Me saying, 'As you wish.' Then the image changes to him shouting, the way he looked when he talked about Cherine. His mum told such a different story, but I saw the hurt in his face too. Cherine really did break his heart, but his mum said he was abusive to her. How can both things be true at the same time? And all the while every part of me misses him with such an intense ache I don't know how to keep breathing.

The next day, I say thank you to Esi and her family and go home. It's so weird to be back in my house. Dad gives me a bear hug and a rough pat on the head which is maybe as close as either of us want to get to a proper talk. In Dad's eyes, that's 'girl stuff'. He does say if he ever sees Aaron near me, he'll 'knock his block off', so there's that, I guess.

A week goes past. I stay in my room, mostly, looking out of my old bedroom window towards the sea. Esi brings Cal and Rachael round one day. We go up to my room, and I can't lie: it's awkward. It seems like I'll be spending a long time saying sorry and having people tell me it's not my fault.

But I still feel like it is.

After an hour or so, Cal says, 'Hey, you want to sing something?'

I go over to my old guitar, but all I can see is the other one, the one Aaron bought me. His foot smashing into it.

I can't sing.

I can't even play.

I'm dreaming. Aaron holds me on a beach and whispers in my ear. 'I hold your heart. I'll hold it forever,' he says, as music plays in the background. The sky above us turns luminous and I sit upright in bed, heart pounding. A moment later, the familiar, gnawing ache starts in my chest, spreads to my stomach. I'm so focused on my misery, it takes me a moment to realise I can still hear music. It's faint, but there.

I have to check I'm not still dreaming, but no, I'm definitely awake.

The music continues. Am I going mad? Maybe I really am this time.

Through a crack in my curtains I see a pale glow.

I get up and look out of my window.

The entire garden is covered in candles. They're by the bushes, in the trees. And in front of them, holding a bunch of massive red roses, is Aaron.

He looks like the old Aaron, my Aaron, dressed in a suit. His face open, loving, lit by a thousand tiny lights.

I open my window.

'Gem.' That's all it takes. One look, one word, and my heart feels like it's left my body and travelled to meet his.

I grab my dressing gown and slip downstairs.

The garden is full of light and shadow, and in the middle, Aaron. The tea lights behind him spell out, 'I love you.'

I walk towards him until I'm only a foot away. He has a box in his hand.

'Gem. God, I've missed you,' he says, his voice cracking. He puts the roses gently on the ground and opens the box to reveal a diamond engagement ring, candlelight catching on it.

I don't move. A gust of wind cuts across the garden, making me shiver. A few of the candles at the far end of the garden blow out. I feel the goosebumps rising on my legs, the back of my neck. I can't look away, his eyes capturing mine. I think about soul mates.

'I need you to hear a song,' Aaron says. He hits Play on his phone and the music starts again, louder down here.

It's one of my songs. The one I wrote before I met him. 'Sea Dreams'.

I hear my voice, singing a story of love.

'This is you, this is the Gem I know. I love you. Come back to me,' Aaron's whispering.

I feel myself take a step towards him, and another. He's so close I could raise my head just a little and touch his lips with mine. My tongue is forming around the words 'As you wish'. I can feel the heat coming from his body, my heart, the way it seems to beat in him.

The ring in his hand. The promises in his eyes. I want to believe in them so badly.

As you wish.

What I would give to be able to say those words again.

Slowly I reach out with one hand, place it over his heart. In my mind, we're back on the beach by the waves all those months ago, exchanging something powerful, something that felt like forever.

Aaron's heart flutters under my fingers. His face seems soft in the candlelight, younger.

I know what to do.

'I take it back,' I whisper. Then I look, really look, full into his face.

He takes a quick breath, but he can't meet my eyes.

The wind cuts between us, blowing more candles out, until his face is shadowed.

And I realise the strange truth of it: both Aarons are him. The boy who loves me, the man who hates me. I think about all the fear I've carried, of never being good enough, loved enough. It was there long before I met Aaron. All the ways I've been selfish and unkind. Perhaps the dark places are in all of us if we look hard enough.

I feel something release from me, out into the night sky. I know I'll never be called Gem again.

'Goodbye, Aaron.'

His face is contorting, but I turn away. In the doorway, light spills out. Michael stands there, holding one crutch like he's prepared to use it if he needs to. I walk towards my brother as the wind whirls around me, the candles snuffing out as I go.

Epilogue

Gemma

'So I found this LGBT support group in Portsmouth,' Esi says.

We're lying on her bed. I have to go into town soon; I'm due at my own group. It's called the Freedom Programme. Most of the women are way older than me, lots with kids and stuff who go into a crèche while we sit with cups of tea and workbooks to talk and, sometimes, to cry.

They might be older than me, but I recognise their stories.

I struggle at times with the way they describe Aaron's behaviour as calculating, how he planned all the things he did. I think the truth is more in-between than that. Esi told me a good word: liminal. It means a space which isn't one thing or another. I do think Aaron believed he loved me, in his way. But I understand more now about what love is and what it's not.

After I went to the police, Aaron got another caution and an order banning him from getting in touch with me. I still have nightmares he'll appear in my garden, or in the cafe one day, but I think I'd deal with it. He's moved anyway. Last I heard, he was in Bristol. He left Shiney behind though.

Aaron's dad said I could have her. The day he dropped her off at my house, I held on to her familiar fur and cried and cried while she licked my tears.

I focus my attention back on Esi. 'A group sounds good,' I say.

She bites her lip. 'Would you come with me?'

We've talked a lot recently about what being bisexual means to Esi. How for such a long time she figured she had to be straight or lesbian, like sexuality is some kind of set menu, rather than something that's just you. She told me about always knowing she had the potential to be attracted to more than one gender, her sadness whenever she saw people in books or on TV turn out to simply be 'gay all along', the way it felt like she disappeared a little every time that happened. And more than anything else, how terrified she is of telling her parents. 'I mean, I hope they'll be OK, but it's going to be a massive shock. To be honest, I'm having a hard enough time with it myself, but I spoke to one of the church pastors and it wasn't as bad as I thought it would be. I guess even if it had been, well … I want to feel like I can be me too.'

I kind of knew what she meant. Right now, I reach over and touch her hand, for reassurance. 'Of course I'll come with you,' I say. I'm learning other things too, like how to actually be a good friend, to think about other people as well as myself. Sometimes I'm amazed we're still friends. Maybe it's because we're both figuring things out about who we are, and even though I don't understand everything she's going through, I can at least try. It makes me ashamed sometimes, to think how I used to act, how little I listened, but like Esi said, feeling guilty is pretty pointless. In the end, it's just another way of making it all about you.

After Michael's boot came off, he went back to training but he can't do a full week yet. We're still waiting to find out if this means he'll get kicked out for good. I hope not. And if he stays, I've promised I'll be cheering the loudest at his first match. I've figured that much out at least.

What I don't know is what to do next. I still haven't written a song or even sung a note since the second audition. It feels like I'll never listen to another country song again, like that part of me has died. If I could just sing one thing, anything, then maybe I could stop feeling so frozen.

We've talked about me going back to college or even going to Portsmouth and starting their Performance course, but I'm not sure. And sometimes, on the beach walking Shiney, I'm so lost.

Yesterday, Dad surprised me at the dinner table. He'd just finished a long explanation of why Gareth Southgate was the best England manager in decades, which was not exactly a conversation we've never heard before. Then he said, 'I saw a singing group – what do you call it? A choir thing in the town magazine the other day. You just turn up and sing. You fancy it, Gemma? I can drive you down. I used to sing a bit when I was younger. I could always come in, keep you company?'

Three forks stayed in the air.

'What?' Dad said.

'Maybe next week,' I said.

But I did smile.

Aaron

My Gem,

I wanted to write you a proper letter, but the police would say I'm not allowed to send it. I want you to know I'm not angry with you, I understand your parents and Esi and all the others put pressure on you. I need to see you. I miss you …

I slam the laptop shut. I was going to send it this time. Set myself up in a cafe with a new email so the IP address couldn't be traced. I know she misses me as much as I miss her. I feel it like a bullet to the chest. Nothing went the way it was supposed to that night at the flat. I guess things got out of hand, but she needs to take responsibility too, for pushing me. She was the one who blew hot and cold. Nothing I did was ever enough for her …

I rub my hand over my eyes.

She wanted to come with me, the night I went to her house, I know she did. If her brother hadn't come out and interrupted us …

I still don't understand how she could do this to me, that she can't understand how much I've been through. How much I love her. I cycle through anger and pain, disbelief and hope every day. She has to know what she's done to me.

'Are you finished?'

316

I look up. This girl has a laptop bag slung over her shoulder. She's smiling, and with the sun coming through the window behind her, she looks angelic. I feel my heart, cracked and rusted, give a couple of harder beats under my shirt.

'It just looked like you were.' She gestures around the cafe, which is packed. I'm entranced by the way she moves, the way her hair looks in the light. Her eyes are playful, friendly. Open.

'Sure, here you go,' I say, and she slides into the seat I've just vacated.

I pick up my laptop and then I can't help myself, because I can sense she's special. 'Hey, you fancy getting a coffee?'

The girl smiles up at me again, a faint blush on her cheeks. It's adorable. There's something different about her, I can tell.

'I'd like that,' she says.

Gemma

'So, are you going tonight?'

I laugh. 'It would be kind of worth it to hear Dad singing. I mean, can you imagine?'

'Not really.' Esi flips over on to her stomach, hesitates like she wants to say more about Dad. But we've kind of covered it before and I don't think he'll ever stop being a dinosaur. He's trying though, and I guess that counts for something. Esi flicks her phone at me. 'I found the poem, the one you talked about. I don't know if it will help. But I thought you might want to read it.'

I stiffen, but take the phone. I've never looked. I know Aaron used to quote things and pretend they were his. Like even when he was loving me, or thought he was, there was something in him that had to do it through someone else's words.

The poem's by e.e. cummings and it's called 'i carry your heart with me'.

Not 'hold'. It was never 'hold'. I'd already thought as much, but the words seem to stab something deep inside me.

I read the poem and lie back on Esi's bed to think. Did he quote it differently on purpose or realise he'd misquoted it but feel too embarrassed to say? Aaron never liked to admit he was wrong. Which parts did he mean, truly? It's the sort of question that can drive you crazy. Then I realise it doesn't matter. The end result was the same. And I'm not sure I even like the correct version anyway. Who could ever live up to all that love?

'One of these days you need to stop picking it all apart,' Esi says.

'I know. It's like, if I can understand why he did what he did, maybe it's not … it wasn't my fault.'

'The thing is, you might never know. He might never know. And anyway, like they say, an explanation is not an excuse. You don't owe him any forgiveness for what he did.' And she holds my gaze.

'I know,' I say simply. I'm done trying to puzzle it out, at least for now.

'So go tonight. Maybe I'll come too,' Esi says.

Which is how I find myself in an old church hall, in the

318

middle of a community choir, sandwiched between my dad and my best friend while the music starts.

Dad comes in first with the tenors. And he can sing. Esi and I exchange startled looks, then she comes in with the altos. She, well, can't sing, but she's giving it everything she's got anyway.

It's nearly my turn. I don't know if I can. I don't even know if I want to.

The music rises, every voice filling the tiny hall. I want to run suddenly, maybe to Aaron, maybe far out to sea. Maybe to whatever future is waiting for me. The one I'm going to have to build by myself.

For a moment, I'm back on the beach holding on to a pinpoint of light. The choir's song swirls around me and still I don't know whether to join it. And then the moment's here and there's no time left to decide.

I hear past Gemma, Confident Gemma, squealing, 'Geronimo!' as Esi laughs by her side. I feel the notes in the pit of my stomach, a sea of stories waiting for me. If I'm brave enough to sing them.

Am I?

I close my eyes and take a long breath in.

Afterword

I Hold Your Heart has not been an easy book to write. I set out to tell the story of one young woman's experience of coercive and controlling abuse, but the thing that struck me most forcefully while doing the research for this book was just how common Gemma's experience is.

Coercive and controlling behaviour can take many forms, from isolating and monitoring a person, to more overt violence and aggression, such as when Aaron breaks Gemma's guitar. While Aaron displays some worrying behaviour relatively early on in the book, the warning signs are all too often easy to miss, as Gemma's experience illustrates. It is also something that often creeps up over time, and can happen to anyone.

I had to make some difficult decisions over what to depict in the book, and by far the hardest was the issue of sexual assault and coercion. Towards the end of the novel, Aaron initiates sex with Gemma before she has fully woken up and is able to give her consent. While this was hard to write, I felt it was important to include as part of the wider pattern of devaluation and control Aaron has established towards Gemma. I want to be very clear that this is assault and should never be part of any healthy relationship.

I Hold Your Heart is Gemma's story, but I took the decision early on to attempt to explore Aaron's perspective too. I tried to imagine what influences at a personal and societal level might have led him to hold such damaging views of women and relationships. This attempt at understanding how he operates is in no way meant to be a sympathetic portrayal: as Esi says, 'An explanation is not an excuse.' There are never any excuses for the behaviour Aaron displays and he is a hundred per cent responsible for his actions. I hope I've succeeded in making this clear in the book.

We are currently at a difficult point in history, where hard-won rights for women and girls feel under threat. While coercive control is now a criminal offence in the UK, convictions and sentencing remain low. I firmly believe we must continue to shine a light on the issue of domestic abuse. We have to find ways to treat each other with dignity and kindness in all our interactions – including online. For anyone who recognises something of Gemma's story in their own life, please know that everyone deserves to be treated with care and respect, and that includes you. If you are worried about any aspects of your relationship or about someone you know, please reach out for help. Some useful organisations are listed on the next page. You are valuable and you deserve to live a life free from abuse.

With much love, Karen

Helpful Organisations

Women's Aid: www.womensaid.org.uk – supports women and children who have experienced or are experiencing domestic abuse, including information on what to do if you are worried about someone else

Refuge: www.refuge.org.uk – supports women, men, children and young people

The above charities run the Freephone 24-hour National Domestic Violence Helpline: 0808 2000 247

Childline: www.childline.org.uk – has a range of information on healthy and unhealthy relationships, and advice for what to do if you are worried about a friend

The Mix: www.themix.org.uk – contains a wealth of information and advice about sex and relationships for under 25s

Acknowledgements

Thank you to the following incredible people:

My agent, Claire Wilson, for all your invaluable support and for your kind words about my writing, which made me (happy) cry at a very difficult moment. Thank you to Miriam Tobin and to the team at RCW for your hard work behind the scenes.

My superstar editor, Hannah Sandford, for always understanding what I'm trying to do and then working your magic to make it a thousand times better. I feel like it's been quite a journey and I'm very glad to have taken it with you. Thank you also to Emma Young for your nuanced and invaluable line edits, and to Nick de Somogyi for your meticulous attention to detail.

Thank you to Rebecca McNally for continuing to believe in my work. Also to Emily Moran, Emily Marples and the marketing and publicity teams for working so hard to put my books into the hands of readers; to Jet Purdie for the beautiful cover design; to Fliss Stevens for all your hard work steering the book through production, and to the entire team at Bloomsbury for basically being the best.

Huge thanks to Henrietta Akesse-Mensah, who patiently

talked me through various cultural issues to do with the Ghanaian–British community, advised me on names and gave me your amazing jollof rice to try. Thank you for your generosity – I hope I have managed to do your comments justice. Thank you also to sensitivity reader Marcus Ramtohul for your time and care.

To my lovely family and friends, I am so very grateful as always for your support. I love you lots. Special thanks to Nikki, who has been through the joys and tribulations of single motherhood with me for all these years; to Lynne, Hannah and Sandy, and most of all to Lexi, for once again holding my hand through the entire process – you are all phenomenal.

The wonderful booksellers, bloggers, authors, librarians, reviewers and everyone else in the YA community: you are all amazing, thank you. There are too many people to mention and I'm worried I'll forget someone, but please know that your tweets and messages of support mean so much and have kept me going on more than one occasion.

Finally, to Naomi and William. I love you both with all my heart.

About the Author

Karen Gregory has been a confirmed bookworm since early childhood. She wrote her first story about Bantra the mouse aged twelve, then put away the word processor until her first child was born, when she was overtaken by the urge to write. Her first  novel, *Countless*, published in 2017, was shortlisted for the Leeds Book Award and longlisted for the Branford Boase Award. Her second novel, *Skylarks*, was published in 2018. Karen lives in Wiltshire with her family.

**Heartbreaking, life-affirming, brave and bold –
discover a completely different kind of love story**

'Is there anything that's concerning you?'
Felicity asks. 'College, home, boyfriends?'
Though she's more or less smiling at this last one.

I don't smile. Instead, I feel my face go hot.
Silence stretches as wide as an ocean.

Felicity has this expression on her face like
she's just seen Elvis. Slowly, she leans forward,
and in a gentle voice I've never heard her use
before she says, '**Have you done a pregnancy test?**'

When Joni meets Annabel, she's sure
they're destined to clash. But sometimes
you find a matching spirit where you least
expect it. And sometimes life asks you
to be bigger and braver ...

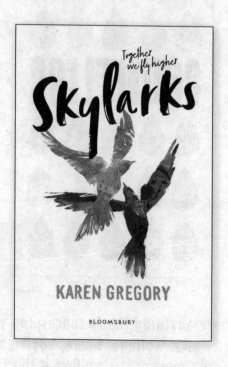

'This moving romance, with its examination
of power, politics and protest, and its clarion
call to make courageous choices, represents
all that's best in British YA'
GUARDIAN